# FULL BEAVER MOON

*a novel by*
*Peter Skinner*

Published by Peter Skinner Books
Copyright © 2023. Peter Skinner Books
Cover by Saana Miklova

ISBN: 978-0-9986740-4-9 (digital)
ISBN: 978-0-9986740-5-6 (paperback)

*For Graham and Rachel Lilly*

The dirt was fresh—that was the first thing—then the middle name. Smelling unsettled earth, he took a deep breath and looked up. The cloud that had followed him passed over a brick wall against which the grave had been dug. Moses would have known what that meant, what larger truth it implied, but the old man was finally gone.

MOSES EZRA HENRY

Born: July 4th, 1854

Died: May 2nd, 1954

The University Bell Ringer

Head bowed, eyes flooded with tears, he knew nothing would change the way they felt about each other. He wanted to tell him that—to tell him everything. Where he'd been. What he'd seen. What he'd learned about himself and the people he'd met. About how dangerous and beautiful the world was, just like he'd said, and how small you felt when you were finally in it, especially that. More than anything, he wanted him to know how much he'd missed the old man and kept him in his heart every day, hearing his bells from time to time in the distance. About the fire, Devil's Kitchen, ole Sister Mo, hopping trains to Winchester, Tangier Island, and the Great Dismal

Swamp. How Stick Watson had saved his life on more than one occasion and, only a few days ago, disappeared off the side of a boxcar in a trail of blood. How he'd go to the ends of the Earth until he found him to thank him properly for everything he'd done. For his bravery, his friendship, and for his affection. If Stick was alive, he'd find him and if Stick was dead, he'd let him go. Moses Henry had taught him that. To look for the goodness in all things. To be grateful for your time on this Earth. To hold it in your pocket like a precious thing. Like a keepsake.

Distracted by a burst of sunlight, Willie Graves looked around, realizing where he was, surrounded by death, alive, alone. After a century of living, Moses was finally free, finally with his momma. Knowing that, it didn't hurt so much.

Leaving Oakwood Cemetery, he passed through a pair of dark rusty gates into an expanse of trembling white dogwoods. Exhausted and spent, he'd figure it out in the morning—where to start, get some cash, find Stick. His momma's house was close. He'd visit with Mr. Matt a while, eat something, and finally sleep. That would be heaven: a long and welcome sleep.

A Virginia Stage Lines bus rolled east along Water Street, stirring waves of fluttering pink cherry blossoms in its wake. He admired them as he walked, mesmerized by their capricious swirling movement. "Nothin' but love," he heard Sister Mo whisper as it sped away. "Nothin' but love."

# CHAPTER ONE

Matt Abel stood in the kitchen counting room keys. Willie remembered them from a hallway table the night she came clean. When she pulled her secret cigar box from the cellar chimney and he saw the money.

"Got the box, do ya?"

"Yep."

"Come out easy?"

The boy nodded.

"Count it yet?"

He turned the contents of the box upside down on the kitchen table, creating a large pile of tightly packed one-hundred-dollar bills.

"Holy mackerel! Look at them C-notes, son!"

Willie had never seen a one-hundred-dollar bill. He imagined he might someday if he worked hard enough, but he never figured, if he did, there'd be so many of them all at one time wrapped in his momma's silver hair bands. "That's a lotta nights, Mr. Matt," he marveled.

"Yes, indeed," the old man agreed, lowering himself into a chair, suddenly remembering that she was dead. "They smiled when they left this place, Willie, yes they did! Morning, noon, or night. And it wasn't the goddamn bourbon."

When Willie saw the faded envelope, he stopped counting. Moses had delivered it before he died. Knocking gently at the door, holding his brown paper bag with her favorite drops. The bills smelled of mothballs and Junior Mints, each facing up, extensively wrinkled. It took a long time for a Black man to stuff an envelope so thick. To ring so many bells.

Mr. Matt fumbled with a pair of car keys. "How old are you, son? Need you to sign this thing here to make it official. Now, where-the-dickens did I put it?"

"Sir?"

"How old are you?"

"Seventeen."

"Seventeen!?" He stopped to consider it. "Seems like we were tossin' apples off that back porch just a while back. You remember that?"

"Sure do."

"No bigger than a pound a soap. Hit that crapper right on the money!"

"I was scared 'cuz we had a wager."

"Cost me a dollar."

"And an apple," Willie added.

The old man's eyes lit up. "An apple, indeed! Cranked it up and let 'er rip, is what you did—that was somethin'! Little bitty you, so sure you were on it. All my days…" he reminisced, drifting off.

The kitchen was quiet as Willie counted.

"Now where the hell that thing go?" the old man asked, breaking the silence, shuffling money about.

Willie stopped counting. "What you looking for, Mr. Matt?"

"Paper you sign to make the thing yours. Right here a minute ago." Sifting through a final pile he saw it on the floor. "Jesus Christ!" he protested, reaching down, retrieving it with a groan. "Fore you know it, be losin' my knickers gettin' dressed!"

Willie's face grew apprehensive. "I only drove a tractor, Mr. Matt. And a boat."

"Straight-8 automatic. Got yourself a radio and some fine seats for sleepin'. Or foolin' with the ladies!" he quipped suggestively. His hands trembled as he offered the keys and title paper. "Need to paper-up at the motor place tomorrow. Show 'em what we've done and all. Help you find that friend a yours, like you said." His eyes focused on Willie momentarily, blurry and anxious. "Before it's too late."

Willie was stunned, understanding the significance of his generosity. "I can't take your Buick, Mr. Matt," he replied timidly.

"Why's that?"

"Been with you too long, and I don't know… how you gonna get your groceries?"

"Groceries?" Pressing his hands against the edge of the table the old man pushed himself up, letting go and standing awkwardly. "Only two things matter in this world, Willie Graves." He looked the boy in the eye one more time, pausing for a moment, struggling to remember what they were. "A clear conscience… and a good piss."

The air was stuffy and her mattress soft. Opening the window, he caught a glimpse of a man through the branches below standing at the gate. Maybe he was drunk and wanted a woman or had stopped to button his coat against the fresh evening air. It felt good to see the world again. To stop running.

Lying on her bed with his clothes on, he listened as a car passed and the sink dripped next to the tub where she died. He wasn't afraid or overwhelmed by what had happened. The road had cured him of that. Allowed him to forgive her.

A patter of rain washed over him as his body went slack. Giving in to it, closing his eyes, he imagined her house as a warm and pleasant place, more human than business. What she'd never had.

Matt Abel stood outside the doorway and watched him sleep. The place was shot. He'd burned the last cedar shake. The boy was determined, you could see it in his eyes. He'd use the lecture chair Moses left, the money, the Buick, the house. Everything that had gotten him home. The guts, the balls, his sense of self-preservation.

The kid had always shown promise. If he could hit an outhouse from the back porch with an apple at the age of six, he sure as hell could fix a whorehouse.

The following morning, license in hand, Willie Graves traveled slowly east along Route 250 in search of Stick, learning as he drove, giving in to the idea of it. Like steering Salty's boat across the Chesapeake, he thought. Or slow dancing with Dolly.

Crossing the James at Westover Hills in Richmond, he turned south on Jefferson Davis Highway toward Petersburg, as traffic thinned and the rain lightened. Outside Chester, he sensed something, rolling the window down, inhaling deeply. Creosote. Water. Air. The police report said Ashton Creek. He panicked, thinking he'd gone too far or missed something along the way—until he saw it.

Pulling over, down a small embankment of sumac, stood the enormous tulip poplar where he'd dropped their knapsacks. Beside it, glistening wet tracks led to the opening of a tunnel. Grabbing his flashlight, sliding the door handle back, he jumped out, dropping to the ground.

Descending sideways down the hill, he reached the bottom, facing the tunnel, gathering himself, remembering the cold dark air and the dead deer's eyes that he'd confused with Stick's. Turning his flashlight on, he advanced, tentatively at first, as the skies darkened overhead.

Halfway through the tunnel a splattering of blood skirted the wall over shiny wet gravel, out into the light. Following its direction up a slippery, wet embankment, he reached a row of Scotch broom, stopping to catch his breath, smelling something sweet, honeyed in the air. Turning off his flashlight he heard it in the distance. Through a line of juniper, across a field, water cascaded off an old tobacco barn onto the roof of a rusted-out motor home. If only to stem the bleeding and move on, he imagined, his mind racing as he squeezed through the tree trunks, dashing out. He'd been over it a million times in his head: a roll of cash in his boot, his bandanna for the bleeding, a bottle for the pain.

The padlocked door turned his heart cold. A window, he thought, racing around back, looking for a way in. Did they lock the door later, discovering that someone had been inside? Or take pity on him, patch his neck, and give him a room? He'd seen it on the road firsthand. When they recognized something of themselves in others, people were often kind and generous.

Desperate to find a way inside, he squeezed below the undercarriage with his flashlight, casting it about. A truck passed in the distance as he lay there, muddy and soaked, seeing a wooden ladder. There was no way in. Strands of baling twine clung to his shoulder as he crawled out, swiping them away. The water on the roof intensified, like drums, or a river. His heart pounded in his chest. He'd left the car unlocked with everything in the back seat: some money, a coat, a sandwich. Walking away, sensing his despair, he stopped one last time to take a final look, shaking the rain from his hair. Before he saw it. He'd been too close to notice where the water hit the roof—a partially open skylight.

The ladder trembled as he climbed, one rung missing entirely. It was easier than catching a coal car, but stepping onto the roof, his foot slipped away, grabbing the top rail frantically with one hand, nearly falling.

He could see it now. There was just enough room. Lowering himself, facedown against the roof, crawling sideways, he reached it eventually, securing the edges with his hands, inserting his fingertips. Squeezing through the frame, hanging for a moment, arms trembling, he let go finally, landing with a loud and pronounced splash.

The air was rank and empty. Mold-mottled ceiling panels sagged overhead. Cabinet doors and magazines bobbed about in the water around his ankles. More boat than trailer now. Lost at sea.

An eerie calm came over him as he cast about. Something was here, between this world and the next. Sister Mo would feel it. Her bottle tree would talk. Give it a name. "When it come, when it come, and da light run dry," she would say, tossing powder on his face. "O'shabala! O'shabala!"

Turning, he saw it in the semidarkness draped over the edge of a small kitchen sink, as rain gushed down through the open hatch, splashing all around him—Stick's shirt, torn to shreds, saturated in dark dry blood.

Finding the car, he drove to Goshen. Old Sister Mo was famous now. Two bucks in a dish and, if you were lucky, her eyes rolled back. "There's a tumor in my head." "Will my momma die?" "Make me a poultice for the little baby Joe." Under her tree, among the broken bottles, she'd touch their foreheads and sing the mumbo jumbo, pretending mostly, hoping always for the healing grace of kindness and love, for the veil to be lifted. The lifting was hard now, she'd explain in a squeaky voice. Everything all the time or, with increasing frequency, a cold, dead silence. "Like da blood be still, and duh light go down." Such was her time on this Earth.

She heard tires against the broken stones. The bottles had been quiet. The boy was here. With a shirt. Perhaps her time had come after all. The prayers she'd burned before the fire. Blessings and incantations. Her next adventure to the White Bakula.

Returning a shard of glass into the pocket of her coat, she felt the power move through her. Rising unsteadily to her feet, shaky and nearly blind, beyond the morning mist she saw it clearly- a big black Buick and the seven Gates of Guinee.

Turning the key, Willie gazed out through the dirty windshield. She looked ancient and small, swallowed by time or spells. As he stepped out, stretching his legs, she raised an open hand.

"Ain't gon' fine yo' Stick in no Buick."

Willie was taken aback. "Ma'am?"

"Heard me."

He watched her carefully. She was feisty. "May I approach, please?"

Seeing a bloody shirt in his hand, Sister Mo dropped down, resettling gingerly on the stoop. "What you do?"

Willie's face fell.

"Ain't gon' bite you, boy—com' on," she said, tapping the top step with her hand. She felt the pockets of her coat. "Come fo' da Skinny Man."

"Yes, ma'am," he answered cautiously.

Retrieving the glass from her pocket, she admired it in the light. "Be green one day, den blue... den gone."

Reaching the porch, he stopped, looking down into her leathery black hand.

"Take it."

Crouching down, he placed his open hand next to hers as she tipped the glass perfectly onto his.

Willie sat next to her, enjoying it for a moment.

"We born wid da veil, an' we born wid da sight," she muttered, looking around to get her bearings. It was too early for shine.

"This is real pretty, Mo," he replied after a while, offering it back.

"Nothin' be shame of."

Seeing her distraction, he closed his hand around the glass, resting it on his knee. "Ma'am?"

The old woman turned to him. It startled him at first. Her pearly gray eyes. "Got a place a pleasure."

"You talkin' 'bout my momma's place?"

"Be a world a pain."

He tried to keep up. "Matt Abel's house? That what you mean?"

Sister Mo smiled to herself, reaching awkwardly for her bottle of shine at the side of the step.

"Can I help you?"

"I be good," she answered, capturing it in one hand, dragging it toward her along the step. "Do da pinch, den show da light."

He didn't understand most of what she was saying but admired her persistence. Hoisting the heavy bottle onto her lap, she fumbled with the cork before lifting it to her lips, tipping the bottom, taking a sip.

"Be strong, dis one." She lowered it quickly to catch her breath. "You want some?"

"No, ma'am, I'm good."

"Here," she offered, not hearing him. "Hep wid da nerve."

He took it. The bottle was nearly empty—more petrol than booze, he remembered growing up. A Cherokee from Gumshoe sold it to his momma one summer. She called it Choop. It went down hard, coursing through him like a warm deep wave. "ShhooEEE!" he shrieked.

She cackled, seeing his face change color. "Blue flame be good. Yellow be bad."

He caught his breath.

"In da spoon when it burn."

"Man, that's strong!"

"How's you know be good," she explained.

Willie looked out, head spinning. Her yard was a dusty gray wasteland. Rusted pots, fallen coops, burned branches scattered about. Brooms everywhere.

After a while, the wind stirred. "Where's Stick, Mo?"

She cocked her head to one side and gave him a strange, inquisitive look. "Skinny Man?"

"Can you help me? Why I'm here." He held up the shirt. "Got his shirt."

"Knows why yo' here."

"Yes, ma'am."

"Ain't no bloodhound," she replied coldly.

Willie laid the shirt carefully on the stoop and swung around to face her. He'd need to be patient. "Is he dead?"

The old woman turned away, distracted by something in the yard.

"You wanna lie down? I can sit in the car while you think about it."

Seeing the Buick, a smile crossed her face. "Dat ting got a radio?"

"Yes, ma'am," he answered proudly.

"Got da AM?"

"Yes, ma'am. Nice sound when you crank it up."

Her eyes twinkled with delight.

"You wanna see?"

Helping her to her feet, they descended the stoop, moving

carefully toward the car. He let go of her arm.

"Bring sometin' fo' me?" she asked, shuffling through the dirt.

"Got some money for you, Mo. Thank you for everything you done fixin' me up that time."

She stopped. "Came down duh Kitchen. Two years by."

"The Maury River. Yes, ma'am," he confirmed, stopping as well, watching her carefully. "Fell in."

"Skinny Man git you out."

"He did."

"Bin wid da Devil, you bin. Put you in da flame."

"That's what he said, yes, ma'am."

Her face hardened. "Yo' daddy a mean man."

Willie stiffened.

"Den da bell come."

He was astonished by her eyes. How far they went when you looked into them. "Yes, ma'am." He waited for her to continue. "Moses Henry."

Reaching up, patting the side of his face with a bony, cracked hand, she took him in for a moment, remembering their time together more clearly, feeling the goodness of his heart, the pain he had endured.

"Den you eat ma pone."


Sister Mo perched on her seat, captivated by the curve of the windshield.

"Dis be nice," she cooed, casting her eyes about, running her hands over the velvet-smooth seats. "Git you where you wanna go."

When Willie started the engine, she clapped her hands together, bursting with anticipation as he turned the dial and the sound swelled. WRNL was in the middle of Eddie Weaver's noon Open House broadcast. He swung the dial clockwise, landing on a crackly, slow song.

"Dat's it!" she screeched, closing her eyes, raising a finger in the air. "Make it big!"

He turned the volume up. The song was melancholy and the singer's voice heartfelt and deep:

"Whisper to me… love is true."

She hung on every note. It surprised him at first, watching her face, so alive and innocent.

"Let's pretend that we're together…"

He turned it up a bit more.

"All alone."

She was lost in something. Someone.

When it was over, he lowered a Mickey's Malt Liquor ad, noticing the glove compartment, remembering the money.

"Turn dat off, please."

"Off?" he asked, surprised, turning it off. "You okay, Mo?"

She opened her eyes and smiled contentedly. "Gon' be a sweet life, Willie," she said, staring out, seeing her shack in the distance streaked in a hazy light. "Make no difference 'bout da time. Place da place, no matta. Be long way ta go. Long, long, but you be fine." She touched the window lightly with her fingertips, pressing her open hand against it. The boy was a sign. "You still read dem books?"

"Yes, ma'am."

"Got da chair fo' learnin'?"

"The one Moses gave me?"

"Gotsta fight."

"Ma'am?"

"You understand me?"

"No, ma'am. What you mean by that?"

Withdrawing her hand, she turned toward him to see his face more clearly. He looked stronger than before, handsome like a young man now. "I mean what I say."

"I need to know 'bout Stick."

"Know what?"

"If he made it, Mo, please! 'Bout killin' me, not knowin'! He alive or dead? Came all this way to ask you."

She smiled, seeing his frustration. His worry. "Need some sleep."

Stick was dead, that's all he could think, and she was too afraid to tell him.

She giggled and shook her head. "Ain't 'bout dead."

"What you mean?"

She stopped to admire the dashboard.

"'Ain't 'bout dead.' What you mean by that?"

It took her a moment. "Read dat Bible ever night to yo' momma an' you don' know what I mean?"

"No, ma'am. I do not."

"'Bout da Father, Son, 'n' da Ghost?"

"No, ma'am. I mean, of course, I know all about them, but what that have to do with Stick? Me finding him?"

She sighed to herself, turning toward the door.

"Tell me, Mo."

"Nothin' ta say," she replied, sounding tired.

"Where do I go to find him?"

A catbird perched on the branch of a nearby pine.

"Found his shirt in a motor home outside the tunnel where he ran."

"When da water run blue."

"That's where he is?" he asked quickly.

"Time a da cockle shell."

He had no idea.

"Take da chair he give you."

"You mean Moses? Old Cabell Hall?"

She turned to him, remembering something. "Be girl fo' you too, boy. An' da moon. Lotta dem." Feeling a chill, she drew the opening of her sweater together. "Be Black in dis world, man, remember dat."

The catbird flew away.

"Most time, alls dey can see. Like rope round yo' heart."

He thought about the places he'd run to, people who'd taken him.

They never talked about the color of his skin, but he felt it all the same.

"Gots to hold dat book an' change da world. Trouble yo' sef, you understan'? Ain't nobody do it fo' you."

"Do the best I can."

"Ain't 'nough, 'best you can.' Silly talk."

Willie looked away. Whatever he thought he was there for was turning into something else.

"Got a brain, man." She watched him as she spoke, seeing colors over his head. "Black brain."

"Yes, ma'am."

"Some folk ain't mo den da wolf."

He remembered how it hurt when Matt Abel called Moses a nigger.

"Came down dat river for da reason. Gots to make it right, chile."

"Yes, ma'am."

"Nothin' stop you…"

He waited for her to finish.

"When you know."

He looked at her carefully. "Know what, Mo?"

Dusting off her sweater with the tops of her hands, she turned to him one last time. "Time ta go."

He reached for the glove compartment, taking out an envelope marked "SISTER MO," offering it to her.

She stared at it in his hand.

"Thank you for everything you done. For me and for Stick."

18

"Ain't 'bout dat."

"Just a small thing."

"Got no use for da small where I go."

"Thought it might help," he replied, disappointed by her reaction. "Before you get there."

She smelled of sweat and kerosene. They sat together in silence.

"You want me to go?"

"Get me to ma tree, please."

"Let me stay with you a while, Mo. Make you a pone or somethin'."

"Naw, be fine," she answered softly. "Goin' nowhere I ain't bin. "

"Keep you company."

Sunlight flickered across her lap. She felt the color of her blood change. It wouldn't be long now. That surprised her—the speed of it. "Come in dis world, go out jes' da same."

The bottle tree rustled in the distance.

"Git me to ma tree."

Closing the door, he walked with her, cradling the elbow of her arm lightly in his open hand. She seemed smaller than when he arrived, more fragile. Reaching the trunk of the tree, he let go, stepping back slightly in case she slipped or fell.

She stopped for a moment to catch her breath, resting one hand against the bark, gazing up as best she could, her face flushed with admiration. "Big ole tree, 'n' li'l ole Mo," she marveled, mystified by its size. "Wid me all ma days, ole friend. Hep dem foke… all dem chil'ren… like dey belong." Watching the clouds, her head began to spin. She lowered herself carefully to the ground, landing gently in a puff of dust. "To da place I be," she mumbled, reaching out for his hand.

Willie dropped down beside her.

They stared out together from under the tree, holding hands. The sky was pink.

"You ready, boy?" she asked after a while.

"Yes, ma'am."

The old woman smiled, hearing the calm inside him. The grace.

"Got da shirt. Got da money. Got da house."

"Yes, ma'am."

She closed her eyes. "Go fine yo' Stick."


Sister Mo's neighbor found someone to watch her. They offered him cookies and milk before he left, told him not to worry, that she'd done this before. He gave them the envelope of money. It was hard to imagine living so long and wanting so little. Being free of it all.

Outside Goshen, he pulled over at the Maury to measure their time together. The Black witch, Sister Mo. She'd been more stranger than friend, but there was something else, something deeper. Like Moses and Stick. People who felt as if they'd always been a part of you.

Watching the currents pass, undulating blankets of dark frigid water, he understood the elements of his life more clearly now. Water. Rocks. Mountains. Death. Maybe that's how it worked if you lived long enough. Stood by a river. Listened to where it came from.

The hallway floor was wet. He'd check the roof for leaks, change the locks. Hitting a light switch, he called out, noticing the back screen door ajar. The night was temperate and still. Mr. Matt slept quietly under a blanket in his momma's rocker. The one she used when the shot kicked in.

The porch had fallen into disrepair since he'd left, a lifetime ago it seemed. Fractured ceiling fans, missing floorboards, broken balustrades. He stood there awhile sensing the chaos, the wild neglect. His childhood was played out, the brothel and its ladies of the night. Approaching the rail, he stared out into the darkness, thinking of Stick, where to start, too tired to unravel what Sister Mo had meant.

The window of her room was open, the bed felt warm and agreeable. As sleep set in, tree frogs trilled softly over the empty yard next door, conflating both past and present in his mind. He would patch the roof and fix the walls, the plumbing, the paint, the mortar. He'd shore the porch, secure the floors, and glaze each broken window. He would do this for himself and in memory of his mother, Sadie Graves of Happy Jack, Louisiana. A quiet house, mended and sane, on the streets of the place he was from.

A train passed slowly in the distance. Then tree frogs, more loudly this time, purposeful and insistent. "Here! Here!" he heard their swelling chorus, from the crown of the great catalpa.

# CHAPTER TWO

She'd kept a journal buried in the cellar behind the chimney. Mr. Matt read their names out loud:

"CARLA SALO

PEACHIE PRICE

FARCY GROVER

EVE GRAY

FRANCISCA MACEDO

ALINE MACEDO

BRIGITTE ROSE

LUNA JOHNSON

ANNIKA SMITH

NICHELLE SWEET

TALISA BROWN

SALLY NYE

SPRIGOT GIRL"

Willie remembered some of them, Carla Salo in particular, pushing the porch swing with her long pretty legs, silky red hair. They were exotic creatures in the house next door, making ends meet. When he asked his momma, she kept the answers deep inside. Like a secret. Or an ancient mystery. He watched them when he could, covertly, climbing his tree, peering down between the branches, trying not to fall.

"You remember them, Willie? Kinda young at the time, I suppose. Maybe Salo? Used to babysit when Sadie was..." He stopped to consider how best to put it.

"Wasted?"

The old man closed the book. "Outta sorts."

While the roofers banged overhead, Willie and Mr. Matt stood beside the kitchen table examining the contents of a dented metal box.

"I'm looking for something else. Here, take this," the old man instructed, offering a dark slender book, pulling more contents from the box.

Willie noted its frayed corners before opening it. "What you lookin' for, Mr. Matt?"

"Thinking she put it here with the rest of it. Help us do this thing right."

"What thing?"

His face lit up, seizing a brown paper envelope. "Eureka!"

"What you got, Mr. Matt?"

The old man grinned, checking the contents quickly to be sure, tossing the envelope on the table. "Bingo!"

Willie hesitated, not knowing who it was intended for.

"Well, take a look!" he barked impatiently, sitting down to rest. "Keys to the Kingdom, my boy. Money in the bank!"

Willie picked up the envelope and opened it.

"But on the down low, you hear me?" he cautioned in a lower voice, pointing toward the roof.

"Yes, sir," Willie replied quietly, extracting the papers.

"Case you need it later."

It was a list of names with corresponding dates. They were in his momma's handwriting. "My momma write these down?"

"For twenty years."

Willie looked up for a second, not fully understanding, then back to the list. "Sheriff Joe Hall?"

"Yes, sir."

"Mayor Tibbs?"

"And Judge Preston, see that?"

Willie found "Thomas T. Preston" with several dates to the right. "He some kinda judge?"

Mr. Matt grinned when he heard the question. "Senior Judge, United States District Court, Western District of Virginia. Drank tea and fucked his brains out!"

"A judge?"

"And Jumpin' Joe Smith, see him?"

"The basketball guy?" Willie asked, incredulous, searching for the name.

"Next page." He enjoyed the boy's expression when he found it. "Big head, small hose, what your momma said. Go figure."

"Got a Bishop 'somethin' here. Can't read it very well."

"John Houston."

Willie's expression froze. "Like a real bishop?"

"'Cept the robes."

"How's that work?"

Matt Abel folded his hands, resting them on the table. People weren't what they pretended to be and Sadies's list could prove it. "What you mean?" he asked, toying with the boy.

Willie shook his head in disbelief. "I mean..." he stopped.

"Last page."

Willie flipped to the final page. "What the heck?!"

"Yep. Only once, but still." He let it sink in before continuing, "With Hardley Grove the attorney general."

"University president?"

"Came to thank your momma for her scholarship money. Until the fun started."

Willie looked up, dumbfounded. "What kinda money?"

"For students. Help 'em with tuition. Goin' on twenty years before she died." He watched Willie closely, measuring his reaction.

"Didn't know."

"Your momma was a good woman, Willie. Pretty and wild, but kind sometimes."

Willie looked like he'd seen a ghost. His heart beat faster.

"Not what you think, I know. You got the other side, mostly. When she was hurtin' and feel'n low."

The roofers were quiet.

The old man stopped, relieved to be telling him. "If you were down on your luck, or needed help, or money, or sex, or booze."

"Hard to believe what you're telling me, Mr. Matt," he interrupted.

"I know."

"Knocked me around sometimes."

"I know, son. Your daddy too. Quite the asshole."

"What's the *kind* side a that?" Willie asked, his eyes swelling with despair.

"No good from it, I understand."

"When *I* was hurtin'?" he managed, fighting tears.

It was hard to imagine what he'd been through, being so young. "When you needed a momma."

"Fuck it, Mr. Matt," he snapped, collapsing into a chair. "All I wanted was *her*."


One by one, the roofers descended their ladders for lunch.

Neither spoke for a while.

"Sadie was difficult, Willie."

"You think?"

"Flawed."

"We all got somethin', Mr. Matt, I know that. But she was mean about it sometimes, like whatever it was was *my* fault." He tossed the papers on the table. "Like it was *me* that put her there."

"She loved you most of all."

"Yeah, well... had a *funny* way a showing it. And my father?"

"He was a carny, Willie."

"Don't matter what he was. Matters how he done it."

"She tried to help him."

"Bullshit."

"No, sir."

"Can't save nobody till you save yourself." Willie looked the old man in the eye. "Stick taught me that."

"That right?"

"'Cuz, it ain't no movie show."

The old man smiled, thinking of it. "Suppose you're right."

He looked down at the list. He wasn't stupid. He understood what good the names would be. "I need to find him."

Matt Abel looked puzzled.

"Stick."

"Oh yeah. Your buddy Stick."

"Gonna use my momma's money to fix this place up, Mr. Matt."

The old man slammed his hands down on the table. "*There* you go!" he barked triumphantly. "Make it shine, boy... goddammit!" He placed his hand over his heart, realizing it. "Sadie be so proud a you, the way you hold your head and think so straight, look a fella in the eye. Little young, I understand that, but Jesus Christ, Willie, it's pretty much in your blood, son… and I can help you some, we *all* can, and… I mean, aside from the money you'd make…" He dropped his hand into his lap. "What kinda spanky-tank town would this be without a proper whorehouse?"

"Then sell it."

Matt Abel froze in his chair.

Willie gave him a moment. "I need to find Stick. Go to college like we always talked about. Make somethin' of myself." He heard the roofers moving across the porch.

The old man leaned back in his chair. His breath was weak. The room was blurry. Maybe the boy was right. The university needed houses and the market was hot. 1956 was different that way. Quick news and fast women. "I got you," he replied, sounding deflated. "Need to find your Baby Doll."

Willie listened without understanding.

"Carol Baker."

"No idea, sir."

"Make a man crazy."

He tried not to smile. "She some kinda actress?"

"Sexy little thing. Them Catholics banned her movie!"

"Really?"

"Turned me inside out, that one."

29

A shaft of sunlight angled through an open window onto the linoleum floor below. Willie collected the papers, sliding them back into the envelope.

The old man's voice grew faint. "Like she was a part a me. Like we *had* something, you know? 'Cept, of course…" He looked down, embarrassed to have said it. "Just a silly-ass movie."

Willie thought about Stick and how much he'd loved his Crystal Ann. About Hilda Scarborough on the gas dock pulling in to Tangier Island. And Dolly. How certain women made things bigger.

"Like your momma's house," he added wistfully, noticing the light suddenly. "Bit a magic while it lasted, what it was. Dangerous and fun. Got the names right there to prove it." He pointed to the envelope. "Goes in a bank box, Willie."

"I will. First thing tomorrow."

"Use it when you need to. Very important."

"Yes, sir."

It would take the boy a while to figure out. What he had and what he could do with it. "You never know, son."

Willie placed the envelope in the metal box and closed the lid.

They stared at the box.

"How it all shakes-out."

He took the box and headed toward the hallway door, waiting for the old man to follow. It was two o'clock. He'd leave him at his rocker and drive to meet with Professor Lilly at Old Cabell Hall, then grab some groceries for dinner. "Come on, Mr. Matt. Take you to the porch."

Rising shakily to his feet, he pushed the chair back, finding his balance. The ancient reckoning was upon him. It made him sad sometimes, hearing children play, watching the evening sky fade. Willie's life had caught a spark—lightning in a bottle. The house would be part of it--hell, maybe even the Buick. Moving toward the door, he felt it everywhere, the slanting sunlight, a new roof. Wherever Sadie was, she'd be happy to see it all. Moses Henry too. Sipping their tea on a back porch swing in a world that was their own.

Willie felt uneasy walking The Lawn, lingering under an ancient linden. He wondered if Moses, poorly dressed, the former slave, had felt this way-- at a distance always, in the shadows. Sister Mo had rattled his heart about the color of his skin. Was this such a moment? Such a place? His momma said the students were decent, spoiled perhaps, but generally reasonable and occasionally even kind. She spoke rarely about the other things—the dark asides, the blinding Whiteness. For a young mulatto, an education at The University was nearly impossible, a kind of mutiny. Such was the power of the chair that Moses had left him—the possibilities.

Old Cabell Hall was larger than Willie expected, with six colossal columns out front. Moving closer, he could barely make it out in the dwindling light:

"Ye shall know the truth, and the truth will make you free."

John Clayton Lilly, a former provost of The University, waited patiently at the top of the steps. Moses had spoken often of him. "Different den da rest," he explained one morning, looking down from his bell tower, seeing him passing below. "Kine to me. Kep' ma chair where it be. Let me sit."

"You must be Willie," the man observed softly, extending his hand. He was gentle looking, in his mid-seventies.

"Yes, sir," Willie answered, blood rushing to his ears. It had taken some courage to get there, find the gumption to call. "Brought my letter with me." His voice shook a little. "Case you need it for somethin'."

The professor smiled as their hands met, seeing him for the first time. He was a fine-looking young man with pleasing, inquisitive eyes. "Delighted to meet you," he replied calmly. "Good of you to bring it, but I've spoken to the school and"—his eyes twinkled as he released his hand—"if we don't scare you off, the chair is yours, sir."

Willie was word struck.

"For as long as you like."

When the tower rang, they turned in the direction of The Rotunda, listening to six clangs, each languishing purposely, each one its own call, before fading away.

Professor Lilly admired the sky, steeped in a slight green cyan.

"How about that, Willie?" he marveled.

As Willie looked up, his apprehension faded. Whatever had come before was over now. Whatever remained would be his future. The town. His chair. The sky. "It's real pretty, sir."

The second-tier back corner of Old Cabell Hall was the  perfect spot.

"In and out," the professor explained, nodding in the direction of an adjacent staircase door. "Whenever you wish," he added, handing him a brochure. "After graduation there's a summer session, well attended, more relaxed. You see something you like, just pop in. That's what your friend Moses did. Between his hourly appointment at the chapel. He was a curious fellow—very eager to learn." He gazed out over the empty seats. "That cannot always be said of our students."

Willie looked down toward the lecture podium, imagining the hall bustling with students. "My goodness," he marvelled. "I feel like a bird up here."

The professor smiled and looked around. "Remarkable acoustics. They replaced the annex when it burned. Our very own phoenix!"

Willie thought of his own fire.

A door slammed somewhere, distracting them briefly.

"My daddy died in a fire. Suppose you know that."

Professor Lilly turned to him, thinking how best to respond.

"Accused me of doin' it," he added mechanically.

"Yes, I..." He stopped, remembering how the town had buzzed

with rumors.

Willie moved closer to the railing, admiring The Grounds. "I'd like to be a student here someday, sir."

The professor gave him time.

"Not sure how to put it." He looked up into a skylight imbued with a lustrous light. "Moses tell you 'bout my momma?"

"He did."

"'Bout her business?"

"Yes."

"Been there?"

"I have not."

"Know where it is?"

"I do."

Willie stared into the light. It surprised him a professor would know about The Bottom. Until he remembered the list. He wasn't sure why he'd spoken so openly about his life, about his momma in particular.

"In my experience, people have very selective memories, Willie." He watched the boy thoughtfully before continuing, "They rewrite their own history."

"Like a story."

"From a particular point of view, yes." What Moses had told him was true. The boy could think critically.

"You think they believe what they want, pretty much?"

John Lilly elicited his habitual, thoughtful sigh. "I believe even in the face of concrete recorded facts, many people rewrite their own stories... and everyone else's as well. "

Willie thought about it. It rang true. "As best they can, I guess."

An entrance door below flew open.

"Yes," he agreed, taking a pocket watch from his waistcoat, checking the time. "I've enjoyed this very much, but regrettably," he smiled warmly at Willie, "duty calls."

Two faces looked up suspiciously at Willie from below, but then seeing the professor, quickly disappeared.

Watching them, John Lilly frowned and gestured toward the door. "Shall we take the stairs?"


When they said goodbye, Willie lingered, watching students as they climbed the steps, thinking of his empty chair, the still, almost holy sound of the place. That surprised him-- the comfort of it... the peace. Looking around, he took a moment to see it all. The Grounds. A cosmos of gables, trees, and light. In spite of everything, beyond his own history, hard luck, or race, improbably, it had come to pass. What Moses had wanted most. A gifted seat in the human world—his quiet place for learning.


Driving home, he stopped at Inge's, parking carefully beside a delivery truck. Entering the store, a cashier looked him over suspiciously, taking note of his car through the window, wondering how a young mulatto could afford such a vehicle—a big-ass Buick, no less. Willie looked the other way, sensing it, disappearing quickly down an aisle. Hearing whispers in the distance, he grabbed a loaf of Wonder Bread, then trout.

As he moved closer to the register, the store grew quiet. It was still a small town, petty and judgy in a small-town way. He'd forgotten that part. How they worshipped the rumors, the gossip, the tales. Writing a better story.

# CHAPTER THREE

The roofers were gone and the house was still. He'd fix a meal and take a bath in his momma's tub. He'd been putting it off since he'd arrived. Life was for the living, Sister Mo had said.

Mr. Matt was in his rocker as the kitchen filled with smoke. The trout was fresh, with shiny clear eyes. Standing over the frying pan, he thought about his Tangier shad flopping in the cooler, his friend Auggie's sunlit face.

He lowered the flames and cracked a window. It had been a week. He'd call Sheriff Hall in the morning to see if he had any leads, then a real estate office. The fish was done and golden brown. It didn't matter where he ended up, or what it took to get there. What mattered most was finding Stick.

A bottle of Jack was left by the sink. When he called Mr. Matt, the rocker didn't move. Maybe he was drunk, passed out, chasing rabbits. He put the plates down and went to see. It would be dark soon and time to walk him out again. He enjoyed those moments, their evening sit, where time stood still.

"Got your dinner, Mr. Matt," he announced, appearing at the porch door. The glass had fallen from his hand and his mouth was open. Drawing closer, Willie stopped.

A car passed down the alley.

"Mr. Matt?" he repeated, more softly this time, touching his shoulder.

Matt Abel's body rolled past him in the hallway before stopping at the door.

"The sheriff is on his way, Willie," an ambulance attendant said, handing him a business card. "We'll take him to J. F. Bell and they will give you a call when they're done."

Willie took the card. "Thank you."

"I'm very sorry for your loss," he said, extending his hand sympathetically.

Willie took it, not knowing what to say. His grip was soft and small.

"Cary Buck."

"Thank you, sir."

"Cary."

Their hands fell away.

"If you require something, just call me," he replied obliquely.

He had thin, silver hair.

"Thank you, sir."

Cary Buck's face grew stern.

"I mean, Cary."

"There you go!" he said, joining his assistant at the door. Turning back, he admired the staircase. "I was here with my daddy once."

Matt Abel's feet poked up from under the sheet.

"Stepdaddy, I should say."

Willie tried his best to concentrate.

Seeing his discomfort, he placed a hand lightly on the gurney. "It has been quite a night for you, I am sure, and the last thing you need to be doing right now is going down memory lane with me so... we will be in touch and, as I have said, if you need *anything* you have my card."

He read the card.

CARY BUCK

Interior Decorator

Glencourt 4-3444

"Oh." He realized, understanding it.

Cary Buck looked around. The curtains needed help and the floors were spent, but the place had promise. "You're the young man who grew up next door."

Willie looked up, embarrassed.

"There is nothing to be ashamed of, honey. I'm sure you had your days like all of us, but… for heaven's sake, Sadie Graves was the cat's meow and this town owes her plenty." He paused. "Stem-to-stern, if you know what I mean?"

Willie liked the way he talked.

"And if you don't know *that*… you are not *from* here!"

A police cruiser pulled up behind the ambulance.

Whatever Cary Buck was after, it wasn't his money.

He shot him a sweet smile. "Let it *shine,* baby!" he declared with a wink, pushing Matt Abel out the door.



Willie stood in the hallway, thinking of death. How it touches everything—the walls, the floorboards, the silence. Mr. Matt had been his friend for as long as he could remember. His house. His porch. His apples.

David Sheffield appeared at the front door and looked in. "That you in there, Willie?"

Willie moved closer to the door. "Sheriff Sheffield."

He removed his hat and stepped inside. "Came as soon as I heard."

He looked thinner, older than Willie remembered. He wasn't sure why he was there. "Yes, sir."

"Lot goin' on for you these days, I know. Very sorry about Matt."

"Yes, sir."

"Had the heart thing."

Willie found a nearby chair and sat.

"Good guy."

He felt tired suddenly. "You wanna sit, Sheriff?"

"No, I'm good, thank you, son." He noticed the parlor in the distance. It had seen better days. "Just checkin' to see if you're okay."

Willie rested his elbows on his knees and dropped his head.

"Anything I can do?"

He remembered his open mouth. The stillness around him. "Thought he was asleep."

An early evening breeze moved through the hallway.

"Called him a couple times for dinner," his voice trailed off, "but he was dead."

"Nothin' to be done, son."

"I know."

"Lived a long time. Was a good friend."

Willie wanted to cry.

"What can I do for you, Willie?"

It surprised him how he felt. So broken inside.

"Call somebody? Be with you a while?"

Gathering his strength, he rose to his feet. The last thing he needed was company. "No, sir, I'm good."

Sheriff Sheffield watched him carefully, closing the door behind him. "Let me close the door."

He'd forgotten about dinner.

"Take a couple days to figure out what happened."

"What you mean?"

"Cause of death."

Willie's expression changed. "Died a being old."

"Yes, he did."

"All it is."

"I know."

"There a law against that?"

The sheriff smiled. "Just doin' what they do, Willie. Nothin' to it." He snuck a look toward the upstairs landing, remembering a girl. "Doesn't seem right you being here all by yourself though," he added, remembering why he was there. "Before I forget, nothin' on my end about your buddy."

Willie's face perked up. "Stick?"

"The Watson fella. Doesn't mean a whole lot. Just what we got at the moment."

"Nothin' in Richmond?"

"No, sir."

"Sheriff Hall?"

"Called him before I came, thinkin' you'd want to know. He may have moved on somewhere."

Stick's shirt was in a drawer. He felt the weight of everything all at once.

"Hopefully." He watched the boy, sensing his mood. "Can I ask you something?"

Willie snapped out of it. "Sure."

"You know how people talk."

"Yes, sir."

"Make stuff up." He fiddled with the rim of his hat, working out how best to put it.

"What you want to ask me?"

"You got plans for this place?"

The smell of fish reminded him of Hilda. Rowing home under the stars. In the end, maybe that's what it was, what remained of a life. A scent, a boat, a constellation.

The sheriff leaned back on his heels. The boy would be tricky, but the calls were coming in with increasing regularity. Money was in the cellar. Names were on a list. He'd put them off for as long as he could. It was time to get down to it. "What are we doin' here, son?"

The house had grown dark and the room was cold. He'd fry some okra and boil the rice, pull some chives from beside the walk. His appetite was gone. He thought about his momma. How hard it must have been being who she was: female, pretty, Black. Whatever he decided, there was one thing he could count on. It was his house now and it wouldn't go cheap. "You like some trout?"

When the booze kicked in, the sheriff got familiar. "You still readin' books?"

Willie poured the pot of rice into a colander in the sink. "I'll get back to it. Like to be a student someday."

The sheriff's face lit up. "Atta boy!"

The table was still set for Matt Abel.

"Make your momma proud!"

Approaching the oven, Willie fiddled with a dial. Yellow flames surrounded the pan suddenly. He turned it off. "Need to fix this thing." He peered through the oven window. "Blow myself up."

The sheriff took a hit of Jack. "Well, that ain't good. Want me to take a look?"

Taking two pot holders, he opened the door cautiously and pulled the trout out.

"Look at you, boy!" the sheriff marveled. "Cookin'! Readin'! Where you learn all a this?"

He returned to the sink for the rice. "All a what?"

The sheriff sat back in his chair, admiring the boy, finishing his glass.

"How old are you now, Willie?"

"Be eighteen in November," he answered, chopping the chives on a small block of wood.

"And where you plan to be a student?"

"Virginia."

"The University?"

Willie heard it in his voice.

"What the hell!" he said, more enthusiastically. "Shoot for the moon, son!"

He dropped some butter into the rice and added the chives. "You think I'm nuts?"

"Nuts?"

He found a wooden spoon and stirred. "Only got four of 'em."

"Four a what?"

The chives disappeared quickly into the bowl, swallowed up by puddles of soft melting butter. He wasn't surprised by the question anymore. "Negroes."

"Well…" the sheriff replied slowly, thinking on it.

"You like chives on your rice?"

"Whatever you got works for me, man. Appreciate it."

The room was quiet.

David Sheffield stared at his empty glass. "Know some people… if that helps."

Willie rested the spoon over the rice and retrieved the pan of okra. "Like another shot?"

"Just an inch if you got it. Thank you."

Willie placed the okra by the sink and returned to the table, filling his glass.

"Woah, careful now!" he protested, raising a hand. "Gotta watch my p's 'n' q's."

Willie put the bottle on the table and stepped back. "How much you figure it costs?"

"University?"

"Yeah."

He stared at his glass for a moment, picking it up. "I don't know…"

"Just the classes."

He took a measured sip and put the glass down.

"Be livin' here, I imagine."

The sheriff pretended not to hear him. "Just the classes?"

He was stalling. It had something to do with the house.

"Be a guess, but maybe… eight?"

"Hundred?"

"What I'm hearin'."

Willie returned slowly to the sink and prepared their plates. He couldn't imagine where the money would come from.

"Smells good." The sheriff took another sip. "You got ladders outside."

"Fixin' the roof."

"What I thought. Little early, but good to get a jump on it."

"Was leakin' real bad."

"Get more for the place when the time comes."

Willie filled the sheriff's plate.

"Not too much for me, son," he cautioned, watching him more carefully. "Belt's getting tight."

Willie put his spoon down, understanding, for the first time, why he was there.


A dog barked down the street. They ate in silence for a while.

"Sorry you missed the bell man's funeral."

Willie couldn't eat.

The sheriff put his fork down. "Biggest thing I ever saw. Out the door and down the sidewalk like…" He hesitated.

"Like he was one of 'em."

He looked at Willie, understanding it for the first time.

"Never missed a beat."

"You were up there with him sometimes."

"I was."

He stopped, remembering what she'd said—about their time together. "You were good for each other."

Willie stared at his uneaten trout.

"He left you an envelope."

Willie looked up, surprised to hear it.

"What your momma said. And how he cared for you."

He looked away. He was still raw, still running. "Yes, he did."

The sheriff waited, remembering everything he'd been through.

"I just…"

"Miss your momma."

His tears began quickly. He didn't care what the town thought of him. Her list was in the bank.

"Need to watch your back, Willie," the sheriff warned, pushing his chair back, stretching his legs.

He wiped his eyes with the sleeve of his shirt. "What you mean?"

"You got things people want and they'll do what it takes to get it."

"Things like what?"

"Things she wrote down."

He looked around the kitchen. The window was still open.

"They're sayin' you got names."

"Who's sayin'?"

"People."

"You mean, *certain* people."

"Yes."

"On the list."

The sheriff touched his holster strap to see that it was closed. "Now don't take this the wrong way. Everybody loved ole Matt, but he had a big mouth, God rest his soul."

They stared at each other.

"Your momma flew with some big boys, son."

"I put it in the bank."

The sheriff cocked his head. "I'm sorry?"

"The money. Her list."

"When you do that?"

Willie rose to his feet, taking the bottle, storing it under the sink. Turning around to face him, he leaned back against the counter and smiled. "Gotta be twice as good to get half as far."

"Who told you that?"

"Moses."

The sheriff nodded reluctantly.

It came to him suddenly, easily. "I'm gonna turn this place around so I can get what I need to go to school and make somethin' of myself. *Better* things, like my momma would have wanted. And Mr. Matt." He thought about Stick, the way he handled people when they got in his way. How it fired him up. Made him stronger. "They have a *problem* with that, or they don't *like* what I'm doin', or *how* I'm doin' it… doin' it just the same."

The sheriff took a moment. He needed the list.

"One room at a time."

He waited for him to finish before he smiled. "Eighteen years old."

"Seventeen."

"And no fuckin' clue."

Blood was surging through his head, his whole body. In the morning he'd call a lawyer. Then Cary Buck.

"Well, then…" He stood up slowly from the chair and put his hat on. His momma was right. He had some balls, this one. And brains to go with it. "Nothin' more to say, I guess."

"No, sir, there ain't."

He considered the boy one last time. His determination. The innocence. "Got yourself a plan."

Willie pushed off from the counter, standing upright. The kitchen faucet was dripping. He'd pour himself a glass. Close the window. "Thanks for stoppin' by."

Outside the front door, David Sheffield turned around to say good night. They wouldn't understand, but he'd figure it out. Buy himself some time. After forty years he'd seen it all. But this was different. Being squeezed by a kid.

"Word of advice, Willie."

"Sir?

His nose flushed with pink from under the brim of his hat. He took the boy in one last time. "Need to fix that oven."


When the dishes were done, Willie drank some Jack, and drew himself a bath. Closing his eyes, he let go finally, suspended in warm, delicious water. Floating there, an eerie light passed through her tattered curtains. Sill by sill, room by room, floorboards, mirrors, stairs. A moon of some kind, a quiet epiphany, on the streets of a small Southern town.

# CHAPTER FOUR

Cary Buck was an hour late. "Oh, liquor be the thief of time," he recited dramatically, out of breath, entering swiftly, casting his eyes everywhere. He smelled of sherry. His head swiveled about, identifying rooms quickly. "I had a cousin once, with *something* like this…" he paused, captivated by the parlor, "…but, *Honey,*" he touched his chest delicately with his fingertips, "*that* was Staunton!"

Willie shut the door. He'd never been to Staunton.

"*Show* me," he said eagerly, removing a light blue jacket, tossing it on a nearby chair. "*Absolutely everything!*"

He was funny, with skin as pale as porcelain. "Don't really know what I'm doin'. Where you wanna start?"

Cary Buck turned, mortified. "Doin', gimme, lemme, gonna! In *English* please," he pleaded, "as befits a young businessman."

They looked at each other, as if from different worlds.

Cary Buck collected himself. "If you expect to change this rather *ordinary* house into something *extraordinary...* then, strange as it may *sound...* it *begins* with *language.*"

Willie was lost. "Language?"

"How we *speak.*"

He waited.

"*Communicate.*" He gestured to the chair. "This *chair,* these *words,* create *style,* dear boy. Do you *understand* me?"

"I'm trying to, yes."

"*Color. Intention. Enterprise,*" he recited intently. "In *all* that we do."

Something was making sense but he had no idea what it was.

He watched Willie carefully. "Where we *sit. How* we sit. What we *say.* How we *say* it."

"Imagination?"

Cary Buck's face beamed. "*Anticipation!*" he crowed, placing his hands together as if in prayer. "The *drama* we create. The *scene!*"

Willie waited, watching him carefully.

He closed his eyes. "What do you see?"

He had no idea. The kitchen sink was dripping.

"Tell me."

"Tell you what I see?"

"Yes. Close your eyes."

He closed his eyes. The drip got louder. "Don't see nothin'."

Cary moaned as if in pain. "Darling, you don't see *anything.*"

OK, sorry. *Anything.*" He opened his eyes and looked around.

"Not really."

"I'm trying to make a point, if you would allow me. Close your eyes… and *imagine* the house."

Willie did as he was told.

"What it might *become*."

When his mind eventually quieted, he saw the chair, upholstered this time, in a golden-red fabric. That surprised him. The jacket was gone, replaced by a splendid silver evening coat with black satin lapels. He opened his eyes.

Cary Buck had left the room.


He found him stretched out under the kitchen sink holding a massive wrench. He slid out carefully, bouncing to his feet. His Keds were pink.

"I've been meaning to do that. Thank you."

"You are quite welcome."

"Since you're here, would you mind looking at the stove?"

"It's shit, William. Give it a toss."

"What do you mean?"

"Parts can be found, of course, but…" He stepped toward the oven to take a closer look. "O'Keefe & Merritt, late forties, no fan, steam function, temperature gauge… just a sassy ole bitch with some broken-down parts." He turned to Willie and sighed. "You can do better."

Willie was speechless.

Cary placed the wrench back under the sink where he'd found it and took a pack of Chesterfields from his shirt pocket. "Want one?"

"No, thanks. How come you know so much about ovens?"

Tapping out a solitary cigarette, he stopped to consider the boy. His clothes. The posture. Hair. "Not my first visit, darling, remember?"

"I thought…"

"We *delivered* it."

"The oven?"

"Yes."

"Oh."

"My family sells appliances. I was your age, I suppose. Your mother was very sweet."

Willie's face grew tender.

"Gorgeous, actually."

It was strange to hear.

Cary's face brightened, thinking of it. "We came through the back door. She gave me five dollars."

"Really?"

"And a Lorna Doone."

Willie shook his head, thinking of her cruelty.

Cary smiled mischievously. "It wasn't for a bonk, William. If that's what you were thinking."

He conjured his mother as best he could. How people could be one way to some and another to others.

Cary Buck's blue eyes sparkled behind the lighter as it fired up. The boy was pretty in a feral sort of way.

"My name's Willie, by the way, not William."

"Oh, don't mind me, honey," he answered softly, flipping the lighter shut, noticing the faded walls. "I like to stir things up." He took a deep, sensual drag of his cigarette, exhaling slowly. "Then knock it all down."


Their tour began in the cellar, moving slowly, deliberately through each room, up the central staircase, ending on the third and final floor. The house was a farrago of Federal, Colonial, and Jeffersonian styles, cornices, mantels, pine floors, porches, and windows. It was a hodgepodge of materials, but not without grace and charm.

Returning to the front hallway, Cary Buck was undone.

Willie laughed, seeing his reaction. "You want some Jack?"

"*Please.*"

As the kitchen filled with cigarette smoke, they drank.

"You're not selling?"

"No."

"And you've decided."

"Told the sheriff last night."

Cary's face flared with admiration. "Well, look at you!"

Willie blushed, feeling the Jack.

"Do you have girls?"

"No."

"Someone to run it?"

"No."

"Money to fix it up?"

"I got seven thousand dollars."

He winced hearing a past participle.

"*Have,*" Willie corrected quickly, refilling their glasses. "And the title."

"With a mortgage?"

"The bank said it's free and clear."

"Which bank?"

"First National. My mother knew the manager."

Cary took a quick sip. "I bet she did."

Willie did the same.

They looked around the kitchen.

"You think that's enough?"

"Is that enough of what?"

"Money."

Cary Buck stared into his glass, considering it.

Willie waited for an answer before he spoke. "I'd like to turn this place into something special if I can. And I'm not afraid. Of anything. Or anyone. Got a lady to call and she'll know what to do. How to do it."

Their eyes met.

"*Properly.*"

He smiled when he heard it.

"Bring some girls when she comes." It felt good to have him there. Someone to talk to. "You think I have enough?"

He shook his head. "It's *all* here, honey, don't you *see?*" He finished his glass, resting it on the table. "Paint the porch out front. Sand the floors. Replace some fabrics. Mattresses. Add a few lamps." His eyes sparkled as he pushed his glass forward for more. "Mirrors *everywhere.* You can *never* have too many mirrors."

Willie poured their final drink, slowly, carefully, considering it. "Seems like a lot. All the furniture. A new stove." Putting the bottle down, he closed the cap.

He reached out for the boy. "Give me your hands, William."

Willie resisted. It felt odd to be touched so gently by a man.

Cary Buck shot him a peevish grin, imagining it all. The possibilities. "As *God* as my witness!"

His head was spinning.

"We can do it for *five!*"

# CHAPTER FIVE

A warm evening rain washed over the house. He would miss Mr. Matt but it felt good to be alone finally, to imagine his new life. Nothing had been the same for as long as he could remember. Since the fire, perhaps. Running. Lost. Disappearing.

He carried the basket of keys up the stairs, testing the locks. They fit perfectly, each one. It was time to make the call.

He tacked the number to the wall, taking a shot, sitting for a moment, finding the courage, how to lay it out the right way. The receiver was heavy in his hand as he dialed, leaning back against the wall. Maybe she'd moved, or found a new calling, turned her life around. The men he'd seen her with looked rough. Dangerous. When would he ask? How would he put it? The final number spun and stopped. He heard a ring. Maybe she was dead?

"Hello?"

She sounded close.

"Hello?"

Pressing down with his finger the line went dead.

As the rain intensified, streaks of water trickled down the window above the sink.

He stared at the phone, took a deep extended breath, and lifted the receiver.

She answered on the fourth ring.

"It's me Willie, sorry." He waited. "Been meaning to call and say hi." He heard a chair move. "Wasn't sure that was you."

She lit a cigarette. "My little Willie?"

"Yes, ma'am."

"From The Spot?"

"Jimmy's place." He heard her take a drag. "Had that birthday dance."

"'Course we did, you sweet little thing. Been thinkin' you were long gone."

His heart raced with relief.

"Had to go."

She laughed. "Bet you did from what they say."

He wasn't sure what she meant. "What they say about what?"

"'Bout what you done."

His spirits sank.

They listened to each other.

"Was an accident. Never meant to do nothin'," he said, eventually.

"Said you killed your daddy in a fire."

Willie stared at her number on the wall. "Fire killed him, not me."

"Said you hit him with a candle."

"Yep."

"'Fore he hit you."

He found a chair and sat down. "Somethin' like that."

"Ran like a rabbit."

"Wet rabbit."

She grinned, not understanding entirely. "What you mean?"

He relaxed, hearing her voice, remembering how their bodies moved together with the music. "Fell into the Maury near Goshen."

"Poor thing."

"Shot through that sucker like a wet sponge."

"Lord have mercy."

"Stick Watson found me."

"Tall fella? Oscar's friend?"

"Yes, ma'am." He unscrewed the Jack and poured himself a drink. "Pushed the water out and took me down the road."

Hearing his glass, she poured herself some wine.

"Old lady saved me."

"Like it was meant to be."

"What you mean?"

She took a sip. "First saw you on that porch, thinkin', this boy's got some spark." She looked around for her dog. "Got a world inside him."

Willie took a short breath and let it fly. "You wanna move here and run my momma's house?"

Dolly withdrew the receiver momentarily from her ear, unclipping an earring. "What house you talkin' 'bout?"

"The one in Charlottesville. My momma's house... Sadie Graves. She left it to me."

She took a deep drink. "Your momma left you a working house?"

"Yes, ma'am."

"With all the ladies?"

"Well, no, not like that. I mean, not at the moment. They left when she passed, but I wanna fix it all up and bring 'em back. Get the place goin' again. Need someone to run it."

Dolly slid her shoes off, leaning farther back into the sofa.

"Got five thousand dollars to make it right and two to get you here. Cash."

She listened to him, lifting her legs up, shifting sideways against the pillows.

"Hello?"

"I'm listenin'."

He waited, hearing the fridge struggle. "Got the bank and a lawyer. Need six ladies and a bouncer. Someone to clean the placc. Give you half a what we make."

"Half?"

"Yes, ma'am. After expenses."

She wanted to laugh but took a sip instead.

"Everything I'm sayin' I heard growing up. How to keep 'em. When to let 'em go. And she left me a list."

"What kinda list?"

"Important people on it."

She lit another cigarette.

"Can use it if we need to."

She heard her dog scratch against the door. "How old are you?"

"Be eighteen in November."

"Couple months."

"Yes, ma'am."

"What day?"

The question threw him. "Thirtieth."

"November thirtieth."

"Yes, ma'am." He wasn't sure why she was asking.

She took her time, drawing thoughtfully from her cigarette. "Full Beaver Moon," she said eventually.

The fridge went silent and the line crackled. She was speaking in riddles. "What you mean by that?"


Halfway up the Lucky Bean tree, he found a dry spot, settling back against the trunk, looking down into an empty field of weeds. The rain had stopped and his shoes were wet. He felt further from the fire now, from the rubble of their lives. Maybe that was a good thing, in the end, the way it was supposed to be.

Looking out through the darkness, beyond the dripping trees, he saw it hanging in the distance, remembering her words. Stark and holy, extant and luminous. A waxing moon, diaphanous, in the alchemy of light.

# CHAPTER SIX

The Penn Central Crescent arrived in a grimy cloud of smoke, scattering pigeons, upsetting the gray October sky. Buttoning his jacket, Willie locked the car door, descending quickly down a rickety wooden staircase toward the Union Station platform. He'd been up since dawn, checking everything, putting flowers in their rooms, sitting on their beds. Downstairs in the front hallway, he went over it one last time: lights, booze, pimento cheese sandwiches. Cary Buck would serve them drinks. He'd show them 'round the house.

It felt odd to be standing there finally, after everything, watching the doors, anticipating the scene they'd make. Dolly and her four girls rolling down Main Street in a '52 Buick.

The first thing he noticed was their hats. A silver toque, a coral velvet turban, feathers, veils, and ostrich plumes. They appeared in a swirl of polka dots, brightly colored chiffon scarves, powdered cheeks, and stockinged legs. Exotic creatures descending carefully from the train, one by one, a spectacle to see. Willie stood, frozen, gawking like a schoolboy as a Black porter scrambled about frantically, locating a trolley, loading their luggage. Eventually, a crowd of men gathered around them, mesmerized by their outfits, scrutinizing their bodies more closely, furtively, enjoying their perfume.

As Willie approached, the women were surprised by his youth. Suddenly, a bitter gust of wind shot across the platform, scattering leaves and dispersing the crowd. Drawing nearer, inspecting them more closely, he stopped, confused. Something was wrong. He counted again. Four. How could it be? His heart sank. Dolly was missing.

Some looked away nervously, seeing his confusion.

"You must be Willie," one of them said, raising her veil, stepping forward.

Her eyes were captivating.

The woman smiled easily. "Dolly couldn't make it."

Willie was undone.

"I'm Josie." She extended a silk glove. "Josie Carr."

Taking her hand, he wanted to scream.

"Something came up."

Willie took his hand away. "Like what?"

"A legal matter."

The women became anxious.

"We had a deal."

"She told me."

"Well, then you *know*."

"I do," she answered, watching passengers board the train.

"She was supposed to run the place."

She glanced at the women before she explained it. "Dolly killed a man."

He froze, hearing it.

"I'll explain everything, but we should probably move along." She turned quickly to her group. "This is Carolyn."

A tall sultry woman with peach-blond hair took a timid step forward. "Hello, Willie."

He gave her a smile of some kind. "Ma'am."

The ladies laughed.

"I mean, Carolyn," he said quickly, hearing them.

"And Amber."

A handsome Black woman in a long red cape shot him a provocative smile, stepping closer. "Pleased to meet you, baby," she replied with a wink.

An Asian girl approached cautiously, handing him a single silk rose. "I'm Poppy," she explained softly. "I brought you this."

He took the flower, not knowing what to say.

"Truth be told, a guy on the train gave it to her," Josie Carr explained, interrupting.

Willie stared at the thing, then the girl. She was very pretty. "Thank you."

They stood for a moment, watching the train doors close.

Willie looked around, noticing the loaded trolley. Whatever Dolly had done, whatever treachery she'd been up to, it didn't matter anymore. He'd talk to Cary and figure it out. There was no turning back.

Releasing the brakes, the mighty Crescent let out a mournful cry. Willie watched them as they tipped the porter, admiring their beauty, the risk they'd taken. He remembered Stick's song about the rivers he loved, what you did with a life when you lived it. Like Josie, Carolyn, Amber, and Poppy, perhaps, leaving their worlds behind.

A raindrop touched his face. The air grew colder. They followed him as he led the way. Cradling the rose between his fingers, he pushed their trolley toward the stairs, hearing it in the distance. Fast trains to better things, to places of the heart.


To a New York hooker, Charlottesville was heaven on earth. Cruising up Water Street, sensing their good fortune, they rolled the windows down and screamed. It startled him at first, the emotion of it, their wild abandon. He focused on the road as best he could, each stop sign, ignoring the sidewalks and passing cars as people gaped, honked, or sped away. The roof and trunk were stacked with luggage. He wondered where they'd sleep, which key he'd give them, or, if they'd choose their own rooms. Josie would help, he imagined. He turned the radio on.

They wove their way toward Rugby Road, down Water Street and West Main. Passing The Rotunda, surrounded by a sea of students, he slowed the car to give them a better look.

"Mm-mm," Amber purred, lighting a thin, dark cigar, tossing her match out the window. "Won't you look at *all them boys!*"

They fancied the houses most of all, their tidy gardens and turning trees-- maple, sweet gum, bursting in the fading sun. At the final intersection, mountains appeared in the distance. That surprised them, the power of it. How a place so small could feel so big.

When he pulled up, they grew quiet, seeing the house through the windows for the first time. He turned the radio off and stopped the engine. Josie was the first to decide.

"Very nice."

He enjoyed them as they spilled out, retrieving their bags, admiring the wide front steps. Clearing the roof of luggage, he joined them at the curb, looking up as well, noticing the place.

"Cary Buck's inside. He did a real..." he stopped. "a *very* fine job with everything."

Amber rocked her head from side to side. "Made a sweet place, Willie."

"Thank you," he answered quietly, seeing the front door open. "That's Cary inside, so, run on up, he's dyin' to meet you."

She looked him over one last time. He was a handsome little thing. "Well, let's get a move on, baby!" she said, flashing her smile. "'Cuz, *Amber* needs a drink!"

A woman stood in her driveway across the street noticing the luggage, stray cats flying everywhere. He took a moment, admiring what he'd done, three floors glowing in the early evening light. He'd need to be careful, find some customers. *Discreetly*, in Cary's words. But he had a good feeling. A certain confidence suddenly. It was the girl's house now, in a town they'd come to know.

They liked Cary and Cary was smitten. On the second pour, Josie took Willie upstairs.

"You've done a nice job, Willie," she began, seeing the bags at the end of the hall.

"Didn't know where to put your things. Figured you'd tell me once you looked around."

She took a sip of gin, noticing a nearby bedroom door. "Let's sit in here, so we can talk."

Willie followed her. His Coca-Cola bottle was nearly empty.

Entering the room, she surveyed the wallpaper,  then curtains, bedspread, a separate bathroom.

"Cary did all this."

She turned and smiled, seeing his youth for the first time.

"My momma always said a place was made by where you start. I never understood what she meant. Until now."

The parlor below exploded in laughter. They smiled at each other, enjoying the sound.

Josie pointed toward the bathroom. "I'm going to step inside here, so why don't you get yourself another Coke, come back, and then we'll talk."

When he returned, she was on the bed, tucked up against the pillows with her boots off.

Willie perched on the edge of a chair and took a sip of his Coke.

When Cary raised his voice, the ladies laughed again.

"They seem to be having fun down there," she said, drawing her knees up, sitting sideways.

"He's tellin' stories."

She took a sip of her drink.

"Used to drive an ambulance, so…"

"Has some to tell, I would imagine."

"Yes, ma'am."

"Josie."

Willie noticed her beautiful long fingers. "Josie, sorry."

She finished her drink and put the glass down on a nightstand.

"Want me to get you another?"

"I'm fine, thank you."

"Got some sandwiches if you're hungry. Wasn't sure what to do about food. Thinkin' you'd want somethin'."

"Thank you, darlin', that's very kind."

Willie's face grew more serious. "Least I can do. Come all this way."

They looked around the room, buying some time, sensing one another.

He could see she was impressed. "I couldn't have done this without Cary."

"He's very sweet."

"Not sure what I'd do without him."

"And funny."

He thought about the night they met. Matt Abel's body rolling out the door. "Did everything. I just…" He stopped, realizing it again. "Gave him the money and he did what he promised."

Josie would need his full attention.

"Used the rest for Dolly…" he paused. "I mean, you." He watched her, hoping she'd explain it once and for all.

The house was quiet.

"I'm sorry about Dolly." Josie took him in, appreciating his situation. "Not what you expected, but here I am."

"It's okay."

"No, it's not. I'm sorry to surprise you like that."

They considered it together.

"Who'd she kill?"

Josie adjusted a silver bracelet around her wrist, twisting it around.

"Don't need to know, I guess. Just… hope she's okay."

"Her ex-husband."

It was hard to imagine.

"Owed her money."

His heart was pounding.

"Wasn't *that* so much…" She considered it again, "as the beatin's."

Willie stared at his bottle.

"My sister wanted this very much. To have something of her own. Like Sadie did." She stopped.

"She knew my momma?"

"No, but you know… your momma did well, so the word got out."

He noticed her eyes. They looked familiar. "I didn't realize."

"Not a lot of secrets in this line a work, honey. "

He took a deep breath. He'd waited long enough to ask. "Can you help me?"

She waited to answer him.

"Show me what to do?"

"Not the kind of world a young man needs to see. You know that."

"I do."

"Then why you doin' it?"

He'd been waiting to tell her, explain himself. "Wanna make some money. Go to The University someday."

"There're other ways to do it."

He smirked in disbelief. "For me?  Come on, Josie. The army, maybe."

She was taken aback by the way he put it.

"It's my best shot."

She shook her head, seeing his sweet face.

"My momma built somethin' special. It's all I know. What I was raised on."

She saw the hurt in his eyes. A certain sorrow.

Willie looked down. He'd never spoken of such things. Realized it so clearly.

When he looked up, finally, she could see that he'd decided.

"Like to show them what I got."

Josie took a moment, admiring the room again. The way he'd put it. "Not doing this like your momma."

He sat up.

"We'd have a modern house."

"Yes, ma'am."

"First class."

He smiled when she said it.

"Private club."

He didn't understand.

"Nothing comes back to us. To you, me... anyone who works here."

Willie liked whatever it meant.

"Keep it small, keep it smart. Heard your momma got sloppy."

"Charge more."

She laughed when he said it. "Twice the fun."

They laughed together.

She considered it further. "Money at the door to get in."

"How much?"

"Twenty dollars."

"What about liquor?"

"We're a private club. They bring it, we keep it."

Willie nodded.

"I need clean girls in a safe house. Guy at the door. Lawyer. Housekeeper. Cook. I keep the books."

The back porch door slammed downstairs.

"We split the take after expenses. Girls get five percent of mine."

"How come?"

"Show them I care."

Willie listened, trying to make sense of it.

"It's complicated, Willie."

"Yes, ma'am. See that now."

"Gotta have a plan. Stick to it."

He thought about the list.

"Only way it works."

"I understand."

"Vacation time. Not running a tired house."

"No, ma'am."

"Fresh linens every trick. Doctor twice a month."

He looked down.

"Nothing to be ashamed of. Look at me."

They took each other in.

"Doesn't matter what you call it, just a word. Way to say it." She stopped to give him time, relax into it. "I take care of people and they see it by the way I run things—that's why the girls came, why they'll stay." She took an easy breath. "There's nothing wrong about what we do, baby. What we call it."

Willie's spirits brightened.

"We bring pleasure to the world."

"What my momma said."

"She was right."

He missed her suddenly.

"One thing, though. My girls do drugs in this house and they're gone. Customers too. Out the door."

"Yes, ma'am."

"Josie."

"Josie." She looked tired. "Would you like another drink?"

She put her head back against the pillow. "Please."

Willie took her glass and hurried to the door, turning back. "Gin and tonic?"

She saw the sweetness in his face. "You have vodka?"

"Yes, ma'am."

"On the rocks, please."

He looked confused.

"Half vodka, half ice," she explained, watching him leave. "And, Willie?"

He turned back. "Yes, ma'am?"

"You're eighteen next month?"

"Couple weeks."

"Been with a woman?"

"No, ma'am."

She couldn't tell from his answer.

"Once almost."

"With Dolly?"

He was embarrassed. "I was a little drunk."

"At The Spot?"

He looked down. "Danced on my birthday."

She considered him carefully before she thought of it. Poppy was closer in age, with skin as smooth as silk. She'd light a candle and put some music on. Take it slow. "Look at me, baby."

He resisted for a moment.

She smiled softly before closing her eyes. "Let's see what we can do."

The bucket was empty. He hustled to the kitchen for ice. They were standing at the porch rail smoking, listening to Cary on his rocker. Filling the bucket, he removed the platter of sandwiches, taking some for Josie, stopping to listen. A cat... boyfriend... something about Omaha. He placed the platter on the kitchen table, knocking on the window to let them know. When they saw him, they froze, startled at first, exhaling gray-blue smoke into the cold evening air.

Josie's eyes were half-open.

"They're smokin' on the back porch." Handing her the drink, he put the sandwich plate on the nightstand. "Brought some sandwiches in case you're hungry. Pimento cheese."

Her eyes came to life. "Aren't you sweet. Haven't had one of these in a while."

"From Timberlakes." He watched her enjoy the drink. "That enough ice?"

She took a deeper sip. It was strong. "Perfect," she replied, patting the edge of the bed. "Come sit with me."

Willie stood still.

"Not gonna bite you," she said sweetly. "Come on."

He found a spot near the corner of the footboard.

"There you go." Her sister was right. He was kind and gentle. She put her drink down, lifting the plate to her lap. "Timberlakes?"

"Yes, ma'am. Counter at the back of the pharmacy in town. Been around forever."

She looked at her plate, noticing the bread. "Removed the crust."

"How they do it."

She lifted one to her mouth and took a bite. "Mmmmmmm."

"You can tell a place by the way they make 'em. What my momma said."

"They make you use the side door?"

"No, ma'am."

She was surprised to hear it.

"Depends on who you're with."

"Movie theaters?"

"At the Paramount," he answered, realizing it. "Gotta Third Street entrance for Coloreds."

Josie leaned back, lost in the cheese. "Are the girls behaving?"

"Yes, ma'am."

They looked around the room.

"Just the way it is."

"What is?"

"How they treat us sometimes."

He nodded. It made him sad to hear it.

She finished her sandwich. "I like Cary."

"Me too."

"Need to keep him if we can. Kind of thing that makes a place. Gives it character."

"He's real sweet."

She looked at him to see if he understood.

He looked down, embarrassed. "Well, not like *that,* I mean."

She grinned, seeing his innocence. "Just what we need, actually."

"How come?"

"Keeps it light. Easy."

He looked up, trying to imagine it. "Oh."

She handed him her plate.

"I'm okay."

"Been a long day, sweetie, come on."

"Thank you," he said, taking it, enjoying the last sandwich.

Finding her glass, she settled back against the headboard and watched him eat. Everything made sense now. The house. Willie. The town she was in. "I'm Dolly's younger sister."

Willie stopped chewing.

"I ran a house in Atlanta for a while."

Her skin was lighter than Dolly's.

"The cops came, so she offered me a room at her place. Was there when you called."

"Where you from?"

"Georgia. Little town called Bainbridge."

"Got family there?"

"Parents left us with a cousin when I was five. Gave us what he could."

"Just you and Dolly?"

She took a sip. "Till death do us part."

He thought about his own life. He'd never had a brother or a sister.

She stirred her drink with a finger. "Dirt poor, but we got by. Worked some."

"Doin' what?"

She licked the vodka off her fingers and gave him a wink. "Climbin' trees."

Willie thought he understood what she was saying.

"Wasn't so bad. Little rough sometimes, but we were lucky. Not like some." She paused to remember it. "The town kept German prisoners during the war. Nasty. Half-dead. Watched them sometimes at night when they moved 'em around." Her face grew melancholy. "Like cattle." She saw his empty plate. "Give me your plate."

He handed it back. "Sorry, I ate it all."

"Nothin' wrong with an appetite." She put the plate on the nightstand. "What my sister would say." She finished her glass and put it on the plate. "Her name's Georgette."

"You mean, Dolly?"

Rising from the bed, Josie left the room, returning quickly with a large square bag, laying it down beside the chair, opening it. She found a small envelope in a side pocket. "Here," she said, offering it to him.

He stepped off the bed and took it, not knowing what to do.

"They're pictures of my family," she explained, moving to the chair and sitting.

He perched on the edge of the bed. It surprised him at first, seeing her life that way.

"We all come from somewhere, honey."

He held up the photograph of a woman beside an automobile in a slinky red dress. She looked like Josie. "This your momma?"

"It is."

Her young face was round and pretty.

"Had me when she was fifteen."

They looked at one another.

After a few more, he found one and held it up. "This your tree?"

She smiled. "Yes."

It was twice the size of his catalpa and mossy like the Dismal Swamp.

She watched him, enjoying his reaction. "Made me feel good bein' up there."

It was bathed in the light of a nearby shack.

"Safe."

"I had one too."

"You did?"

"Wasn't so big. Felt the same when I was up there." It came to him when he said it. "That's what you want this place to be."

Georgette was right—he was different, the Juke Joint Boy. Wise beyond his years and clueless as a mouse. Things happened for a reason, she'd learned over time. There was a purpose to it all. Places that called you. A stack of faded photographs and oak trees in the night.

They heard voices on the stairs.

He gave her a funny look.

"What is it?"

He thought about Sister Mo and how she'd spin the world around until everything stopped, crashed together.

"Tell me."

Standing up, he moved closer, offering the envelope, seeing it more clearly in the light. "You got my momma's eyes."

When he came down, Cary Buck was on the front porch pacing about. When he saw Willie he turned, approaching him quickly. He said he loved the girls, that he'd been waiting all his life for something like this, something *bigger* than the town.

Willie was happy to hear it. Relieved. They were more than just acquaintances. He was a part of it now. "You sure 'bout this, Cary? Scares me a little. Gonna be trouble at the door sometimes. You know that, right?"

Hearing his worry, he flashed a mischievous grin, reaching for his car keys. "We've got this, Willie Graves."

"You think?"

Turning to go, a delightful wildness came over him. A certain mutiny. "Can't never could!" he shouted, leaping off the front steps, bounding away.

The rooms were easy to choose between, each with its own personality, color, and light. Willie took the top floor, with bookshelves and a small safe bolted to the floor. Cary said he'd need one for the money. And a pistol. He'd be careful moving around, avoiding the rooms as best he could, the hallway below his stairs. Josie chose Sadie's room, with Amber across the way. Carolyn and Poppy were down the hall in smaller rooms with pale yellow walls and thick floral curtains.

They had a few weeks until Willie's eighteenth birthday. That was the deal before they opened, Josie said. Linens, maid, doctor, cook. Then, show the girls around.

Their first outing was the Apple Harvest Parade, down Main Street. Standing on the Belmont Bridge, wrapped in exotic winter coats, they marveled at the swirling crowds, marching bands, and floats. Willie positioned himself at a distance, blending in, leaning back against a streetlight. The ladies were hard to miss. He wondered if they felt it too, like circus cats, or German prisoners. A marching band passed by loudly, then clowns, Clydesdales, a Carter Mountain Orchard truck, its sides filled with fresh-picked apples. He thought about the Pettits' place, their gentle ways and kindness. How much larger the world had become since then.

A pretty red-haired girl crossed the street between two floats, disappearing into the crowd. Could it be? He moved quickly to get a better look, losing her at some point and stopping. Her knife was always in his pocket. Or, was it? Reaching into his pants he felt it, oddly, next to something tiny and hard, pulling it out.

"What you got there, honey?" Amber asked, coming up from behind, surprising him suddenly.

He held it up into the sun, watching it shimmer. "From bones we come and dust we go, to all dem stars we see," he heard Mo say. "Friend gave it me," he answered finally, letting her hold it.

She took it carefully into her open hand, examining it more

closely. "Pretty little thing, all sparkles, ain't it?"

He looked with her. "It is."

"Some kind a glass I s'pose." She admired it a bit more before dropping it back into his hand. "Don' lose it, baby."

"I won't." He placed it carefully in his pocket as the wind kicked up. It was getting cold.

A young lady in a shiny fake tiara waved absently from the boot of a passing convertible. Her sash said, "Apple Harvest Queen."

When they saw her, Amber laughed, realizing where she was.

"Kinda different here, I guess." Willie said, seeing her reaction.

Tightening her coat, she filled her lungs with fresh autumn air, looking around. There were families everywhere. An innocence she'd never known. "Like another world."

Cary met David Sheffield at the front door.

"Good morning, Sheriff." He sounded sleepy, adjusting his eyes to the light.

The sheriff removed his dark glasses and smiled. He liked Cary.

"Figured you'd be downtown." He watched a car pass down the street, squinting into the sun.

"Came for the boy. Got some calls about his buddy."

Cary's expression changed quickly. "Stick Watson?"

"Yep."

He couldn't tell if the news was bad.

"Good news, bad news kinda thing," the sheriff explained, looking past him into the front hallway. "He around?"

Cary backed away, holding the door. "Took the ladies to the festival. Come on in."

The house smelled of flowers and fresh paint. He took his hat off and looked around.

Cary watched his reaction carefully. "All spruced up."

The room keys were in the basket. He'd had calls about the construction, the scene they'd made at the Main Street Station.

"Kind of early, but can I offer you a drink?"

He'd heard about the private club, how they'd dodged a license. "I'm good, thank you, Cary." He looked him over. He'd always been different—bit of a renegade. "Did a nice job with this place."

"Thank you, sir."

They sized each other up.

"This ain't gonna fly on my watch. You know that, right?"

Cary's face went blank.

"Whole town's talkin'. You know that too, don't you?"

"I do."

He ran his fingers through his hair. "Puts me in a bind, is what it does."

"Not what we wanted, Sheriff."

"The whole thing's wrong and you all know it... so better not push it, boy." He stopped to let it sink in. "You get this thing rollin', gonna shut you down and lock it up. Tell'n you now." He glanced upstairs. "Not up to me anymore."

They heard a car pull up, radio blasting.

"Never was."

Cary assumed a poker face. "I understand, sir."

Willie's car doors opened and closed.

"Well…" He put his hat on, hearing it. "Said what I need to say."

Cary smiled politely.

They looked at each other one last time.

"Rest is up to you."

Josie was the first to arrive on the porch. "Hello, Sheriff," she said cheerily, offering her hand.

She was a pretty woman, no doubt about it. "David Sheffield," he replied, seeing Willie in the distance.

Josie let her hand go, looking back at the girls as they approached. "Let me introduce you to my friends," she offered, stepping aside.

Carolyn, Poppy, and Amber approached the top step, out of breath, filled with excitement.

"Lord have mercy, we in it now," Amber teased, seeing the sheriff's shiny big badge.

"Hello, ladies."

Amber looked him over carefully. "My name's Amber." She flashed her smile. "I like your gun."

He wasn't sure if she was serious. "Hello, Amber."

"And this be Poppy on my right," she added playfully.

"Hello, Poppy," he replied, tipping his hat in her direction.

A tall White woman was next to Poppy.

"Carolyn Smith."

She had long blond hair and pale blue eyes. "Ma'am."

"Sheriff."

They took each other in.

"Where you from, Carolyn?"

She could see he liked her. "Originally?"

"That works."

"Seattle, Washington."

His eyes lit up. "Well, my goodness."

She took a box of cigarettes and a lighter from her coat pocket.

"And how'd you end up way out here?"

Lighting a cigarette, she raised her mouth slightly to one side, exhaling slowly. "Runnin' from the law."

When the girls laughed, the spell was broken. They said their goodbyes and headed to the parlor.

Josie watched them go. They looked happy together. "Join us for a drink?"

"No, thank you."

She touched his arm lightly. "Well, nice to meet you, Sheriff," she said, heading for the door.

She had a nice figure. Pretty hair. "Last question."

She stopped to turn back.

"You stayin' a while?"

"Me, personally?"

"The whole package."

Willie stepped up to the porch. He'd been listening from the middle step.

Josie looked at Willie, then the sheriff. She knew when to flirt and when to swing.

The parlor exploded in laughter.

She gave him a sultry smile. "Don't be a stranger, David Sheffield."

When the door closed, he took a piece of paper from inside his jacket and gave it to Willie. "That him?"

Willie's hand shook when he heard the question, holding it up to get a better look.

"Joe Hall sent it this morning."

He was handing money through an open window. A scar was visible on the right side of his neck.

"Outside a place called the Black Pearl."

Willie looked up.

"Gambling hall. New Orleans."

He looked again, not recognizing his clothes.

"Showed his ID at the door. Used a Richmond address. Man was killed inside."

Willie lowered the paper finally, looking out over the balustrade, into the trees.

"A guy named Hook."

His heart stopped.

The woman across the street was watching.

"Told Sheriff Hall I'd show it to you, see what you thought. Need to call him back."

Willie stared at the sky.

The sheriff joined him at the rail, noticing two strange clouds side by side, their edges blazing in sunlight. "Well, look at that."

Seeing it, his eyes filled with tears, remembering Stick's hands pressing down against his heart, how they'd brought him back to life.

"Yes, sir," he said, checking the photo one more time to be sure. "It's him."

# CHAPTER SEVEN

In a few short weeks they'd made peace with the place. It was time to hit the road. He explained everything one last time. How Stick had saved his life. It was up to him to do the same.

"Take your time," Josie said, walking him to the front porch. "We'll be here if you need something." She offered him an envelope.

"What's this?"

"It might help."

Willie looked at it, hesitating.

"Got plenty left from what you gave us. Take it."

"Don't think I need it."

She put it in his hand and gave him a tender smile. "Then bring it back. We'll use it for cat food."

Willie grinned, looking for them. "How many we got?"

"Five, maybe more. We ran out of bowls."

He wanted to thank her but didn't know where to start.

"Stop to sleep, get some food."

"I will."

"You have a map?"

"Got one when I gassed up."

Amber, Carolyn, and Poppy joined them suddenly, looking solemn.

"Need me to come along?" Amber asked, adjusting her robe suggestively. "Tell you where to turn?"

Carolyn put her arms around him. She smelled of rosewater. Then, Poppy.

"I left some money under your door for the cats," he said, feeling her warm body under the fabric of her nightgown. "Thanks for takin' care of 'em."

Josie thought of his birthday. Wherever he was headed, it would take a while. "Call us on your birthday."

Willie stopped to consider it, realizing he'd forgotten.

"We'll be fine. Cary's here, house is ready."

"I didn't say goodbye to Cary. Called his number just now."

"He's buying booze. Left this morning."

"Tell him I'll call when I can."

"I will."

His face grew anxious. "The lawyer call you back?"

"He's on it." She gave him a sweet look. "We're ready, honey. It's almost ten and you need to go."

Amber's eyes glistened in the porch light. "Don't want nothin' happenin' to our Birthday Boy, you hear me?"

Her tenderness surprised him. "I'll be fine."

"Need you back here once you find him."

"I will."

"And bring me those sinkers."

He had no idea what she meant.

She gave him a fierce look. "Child, you don't remember nothin'!"

"Sorry."

"Beignets, Café du Monde." She paused, waiting for him to remember.

"Sinkers."

"Twelve box, baby!" She flashed her epic smile. "Tell 'em 'Rosie' sent you."


He drove all night, imagining the expression on Stick's face when he realized who he was, wrapping his arms around him like he'd always meant to do but never did. At a truck stop on the Tennessee line, he stopped for gas and to pee. It surprised him how awake he was, how little he cared about the days ahead or noticed the people around him. How things made more sense the farther he drove.

When the sun hit the windshield he pulled over, feeling the weight of his arms and legs, stepping out slowly, beholding the Tennessee River. He'd never seen water so big, or move with such power, its downstream reaches steeped in a deep bluish green. He imagined Indians on the shore with nets of fish, clay banks wet with mussels. He'd read about such things, such noble encampments. Before there were borders, cities, or roads.

By 2:00 p.m., Meridian, Mississippi was the end of the line. He parked near a Confederate Inn billboard sign, setting the brake, locking the doors, and closing his eyes. An hour of sleep, 59 South to US 90, then eastbound to Third Street and the Jefferson Parish. Stick might be there, or hiding somewhere. He'd find a room and ask around. See what he could find.

A hard knock shattered his sleep.

"Window down" Something struck the glass two more times. "Window!"

Half-asleep, Willie fumbled for his keys, turning the ignition, lowering his window.

A Mississippi state trooper stood outside holding a baton. "*All of 'em!*"

"Sir?"

"*Every window!*" he shouted, face reddening. "*License and registration, then step out of the vehicle!*"

Willie's hands shook. His money was in the trunk. He'd read about the Hangin' Bridge in nearby Shubuta. How they'd lynched two boys for talking to a White girl over the Chickasawhay River. "Yes, sir," he managed, seeing the flashing lights, reaching slowly into the glove compartment.

His car door opened.

*"Outta the car, nigger!"*


Poppy loved Snow White. She named the last cat Doc. One sneezed, one was sleepy, one grumpy, another shy. She watched them from the kitchen window, sipping tea, enjoying their antics: chasing leaves across the porch, diving in and out of balustrades. A scrawny white kitten with pale blue eyes appeared one morning, fearful and tentative, sniffing at the air, disappearing as quickly as it came. She watched for it each day, hoping to get a better look eventually. Perhaps it needed milk, a soft blanket, or the smell of her warm silk nightgown. Cats were essential to her world, eternal, and wise. She'd had one in Saigon when she was little, before her parents sent her away. His name was Ki and he had no tail. The day she left, they said he ran away.


When Willie didn't call, they knew something was wrong.

"It's Josie, Sheriff."

"Hey, Josie. Hear you're on fire over there."

She paused, considering her response carefully. "We have a problem and I need your help."

He put the heel of his boot on the edge of the desk. "Not sure I can, but it doesn't hurt to ask."

She considered it one last time and sighed. "Willie's gone."

"Willie's gone. What you mean, gone?"

"Missing."

He leaned back in his chair. "Cary said he went for Stick."

"The night you came over, yes. Drove to New Orleans."

"Last Sunday."

"Sunday, I suppose." She counted the days in her head. "You're right, Sunday." She looked around the empty kitchen.

He raised the other boot, crossing his legs. She sounded tired.

"Been a long week."

He wanted to laugh. "Bet it has."

For a moment, she'd forgotten who she was talking to.

"So, what you mean, he's missing?"

She lit a cigarette. "He was supposed to call us on his birthday."

"What day was that?"

"The thirtieth."

He checked his desk calendar. "Last Wednesday."

"Been five days. Something's wrong."

He thought about it.

"Not like him not to call, I'm thinking. Haven't known him long, but I'm worried."

"Maybe he's just caught up in somethin'. On the road… you get there, ask around… then what? Not sure he thought about that part."

She took another drag.

"Maybe he forgot."

"To call?"

"Yeah."

"Was his eighteenth birthday. Our first night open. Said he would."

She was right.

"Something's wrong and I know it. We all do."

He pulled his boots off the desk and sat up. He'd need to make some calls.

"Told us he was driving straight. Twenty-four hours, give or take. Good car. Plenty of cash." She put her cigarette out. "Amber knows some people down there, but figured I'd call you first."

He pulled out a drawer of files, taking one marked, 'GRAVES'. "Give me a couple hours and I'll call you back."

Hearing him say it made her more afraid. "Thank you, David. I mean, Sheriff."

He opened the file. "And have Cary call me." He found it under 'SPORTING HOUSE, 313 West Main Street, Charlottesville, Virginia.'

"I will. Thank you."

"See you got the booze figured out."

"Excuse me?"

He smiled, hearing the worry in her voice.

"Don't say nothin' 'bout the girls."

# CHAPTER EIGHT

His mouth was dry and the cuffs hurt. The room had no windows. The questions were all the same.

"So, how the fuck does a young ass nigger like you come up with one thousand dollars in his wallet?"

"Told you."

"Well, then tell me again."

"I'm on my way to New Orleans to help a friend."

The officer smirked, moving around the table, approaching him from the side. "Those cuffs too tight?" he asked, more sympathetically.

He checked his wrists. "Little bit. Yes, Sir."

"Let me fix 'em."

Willie hesitated before raising his hands, feeling a fist against his face, flying backward off the chair. When he came to, he was on his knees curled up. The floor smelled of Clorox.

Someone brought water.

The officer sat down and waited. "Can't raise your hands when we're asking you questions, boy. You understand me?"

Willie didn't move.

"You get me?"

He tried to breath.

"Come on, get up." He opened a file, flipping through the pages.

Willie sat up. His cheek was throbbing.

"Brought you some water."

Willie saw the glass. "I need a lawyer."

"We all do."

They looked at each other.

He stood up slowly, getting his balance. His eye throbbed. It was hard to see straight.

"Happy to get you one. Just need to ask you a couple questions, that's all. Tie this thing up if we can." His eye looked bad. "Come on, boy. Have some water. Been a long day and you must be tired."

When he sat, he drank the whole glass, wiping his mouth with the sleeves of his shirt. The water was cold.

"There you go." He took a piece of paper from his file, laying it on the table, giving him a moment. "Get you more when you need it. Just let me know."

Willie stared at the thing, unable to read it.

"My name's Officer Foster and I'll be asking you a couple questions about some of the answers you've given us." He sat up and smiled. "You okay with that?"

"I guess."

"Simple really, just… you said, he said, kinda stuff… you know… case there's somethin' we got wrong. Somethin' different than what you *meant* to say."

"I get a lawyer, right?"

He smiled again. "Soon as we're done. Call him right away."

Blood was rushing around his eye.

"Get you some ice while I'm at it."

It was hard to say. "Thank you."

"Let's start with the money."

Willie waited for the question.

"Where's it from?"

"Told you. My mother died, left it for me."

"In cash?"

"Yes."

"From her business."

"Yeah."

"What kinda business was it?"

Willie hesitated. "Social."

"What's that?"

"Like a club, I guess you call it."

The officer studied him carefully, not understanding.

"Where people get together."

He thought about it.

Willie started to sweat. "She charges twenty at the door."

"Twenty at the door," he repeated.

"With a bar."

His face brightened. "Well, that makes sense."

"Lotta folks on weekends."

"I bet."

"College town and all."

"Charlottesville."

"Yes, sir."

He remembered a book in school. "Thomas Jefferson."

"Yes, sir."

The right side of his face hurt.

"You need water?"

"I'm okay. Like to get outta here. Get on the road."

"I'm sure you would... so would I."

"No reason you had to bring me in here as far as I can tell. Pull me outta the car like that for no reason. Tow it somewhere, like I'd done something wrong."

"Never easy these things, I know."

Willie tried to be calm. "What things you talkin' about exactly?"

The officer placed his hand on the file. "Says here, you didn't signal when you pulled over."

Willie shook his head, understanding the game.

"Right tail and plate lights are out."

"Heard him break it after he put me in his car."

"Back tire treads too thin."

He exhaled slowly, trying to make sense of it. "So, you tow my car, bring me in like I robbed a bank or somethin'?"

"Just doin' our job, Willie, that's all."

"Call me a nigger, knock me in the head."

"I'm sorry about that, really I am. Raised your hands. Gotta keep 'em still."

The lamp cast a bright, shiny circle over the table. He stared into it with his good eye. "You know what they call this?"

Officer Foster put the paper back and closed his file. His patience was running thin. "Call what?"

Willie's cheek throbbed. A wall was splattered with blood. He took a deep breath, considering it carefully. The trouble he was in. "I need a lawyer, please."

He gave him a look and grinned, taking the file, standing quickly, moving to the door, knocking twice. "Your eye looks bad. Let me get you some ice."

The door opened and closed.

Willie heard voices in the hall, then silence. His mind was racing, his heart. What would they do to him? Who was coming next?

Sitting back against the chair, he closed his eyes, imagining sunlight, what they could not take. Oceans. Valleys. Sky. A glistening stream, with Indian grass, bending in the wind.

The cell was cold. His eye swollen shut. He heard conversations from time to time. A train passed occasionally. He found a magazine on the floor dated 1951. He stared at the pictures, advertisements mostly. The dogs looked happy. Everyone was smiling. In the morning they brought him grits and a stale biscuit. They told him his lawyer was coming, that he'd been delayed in Jackson with a big trial. They were out of ice.

Willie's Buick was in a stall, seats removed, stuffing pulled out, carpeting and panels everywhere. The radio was on. Hearing the front door slam, two men slid out from under the carriage, their faces splotched with grease.

"Afternoon, boys!" Officer Foster barked, seeing the mess they'd made.

When the radio stopped, the two men joined him.

"Find anything?"

They shot each other a look.

"Need to wash up," one said, leaving quickly.

The other man wiped his hands with a dirty blue cloth, nodding toward a row of windows. "Put it on the table."

"Thanks, Jerry. Anything I need to know?"

He considered the question, turning back, admiring the car one more time. "Got a sweet radio."

When they left, he circled the car, poking his head inside from time to time, pressing down against a slashed tire with his boots when he was done. The table was littered with ashtrays, soda cans, and dirty rags. They'd pushed everything aside to clear a space in the middle. It was a book. The title surprised him. Then a manila envelope ripped open at the top. He picked it up, sneaking a look, sliding it into his coat.

Willie was asleep when they came for him. Their faces were harder this time. He asked them where he was being taken. They told him to put his hands behind his back, applied handcuffs, and led him out.

The cell doors had faces behind them this time, all Black, stone-faced, or ravaged with fear. A few whistled.

"Hey, li'l Sugaboy! Lemme have a lick!" one shouted, sending shivers down his spine.

"Shut the fuck up, Antoine," an officer replied quickly, moving Willie along.

Officer Foster sat, without looking up, going over his notes. Willie's book was on the table.

"Lose the shackles, Ernie."

The officer gave him a look.

"Take 'em off, please."

Willie stood still, staring into space, feeling the pins unlock. When the door shut, he sat down. His clothes smelled and his eye was a mess.

Officer Foster checked his wristwatch before closing the file, picking up Willie's book, admiring the cover. "*The Grapes of Wrath,*" he read out loud, opening it. "'A portrait of the conflict between the powerful and the powerless...'" He skipped down a few quotes. "'Of one man's fierce reaction to injustice.'" Closing the book, he slid it across the table, noticing Willie's eye. "Thinkin' it's not just a story, now is it?"

He wasn't sure where this was headed.

"'Bout the 'haves' and the 'have-nots,' I'm think'n."

Willie played along. "Somethin' like that."

"Like you." His face hardened. "Or me."

Something had changed.

"Time to go."

Willie's heart stopped.

Bud Foster grinned. "Get your car in the morning," he said, grabbing the file, standing up.

Willie stood as well, retrieving his book, waiting for an explanation.

He walked to the door, knocking twice. "Your book's banned in the state of Mississippi, son."

"Why?"

When the lock clicked, he opened the door, flooding the room with light. He liked his job. The town he was in. The way it made him feel. He shot the boy a final look and got himself to smile. "Guess they didn't like the movie."

When he saw the car, he knew what they'd done.

Jerry Trout stood in the doorway. "Patched your tire as best we could. Put the spare on."

He placed his bag in the trunk, lifting the edge of the carpet. The envelope was gone.

"Left the keys inside."

Stick's half-ripped photo was on a floor mat under the steering wheel. Getting in, he shut the door, settling back against the seat. His eye was purple in the rearview mirror.

A knock on the glass made him jump. He turned the key and lowered the window.

"Need to sign this before you go. Got a pen?"

Willie gathered himself, taking a pen from the glove compartment, signing the release. Seeing the hole in his dashboard, he hesitated before handing it back.

"Ready to roll."

He turned the engine on. His eye was throbbing.

"Hang on."

He released the brake and put the car in drive, looking up. "Come on, man, what is it?"

Jerry Trout handed his pen through the window and smiled. "Have yourself a day."


The windshield was dirty and he needed gas. He drove as fast as he could, stealing glimpses of his car. He was lucky it still worked, to be driving, breathing again. The money in his wallet would get him there. Foster had the rest. He didn't care. He was on his way to Stick again, one eye shut, with Steinbeck on the dash.

The Black gas attendant gave him a menacing look, topping his tank and closing the cap. It surprised him at first, until he realized where he was, what he was learning.

"Be five dollars and fifty-three cents."

Willie gave him a ten-dollar bill.

When he saw his wallet, he blinked.

"You need somethin' smaller?"

He took the money from his hand, looking at the bill more closely. "Naw, we good," he answered. "Get yo' change, Boss."


An hour down the road, the air turned warm and humid. He closed the window, missing his music, trusting no one. What Stick meant about people, their kindness and their thievery. How hard it was to tell the difference sometimes.

Crossing Lake Pontchartrain, the sky turned smoky gray, with trees frayed from time to time. He'd find a room on Metairie Road near the police station, get a meal somewhere. Wherever Stick was, it could wait. It had to. He'd aged a hundred years since Charlottesville, since turning eighteen. It was time to call the house.

"Heavens-to-fucking-Betsy, William!" Cary Buck shouted. "This better be good!"

Scrambling for a phone, they all listened while he explained it.

Josie was the first to ask, "They treat you White or Black?"

"How you *think* they done it, girl?" Amber replied, interrupting.

"I'm fine," Willie explained, hearing their worry.

"Some Blacks hate your ass more than Whites, what I know."

"Amber!" Josie protested.

"Jess sayin', honey. You know that."

"I'm good, really, I am. Eight o'clock and still warm down here," he said, changing the subject.

Poppy snatched the phone from Caroline. "Where are you?"

Willie smiled, hearing her tiny voice. "Hey, Poppy! Little room in New Orleans. You ever been here?"

"No."

"It's warm, man. Streets full a people. Got the windows open. Lady said they had a hurricane last September. Trees look bad. Tore the coast up pretty good, what she said."

She imagined it in her mind.

"Cats everywhere."

Poppy smiled.

"Some big bruisers too by the look of it."

When his quarters ran out, they said goodbye. He could hear their relief, knowing he was safe.

Resting on his bed later that evening, testing his eye gently with his fingers, he listened to the streets below, the racing sounds and breaking glass. He felt the wildness of it all, the chaos. Fierce and unpredictable.

A street band danced along the sidewalk, disappearing into the night. The air was soft and enticing. He was learning about the world—surviving it as best he could. Letting go of his book, he closed his eyes finally, giving in to it, hearing trombones and alley cats, a distant siren, dreaming of salvation.

The sheriff was a big deal. You could tell by his picture on the wall.

"I'm here about a friend of mine," Willie explained at the desk when he arrived.

"With you in a minute, son," an officer replied, preoccupied with paperwork.

The station was quiet. He looked around to get his bearings. The photograph was in his pocket. "A guy named Stick Watson."

Stamping a form, the officer looked up finally, noticing his shiner. "How can I help you?"

"I'm trying to find a friend."

"Aren't we all."

They looked at each other.

"Guy named Stick Watson."

"You the kid from Charlottesville?"

Willie flinched when he heard it. "Yes, sir."

"Hang on." He lifted his phone and pressed a button, checking Willie's eye while he waited.

Willie looked down, listening carefully. His sneakers were a mess.

"Got the kid from Charlottesville out front. You want him?"

His mind was racing.

"I'll send him back... and hey, got that Baxter file on the blood work you needed." Hearing the response, he hung up and pointed to his left. "Round the corner, down the hall."

On his way, Willie took the paper from his back pocket, stopping at the corner to get it straight.

The officer watched him, noticing his dirty clothes. He had an aunt in Culpeper, Virginia. It seemed like the end of the world when he was little. "Johnny Boudreau. Name's on the door."

Standing outside the door, putting the photo back in his pocket, he took a deep breath and knocked.

"Where y'at!?"

The room smelled of shrimp and cigars. He was on the phone.

"I understand you, Earl, but I left it by my house. Don't you get it?" He looked up, recognizing Willie, waving him in as he listened.

"Awright."

Willie stepped in cautiously and stopped.

"Awright."

A big blue fish was mounted on a wall behind his desk, papers and files everywhere.

"Last time I'm gonna say this…" He waved Willie closer, pointing to an empty chair. "So you say."

Willie found the chair and sat.

The sheriff rolled his eyes… "Been down that road a time or two, now ain't we?" He shook his head, exasperated. "*Goddammit, Earl!*" he shouted, slapping his hand on the desk, sending papers flying. "You better pinch the tail and suck the head on this one, 'cuz I don't like it! You understand me?!" He paused to listen, catching his breath, calming down. "There you go." His voice was softer now. He gave Willie a little wink. "Then we'll see—all I'm sayin'. Gotta go. How's ya Boo an' them?" He noticed all the papers on the floor. "Well…" He smiled to himself, hearing the answer. "Tell her, hi and to stop growin' till I get there. Gotta go." Standing quickly, he hung up and extended a large hand over the desk. "Willie Graves from the Ole Dominion. Lord have mercy, look at you, boy!"

Willie stood as well, shaking his hand. His grip was strong.

"Come a long way. Now sit down and tell me," he said, sitting, tapping the edge of his desk with his hand. "Where you stayin'?"

Willie dropped to the edge of his chair. "Got a room real close on Maple."

His eyes lit up. "By the Prague Church?"

"Next to a church, yeah. Don't know what you call it."

"Tessula Cambridge. Old Black lady from St. Vincent?"

"Yeah, guess so. Kinda tired when I rolled in."

"Long drive, now ain't it?"

"Yes, sir." He looked past him. The fish was huge.

"Little trouble comin' down, I heard."

It surprised him, hearing it.

Johnny Boudreau leaned over his desk, shuffling papers, casting his eyes about. "Here the other day. Swear to God, if you're hidin' from the law, this be the place to do it!" he joked, finding it suddenly. "Here 'tis!" He lifted up a copy of Stick's photo, looking at it carefully before showing it to Willie. "Figure you've seen this?"

"Yes, sir."

"Sheriff up in Charlottesville?" he asked, reading it again.

"Yes, sir."

"David Sheffield. Nice guy."

Willie smiled politely. "Yes, sir, he is."

He looked up, suddenly concerned. "Said you might be in some kind of trouble. That's why he called. Supposed to call the house. Said he goes back with your momma."

His body tensed.

"It's okay, son. Not my first whorehouse."

Willie relaxed, understanding the world he was in.

"You know, so… I mean we got ourselves some churches, don't misunderstand me… lotta good folks doin' right, but…" He tossed the paper on his desk, rocking slowly in his chair. "Hard to miss a good time."

Willie liked the way he talked.

"You're lookin' for Stick Watson?"

"Yes, sir."

"Friend a yours."

"Yes, sir. He helped me out a few years ago and I'd like to do the same. Find out what happened, mostly, but also…" He didn't know how to say it…

"Return the favor."

"Yes, sir."

Sheriff Boudreau reached into a drawer and removed a file. The cover said 'HOMICIDE.' "Let's see what we got." He scanned the top page. "'October seventh… Black Pearl… pay booth photo… 7:05 p.m.… with ID… 10:50 p.m. EMS gunshot wound to the chest… John Cheshire III… three witnesses… fifty-five-year-old male Caucasian suspect… Richard Allen Watson.'" He looked at Willie. "That him?"

The name was strange. "I guess."

"Not what you call him, probably."

"No, sir."

He kept reading, finding something of interest, then closed the file, leaning back in his chair. "Get you a soda or somethin'?"

"No, sir, I'm fine, thank you."

The boy looked whipped. "Have Tessula make her Po' boy. Tell her I said so."

Willie barely heard what he was saying. "I will. Thank you."

"Crisp on the outside, soft in the middle. Break your heart, man."

"Can I ask you something?"

The sheriff folded his hands together. He'd need to wrap it up. "Talk to me."

"How come they think Stick did it?"

"Must a seen it. Said he and the..." He stopped, trying to remember. "Cheshire fella had some history together."

"Knifed him on a train."

The sheriff's eyebrows lifted. "Well, there you go."

"Guy named Hook."

He wanted to smile, hearing the name.

"Not too long ago with a bunch a fellas. They tossed him out and ran. I was there."

"What your sheriff said."

Willie looked up, tired suddenly. "Been lookin' for him ever since."

He took a moment, unfolding his hands, sitting up.

Tears raced down Willie's cheeks suddenly. "Need to help him if I can."

"A course you do, son. I understand." He looked around for a tissue box.

Willie wiped his nose with the inside of his arm, embarrassed, noticing the fish. "That's a big fish."

Johnny Boudreau swiveled around to sneak a look, then back again, grinning. "In a small pond, my wife reminds me." He stood up, feeling his pants pocket for car keys.

Willie stood as well.

"Need to skedaddle I'm afraid. Wish we could talk."

Willie's face dropped. "I understand."

He paused to consider the boy. He looked rough. "Guy who runs the Black Pearl said his voice was messed up… somethin' about shrimpin'."

"Shrimpin'?"

"Yeah."

"That mean somethin'?"

The sheriff laughed. "Not unless you're a shrimp."

Willie pressed him. "No, I mean… where they doin' that?"

"Ain't where he *was,* son. Gonna be where he's *goin'*—that's how it works."

Willie considered it.

"What a man does when he kills a man."

"*If* he kills a man."

He pulled two cigars from a drawer. "My two cents." He offered one to Willie. "Your buddy's done gone. Plain and simple."

He stared at the cigar.

"For the trip home."

"Thank you," he said, taking it.

"Hear you got a house up there. Brand spankin' new, sheriff said."

He cringed, turning the cigar with his fingers.

"Nothin' to be ashamed of, son." He waited for their eyes to meet. "Like my marlin up there."

Willie looked up. It was smiling.

"Catch it goin' by."

The sidewalk was alive when he came out—accents, faces, smells. He stopped on a corner to take it all in. Watching the world he was in. He'd never known a place like New Orleans, so mixed up and loose. He'd ask about Stick in the bars and grab some dinner, leave first thing in the morning. Something about shrimp. A gun. A card game. What happens when you kill a man. Wherever Stick was, he'd be there awhile. Of that he was certain. On the first ride gone.

# CHAPTER NINE

By the first frost, the house was printing money. Cary Buck explained it over the phone: the cars, the crowds at night. He said the hardest part was turning them away at the door, students mostly, drunk and boisterous. "Honey," he boasted, "we're busier than a moth in a mitten!"

Hearing their time elapse, Willie added quarters.

"But enough of that…" He lit a cigarette quickly, blowing smoke across the kitchen. "Have you found your friend?"

"No."

A truck flew by.

"Where are you?"

"Phone booth outside Biloxi."

Cary inhaled, conjuring it in his mind.

"Mississippi."

"And here I was thinking Kansas," he teased, exhaling too

quickly, coughing.

Willie laughed, hearing him sputter.

"I'm lookin' for my momma's grave."

The line went quiet.

"Since I'm down here."

He tapped the end of his cigarette into an ashtray. "Where is she?"

"That's the thing of it. Heard she had a sister in Biloxi once. Matt Abel told me, I think. Or maybe Sheffield. Was headed home and figured I'd take a look."

"Good for you, honey."

"Thought I'd ask around when I get there."

"Let me call Sheffield. He might remember."

"Matt Abel did the whole thing. Put her on a train."

"Let me find out. Call me tomorrow."

Willie looked out through the open door. His car was a mess.

"The mornings are best. You okay for cash?"

"I'm fine."

"Where you staying?"

"No idea. Bought a Green Book at the last station. What's the weather like up there?"

"It's cold as all get-out."

"Really?"

"I'm jealous that you're down there."

"Don't be. It smells like rotten eggs."

"Eeww."

A tanker raced by.

"And gasoline."

The connection faded in and out. "I'll find out about Sadie. Call me in the morning. Some other things going on, but we're out of time and it's hard to hear you."

A car pulled up to the phone booth, idling next to him.

He reached into his pocket. He was out of quarters. "Things like what?"

The line beeped three times.

He closed the door quickly, hoping for an answer before the line went dead.

"Poppy left."


Biloxi Bay was ruffled and green, with bone-white sandy beaches. He wanted to run, to scream, eviscerate everything inside himself. Pushing against the car door, the wind was up, rattling fronds overhead along the bluff. A cop watched him from his patrol car at the end of the lot. Or was he sleeping? There were people on the beach below, dogs barking, birds diving about. He locked the car and disappeared down a long, rickety staircase, reaching the final step, dropping into the sand, removing his shoes. He sank as he walked, feeling its warmth, giving in to it finally and running.

When he reached the water, waves swirled around his ankles, sand washed over the tops of his feet. Catching his breath, finding his balance, an endless blue hovered in the distance. Lustrous and clear. She would be there, he imagined, drifting in the warm and gentle currents. South and away. Such would be her resting place, her final, endless heaven. Past the rocks of Dry Tortugas, into the lights of Pinar del Rio.

The sign was broken. He checked the Green Book. It looked like a dump, but the cars said otherwise. He changed his shirt in the front seat and checked his eye in the mirror, surprised when he saw it. It was the color of shrimp.

Tempy Keys was standing where she always stood. "Welcome to Chesters," she said, reaching for a menu, noticing his sandy shoes. She looked him over one more time and smiled sweetly. "Got a nice table by the window, young man. Come on." Willie followed behind, trying to blend in. A customer lowered his voice as he passed, checking him out.

She placed the menu on the table as he sat down, stepping up to the window, admiring the midday sky. "Pretty day out there."

"Yes, ma'am," he agreed, opening the menu, hearing his stomach growl. "Nice and warm on the beach. Heard you had a hurricane a while ago."

A deep voice called out from the kitchen pass-through. "Hang on, sweetie," she replied. "Be right back."

For forty-some years, Chesters' food was simple, fast, and cheap.

Catfish, chitlins, sweet potato fries, short rib meatloaf, Johnnycakes, and shrimp, spiced rice, fatback, ham hock, and sprouts, hog jowl, crawfish, fried peach pie, turkey neck and collard greens, okra, cabbage, peas, cast-iron biscuits, buttered grits with cheese.

When she returned, she could see he needed help. "Special on the gumbo: sausage, rice, and shrimp. Fried chicken, if you like. Soup today's our ham and bean."

Willie was overwhelmed.

"Look it over. I'll be back. Bet you like your pitcher sweet," she said with a wink, walking away.

The fried chicken melted in his mouth as he looked around. The place was packed. When the collards, mac and cheese, and fried peach pie were done he could barely move.

Tempy giggled when she saw his plates. The pitcher of tea was empty. "Bless your heart," she said, enjoying his happy face. "Take the bones in a box?"

As she cleared the table, he looked around again. Half the room was gone. "Everything was so good, ma'am."

"Glad you liked it." She glanced out the window. "That you out there with the Virginia plates?"

"Yes, ma'am."

"Nice ole Buick you got there."

"Needs a wash real bad."

She turned toward the kitchen, balancing the plates perfectly in her arms. "Bring you somethin' for the road."

Willie liked her face, the way she listened when he spoke. He figured she was his momma's age before she died, give or take a few years. "That's very kind of you, but I don't need a thing after all that. 'Cept the check, maybe." He noticed his greasy hands. "Need to wash my hands."

"Door's back there by the highchairs." She indicated with her head. "Take your time."

A few diners watched him as he stood. Passing the kitchen window, an old Black man was washing dishes, singing to himself. It sounded sad and faraway, something about Jesus and the road to Hell. He washed his hands and returned to the window by his table. It had been a long day. He'd need to find the cemetery and a place to sleep.

Tempy brought him a mason jar. "Ham and bean soup, in case you need it," she said, putting it on the table with the bill beside it. "Good hot or cold."

"Thank you, ma'am." It had been a while since anyone had been so kind. He reached inside his wallet.

"Nothin' to it. Little somethin' to remember us by."

Willie handed her a five-dollar bill and the check.

She gave him an inquisitive look. "What you doin' way down here?"

He stopped, not knowing where to start. "I was looking for a friend in New Orleans."

A table nearby listened in.

He looked into her eyes. "Now I'm lookin' for my momma."

Hearing it, she stepped closer, lowering her voice. "Where she live, if you don't mind me asking?"

She was sweet the way she asked him. He took a moment, considering how to say it. Where to start. If there were beans to spill, this would be the person.

When he was done, sunlight touched the side of her face and the place was empty. They both stood. The kitchen was quiet.

"I went on too long, sorry," he said, glancing at his car. "Been all my life and I don't really know who she is. Where I come from."

Tempy's face was filled with questions. "She ever use another name? Tell you anything like that?"

"No, ma'am. Not that I can think of."

"No cousin or relation somewhere?"

His face brightened, remembering it. "She mighta had a sister. Think I heard about one when they put her on the train, maybe." He thought about it. "Sheriff at home might know."

"There you go! Ask *him*."

"Guy who did it's dead."

She watched him think it over. "Well."

"Gave me that Buick out there." The lot was empty. "And my momma's house."

Tempy Keys took a moment to digest it all. Picturing a boy raised in such a place. "Been down a hard road, darlin'." She smiled, admiring his tough, sweet face. "Seem to come out alright, though."

Willie sighed, hoping it was true. He thought about Moses, how their time together had stayed with him. "Miss my ole Moses sometimes."

She shook her head. "Like from a book a some kind, sounds like."

He'd never thought of it that way.

"Little boy and a bell man," she said, enjoying the idea. "Leavin' you a chair."

A car pulled in, parking by the window.

She took his money and check from inside her dress pocket, seeing the car.

"Keep the change, please. I best be gettin' outta here."

She nodded, still living in his story. "Well, thank you, sir."

The front door opened.

"People coming now, so best be gettin' to it." She put her hand out.

Willie took it into his. It was soft and warm. "Thanks for all your help." He looked down at the jar of soup. "And the soup. Appreciate it very much."

She put her other hand over his, resting it there. "Try the cemetery."

"Yes, ma'am."

"Then Miss Alcina on Washington Street. Tell her I sent you. Got a pretty garden."

"Thank you, could use some sleep. Been a long couple days."

She held his hand a bit longer and thought of the Alcina boy, how close they were in age. "Said you like reading?"

"Yes, ma'am. Need to pick it up again when I get home."

"Books be a sweet fruit," she said, letting go of his hand finally.

"Yes, ma'am," he agreed, following her to the door.


When he pulled out, she was in the window taking her next order. Turning onto Highway 90 he watched in the rearview mirror as the Chesters sign disappeared, still feeling her touch, the kindness in her eyes. Feeling less alone.


At five o'clock Gabriel Cemetery was steeped in long dark shadows. He sat in the car, frozen at first. Without her name, it was hopeless. Maybe Cary would know something in the morning. Or Sheriff Sheffield.

Getting out, he walked between the tombstones, passing people he'd never known. Mother, brother, sister, father, unborn child. They were strangers all. Cold and silent. Chambers, Rich, Pablo, Clower, Tucei, Ahern, Hyde. He followed their names, the quick and the dead, searching for his own.

Mrs. A. J. Alcina was in her garden holding a basket of dahlias. He turned off the engine and grabbed his book, throwing it into his bag, closing the trunk.

"That you, Willie Graves?" she shouted over a white picket fence.

He looked up, surprised to hear his name. She had a round, cheery face. "Yes, ma'am."

She smiled back. "Tempy's friend," she replied, moving toward the house.

He met her at the stoop. She was a large, gentle woman.

"I'm Mrs. Alcina," she said, offering her hand. "Welcome to our home."

Willie shook her hand. "Thank you."

"Any trouble finding me?"

"No, ma'am."

She gave him a quick look. "Call me A. J., sweetie." She noticed his car. "A for Angel, J for Jesus."

He tried not to laugh.

"You hungry?"

"No, ma'am. I mean, Miss A. J."

She checked her flowers in the basket, adjusting the stems with her hand. "Tempy said you filled the tank."

Willie smiled. "I did. Don't need a thing after that."

She leaned in. "Fried peach pie?"

"My goodness, yes. That was somethin'!"

"Mm-mm," she murmured, thinking of the crust, heading toward the stairs.

His room was sunny and bright, with windows over the backyard.

"Get some air tonight. Got screens 'n' all, so you'll be fine." She looked out into a large magnolia. "Still standin', my trees, don't know why. 'Bout blew the house down that night. Never seen anything like it."

"You talkin' 'bout the hurricane?"

"September twenty-fourth. Flossy came a callin'."

"See some of it drivin' round."

She opened the window halfway, feeling a breeze. "Sun be down soon. Got an owl about. Might hear him if you're lucky." She adjusted the edge of a curtain. "Bathroom's down the hall. We're full tonight, so you'll hear people. Don't be shy. Need anything, I'm downstairs, room two off the parlor. Coffee, tea, and biscuits in the morning before you go." Returning to the doorway she noticed his bag, remembering Tempy's call. "Got a washing machine in the basement if you need it."

"I'm fine, thank you," he replied, embarrassed that she'd noticed.

"Said you been on the road a while."

"Not too bad."

She saw his eye. "Had some trouble in Meridian."

He'd almost forgotten. "Yes."

"Lucky this time."

He didn't answer.

She liked his manner. The way he thought about things before he spoke. "If I may, how old are you?"

"I'm eighteen."

"*Eighteen.*" She could see he didn't know. "Well... I'm very pleased you're with us tonight, Willie."

"Thank you for having me," he replied, sounding tired.

She put her hand on the doorknob, thinking of her son, his empty room. "Safe 'n' sound."


There was no owl, no voices in the hall. The bed was soft and warm, that was all that mattered. He'd call in the morning to see about his momma, then hit the docks and ask about Stick. It would be a long way to find him, he understood that now. His momma too. Maybe that's what they wanted all along, or dreamed of when they could. To be free of this world, the death and the dying. Without memory. Or measure. To open their eyes in a brand new world, and start their life again.


She told him after breakfast as they said goodbye, standing in her garden, showing him the grave.

WILLIAM HOLLIS ALCINA

1932–1950

loved forever


He'd bumped into a White woman racing for a bus one night. When she found him, they cut the rope, his body crashing to the ground. He wondered how a person could live through such a thing. How such violence would not change her heart forever.

"He was a beautiful boy, Willie," she said, finally. "On his way to see a cousin." She bent over and pulled a weed near the edge of the stone, placing it in her basket. "Liked everybody he ever met." She smiled thinking of it, being with a young man again. "'*Specially* the ladies."

Willie's tears surprised him, then his laughter, how easily they came together.

She stepped back to give him space, time to understand it. "Be a long way in life, but a short way to heaven. "


He felt hollow when he left. He'd heard of such things, read about them in newspapers, but this was different. Her face was loving. Affectionate. They were people from families with flowers and fences. Mothers without children, fathers without sons. Waiting for justice. Listening to the owls.

It took him a while to gather his senses, make his way. He'd locate a phone and walk the docks, find a shrimp boat. Maybe he'd leave, or maybe he'd stay- keep looking. Or was it all the same in the end? He missed his Blue Ridge Mountains, the simple autumn light. Something had changed inside him forever. He knew that now. Something deep within his heart.

When the sky darkened, raindrops trickled down the phone booth. They'd found no papers, or a sister in Biloxi, no records at the Main Street Station, or from J. F. Bell Funeral Home. The trail went dry and she was gone. His name would stay the same, that much he understood. Willie Graves, son of Mopsy and Sadie, born November 30, 1939, in Charlottesville, Virginia.

"Well, thanks for tryin', Cary. Appreciate it," he managed, sensing the end of it.

Cary made smoke rings in the air. "I found something in the cellar."

"What you mean?"

"Write this down."

He took Stick's paper from his shirt pocket and a pencil from behind his ear.

"Ebenezer Baptist Church."

He scratched it out.

"Happy Jack, Louisiana."

"I don't get what you're saying. Found what in the cellar?"

"Behind your momma's brick."

Blood rushed to his head. It was the only place she'd put it.

"On the back of an old photograph."

When the rain came, the boats returned early, raising their nets, docking together. The front would pass by morning, but with so many missing boats, ice plants, and marshes, the season was a bust.

The air smelled of fish. Walking the pier, raindrops bounced against the water. He read the names, hoping to see someone.

*CLIFFORD PAUL*

*CAPT. TOM*

*LUCKY BABE*

*BENDORA*

Near the end, a large scruffy man looked down from the *FAIR MAIDEN*.

As Willie approached, the man's face brightened. "You the kid from Mary's?"

Willie came to a halt. "No, sir."

"Oh," he replied, noticing his eye. "Thought you were the kid she sent."

Willie felt the rain as he listened.

"From the drive-in." He checked a bowline below his feet.

"I'm lookin' for a friend a mine. Guy named Stick Watson. Heard he did some shrimpin' a couple months ago. Not sure where. Figured I'd ask around. Got a picture if you'd like to take a look." He took the photo out, stepping closer to the boat. "Show you what he looks like."

The man stopped what he was doing. "Never heard of him."

Willie approached the boat, raising the photo up over the gunnels.

He hesitated before he took it. One of his fingers was bleeding.

"Maybe you saw him somewhere. Mighta heard somethin'."

He handed it back. "Nope. Can't say I have."

Willie took it and stepped back, returning the photo to his pocket quickly. His shirt was soaked. "Sorry to bother you. Thanks for lookin'."

The man scanned the horizon, noticing dark clouds overhead. "Try the harbor master," he barked, heading aft, disappearing into a wall of netting.


The door was hard to miss.

## HARBOR MASTER

### Rat Stolar

The room was warm and musty, Boats for Sale signs everywhere.

"Dolphin Tours's next dock over. B slip," someone said, hearing the door close.

Willie's shoes made puddles as he entered.

"Whoa!" a man exclaimed, popping his head up from behind a desk. "Man overboard!"

Willie was too wet to laugh. "I'm looking for the harbor master."

"That would be me."

"Mr. Stowlare?"

"Close enough."

"Thank you. I'm lookin' for a friend of mine." He took the paper from his pocket, unfolding it carefully. "Guy on the *FAIR MAIDEN* said you might be able to help me." The photo had dissolved in the rain. "Shit."

"What you got there?" he asked, suddenly curious.

Willie took a moment, folding the paper, slipping it back into his pocket.

"What's his name?"

He tried not to panic. "Stick Watson."

"And what makes you think he was here?"

"Sheriff Boudreau in New Orleans said he heard something about him maybe shrimpin' somewhere. Figured I'd ask around."

Rat Stolar's face grew more thoughtful as he considered it. "Got shrimpin' up and down the coast, boy. What makes you think he's here?"

He felt stupid. "Just a guess, really. I was here anyway, so I figured I'd ask around."

"As a deck hand?"

"I suppose. Don't know."

"Stick Watson."

"Yes, sir."

He grinned for some reason. "Owe you money?"

Willie grinned. "No, sir. Just a friend."

"Good. In that case..." He stood up, dusting potato chips off his pants, shuffling to a cabinet near the back wall. "Not ringin' a bell, but let's see what we got. Pretty quiet since Flossy blew through." He took out a large binder and plopped it on a nearby desk. "Last couple months, you say?"

"Not sure. Six months out, maybe?"

He opened the binder, searching for a particular section, finding it.

Willie took a hopeful breath. "Really appreciate it."

"You're welcome," he answered, reviewing a list of names, reaching the end quickly.

Willie watched him carefully. It didn't take long.

He closed the binder and looked up. "Nothin' on the nigger list."

Passing Biloxi Lighthouse, the light fell grim and heavy. If Stick had been there, he would have felt it, known where to look, or who to ask. He'd never seen a place so callous and smug. So dishonorable. Maybe that's what Sister Mo meant about the world. It was more than a black eye, a stolen radio. There was evil sometimes. Roads you should not take. Watching his speed, checking the rearview mirror, he understood that now, what people did to each other sometimes when no one was looking. When the doors were closed. They called him Rat for a reason.

South of New Orleans he remembered their conversation over the phone. "Same face as your momma, William. And she has your eyes!"

"Least I got somethin'."

"You're speaking like a turnip again."

It felt good to hear it.

"You need to come home."

"I will."

"I should have come with you."

"No."

He lit a cigarette, enjoying their moment together.

"This is *my* deal."

"Poppy's in Los Angeles."

"Los Angeles?"

"Called last night to let Josie know."

"Why's she there?"

Cary exhaled. "Greener pastures, honey."

"How'd she get there?"

"Guy came to pick her up."

"What he look like?"

"Like a father."

He thought he'd misunderstood. "What do you mean?"

"She's adopted. Her daddy has fruit trees."

He tried to make sense of it.

"Oranges. Lots of oranges."

He waited.

"I'll tell you when you get here."

"Tell me now."

He watched the smoke of his cigarette rising up into the air. "She grew up rich and left when she could. Little Miss Poppy."

"Did Josie know?"

"Yes."

He thought of her tiny voice. Her scent.

"Carolyn's daddy is a Lutheran minister."

"Oh, my."

"Up North somewhere. Said her momma sleeps with boys."

"You mean, men."

"You heard me."

The line was quiet.

"Oh."

He took a drag, exhaling slowly. "We drank some shine one night and started talking. Amber plays the saxophone. Josie can juggle."

Willie cracked up, imagining it. He'd forgotten the beignets.

"Cary likes dresses."

He'd never heard him talk that way. "Guess it's not what you think."

"Can't judge a girl by her shoes."

He waited to ask. He was out of quarters again. "How'd they end up where they are?"

He put his cigarette out. His coffee was cold. "Same as you, honey."

"I suppose."

"As did I."

A tiny cat scratched lightly at the kitchen window. Cary watched it.

"The stuff people do."

The line beeped three times.

"You need to go now. When you find what you're looking for, turn that thing around and get your ass home."

After the line went dead, he held the receiver in his hand. He'd wanted to tell him about Miss A. J.'s son. What he'd learned about things, about himself. About the hurricane. How he'd said a prayer for his momma one day and tossed Mo's glass into the sea.

Thirty miles down Route 23, the trees were gone, towns scattered, boats upside down. It was hard to wrap his head around it, mile after mile, the devastation. His fuel tank was low. He'd look for the church and check for names, then find some gas. Watching the odometer, he counted the miles, expecting it in the distance—water tanks, buildings, a sign of life.

When the numbers aligned, he pulled to the side of the road, rolled the windows down, and cut the engine. A Gulf station lay on its side, detritus everywhere. He checked the map to get his bearings: 43.6 miles south of New Orleans, Mississippi River, Long Bay, Chandeleur Sound. He put the map down and looked around. Broken piers. Silence. Maybe that's how it worked at the end of a life, after the singing and the tears. Happy Jack, Louisiana, off the map and outta gas. Her final place on Earth.

He thought about what she'd kept from him, her many secrets. Did she love someone? Did they love her back? Was she faithful? Was she scared? Did she want a better life?

Stepping from the car, he looked out toward the bay into a blinding, brilliant sunset. He stopped when he saw it, surrounded in wreckage, from the storm that was her life. A speck of green flashed above the sun, then again, before it came to him. The peace, the calm, her opal eyes, translucent in the aftermath.

# CHAPTER TEN

When Perlie saw the car, he waved, noticing the license plate. It was white with dark letters.

Coming to a stop, Willie rolled the window down. The guy looked rough.

Perlie lifted an empty plastic crate up towards the window. His pants were ripped and one of his shoes was missing. "Nothin' now, try tomorrow," he screeched, checking out the car.

Willie had no idea what he meant. "You know where I could find a gas station?"

He put the crate down. "Happy Jack Gulf. Close at six."

His teeth were gone and his arms were riddled with bites. "Nothin' much in Happy Jack. Need some gas."

Perlie looked up and down the road.

"Map says I'm near Socola?"

He took a half step toward the car and looked through the

window, admiring the interior. "Got no mail. Come back tomorrow."

His eyes had cataracts. "Mail for what?"

"For you."

Willie wanted to ask him things. About Happy Jack.

He backed away, picking up his crate. The side said US MAIL. "I put it here."

Willie nodded, not understanding.

"First I read it," he explained, grinning.

"Where's it comin' from?"

Perlie scrunched his face up in confusion. "Post office."

"Where's that?"

He pointed down the road.

Willie looked out through the windshield, noticing a large pile of cement in the distance.

"I bring da mail. People stop."

He looked back at the poor fellow. "You need a lift?"

Perlie gave him a funny look. "Where?"

"I don't know, grocery store?"

"Grocery store!!?" he shrieked. "Got mail to read, man. No time fo' no Shop 'n' Go!"

The fuel gauge was on empty. "I get it."

"You get it?"

"I do."

"Ain't 'bout me no mo'," he said, suddenly subdued.

Willie turned the car off. The road was quiet. It would be dark soon.

Perlie looked around, then back at Willie, looking inside the car again, noticing the missing radio. "Stole yo' radio."

"Yep."

"Who done that?"

"Cops."

He smiled when he heard it. "Bang, bang."

Willie had no idea.

"Need gas?"

"What?"

"Gas."

He looked at him, mystified. "I do."

"Come on," he said, lifting his crate, heading down the road.

When the Mississippi River receded in late September, it left a large commercial trawler behind, upside down over what remained of the Town of Socola's post office.

"Watch yo' head," Perlie warned, stooping under a chunk of broken cement, disappearing into a wide expanse of darkness.

Willie stopped. He wasn't sure where he was going, or why, but if he didn't find gas, he'd be spending the night in his car.

"Come on, mista!" Perlie called out from somewhere inside. "Be dark no time."

Giving in to it finally, crouching down, he lowered his head and stepped inside, standing upright eventually, adjusting his eyes, gazing up, incredibly, into the vaulted ceiling of a mighty wood cathedral.

"Get me da light, den we find you da gasoline." Perlie struck a match, lighting the wick of a large lantern. When the flame took hold, he closed the glass cover, pulling down on a long rope, raising the thing up into the air, tying it off to a nearby post.

Willie's mouth fell away, girders, frames, and crutches writhing in the shadows. He was under a boat.

"Name's Perlie."

There were stacks of mail everywhere. "Hey, Perlie, I'm Willie."

Perlie set his mail crate on a long metal table piled with boxes, envelopes, and magazines.

He'd never seen such a thing. His world was upside-down. "Quite a place you got here, man." A makeshift kitchen jutted out at one end. "That a radio over there?"

Perlie grinned when he heard the question. "Get me three stations and the Pelicans. Hear me some baseball."

"Where they play?"

"City Park, New Orleans."

"They any good?"

"Fifty-seven, ninety-four."

Despite his appearance, Perlie was sharp.

"Gotta throw strikes, man."

"Never been to a game, but that makes sense."

Perlie's body seized up. "You never been to no ball game?"

"No, sir."

"Goddamn, you born in a rock?"

Willie laughed, remembering the gasoline. "I know."

"Where da hell you from, boy?"

"Virginia."

Perlie considered it. "What part?"

"Charlottesville."

His eyes lit up. "Got the Senators, man!" he shouted. "Pistol Pete Runnels, Rocky Bridges…" He stopped. "Fast Eddie Yost. I mean, come on! Gots to grab dat shit when you can!"

Willie was astonished. "I suppose."

"Get yo' sef a *hot dog*." Perlie tried to think of something. "Gasoline!" he remembered, suddenly. "Willie need da juice!"

Willie wasn't sure if he'd been drinking, or how his mind worked, but he liked him. There were books on a table. "Really somethin', what you've done with this place. Got books, I see."

Perlie regarded the books dismissively. "Don't read much. No time, man," he explained, patting a pile of mail. "'Nough fish to fry right here, right now."

Willie approached the table, counting the stacks of mail. "Got twenty stacks…" He looked around, seeing more. "And all a that."

Perlie straightened up, rubbing his lower back with his hands. "Bring it in, stack it up. Make it dry." He considered all the piles. "Still blowin' round. Find it where I go."

"Go where?"

Perlie's face softened. It felt good to be telling someone. "Where dey see me."

Willie nodded, understanding how they'd met.

"Get da mail if I got it."

"People from around here?"

"Come back, see what they got. " He thought about it some more. "Take it all in."

"Is this all that's left?"

Perlie looked around, his eyes filled with sadness. "Lady come back, ask me if I seen her dog." He shook his head. "Man stop, give me a picture of his baby girl one day." He found a metal folding chair and sat down.

He looked exhausted.

"Said da wind took her," he mumbled, closing his eyes.

He watched him sleep. When the rain came down, he checked the lantern and covered him with a blanket. If there was gas to be found, it could wait until morning. He was in Perlie's world now, stacking the mail, keeping it dry, waiting for someone to call.

In the morning, a rooster crowed. Willie opened his eyes. Sunlight streaked through the hull. The couch smelled of peanuts.

Perlie was outside next to the Buick.

"Got yo' gas done," he said proudly, holding a garden hose,

spitting on the ground. "Come out real good."

The air smelled of gasoline.

Perlie gathered the hose as he walked away. "Got tanks in da ground over here."

He followed him, seeing a mound of hoses.

"Stack it up fo' next time," he explained, looping the final bit and letting go. He smelled his hands. "Shoowi! Blow massef up someday!"

Willie followed the hose to a tank in the ground. "This a gas tank?"

"Yessir."

"How 'bout that?"

"Don't be tellin'. Fo' da people dat need it."

"I understand, Perlie. Thank you very much."

He walked away toward the opening. "Time fo' some eats, man."


Perlie's fridge was a washtub full of ice. "Got shrimp, got eggs, some pone, hocks 'n' jam," he said, pulling out what he needed. "Fry it up outside."

Willie couldn't imagine how he'd survived. "I'm good, Perlie."

Perlie stopped. "What you talkin' 'bout?"

"Not hungry, thanks."

He grabbed some forks, plates, and a pan off a nearby bench. "Come on."

His grill was a hubcap over two slabs of concrete with a fire below. The smoke smelled of applewood.

Willie watched him, seeing chickens and a garden in the distance. "You got chickens?"

"And da rooster," he bragged, checking him out. "Noisy li'l fucker, but he get da job done."

"That a vegetable garden over there?"

He made a sour face. "Need's ta git on dem weeds. An rabbits. Fry one up someday."

He'd made a broken paradise with what he had. "Where you get the ice?"

"Shrimp man bring it," he answered, breaking two eggs with one hand, tossing the shells into a bucket. "Give him some gas." He shot him a racy look. "Couple magazines."

A line of pelicans flew over their heads, peering down as they passed.

"Pretty day for Mista Pelican," Perlie said, stirring his pan slowly.

Willie looked up. The sky was as blue as he'd ever seen.

"Be divin' fo' dem pogies," he muttered, shoveling food onto their plates.

Climbing a staircase of makeshift steps, they dangled their legs over a concrete ledge while they ate, admiring the river. It was a glorious day, warmed by the sun, washed by the rain.

"'Bout the best eggs I ever had," Willie confessed, stopping when he realized it. "And this pone, man. Give someone I know a run for her money."

Perlie smiled.

Willie dragged the last of it across his plate, popping it in his mouth. "Guess I was hungrier than I thought."

Perlie looked out between bites, noticing things. "Air be fresh after dat rain," he explained, hearing a car pass behind them. "People be comin' now."

Willie held his plate in his lap, watching the river.

"Get da mail."

They were quiet as Perlie ate.

"You seen duh world, Willie?"

"Seen some of it, I guess. More since I left Virginia."

Perlie's face turned resolute. "Got a cousin in Shreveport. Like ta go dere someday. Fish duh Red."

Willie watched the river move.

"You tink it be different here from where you from?"

"Maybe."

"How so?"

It came to him quickly. "Call you nigger to your face."

Perlie nodded, taking a bite of his scone.

Willie handed him four five-dollar bills. "For the gas and

everything. Left some soup inside. Don't know what I woulda done if you hadn't come along."

Perlie's face grew circumspect. "Tinkin' *you* did da come-along," he replied, taking it, counting slowly.

Seeing the condition he was in, Willie wondered about his age. "Where you from, Perlie?"

He put the money in his pocket, taking up his pone. "Cross da road."

Willie turned around.

"Dat ole swamp oak. Little house and da land."

He saw a tree but the house was gone.

"Daddy raised chickens. Momma flew da coop."

"You got brothers and sisters?"

"Told me, no."

Willie grinned. "Me too."

"What you do up dere in Charlietown, man?"

"Charlottesville?"

"Yeah."

"Got a whorehouse."

Perlie stopped eating and looked at him. "Damn."

"My momma had it, so we fixed it up."

He considered the idea. Willie's age. "Never too young for da lovin'."

Willie smiled. "Nice way to put it."

"Got pretty girls?"

"We do."

"Bet dat helps."

"Yeah."

"How much it cost?"

"To be with one?"

"Yeah."

"I don't know? Depends, I guess."

He looked confused. "Like what?"

"How pretty she is? How long you stay?"

Perlie nodded, finishing his scone.

"Twenty bucks an hour, maybe? Somethin' like that."

"Like da mail," he managed while he chewed.

Willie thought he was serious until he saw his face.

Perlie gave him a wink and slapped his legs "Lickin' dem stamps!"

They cracked up, looking away. Then again.


A tow appeared, moving slowly upriver. They watched it for a while.

"Takin' sulfur from da lake."

"Which lake?"

"Grande Ecaille. Up west."

The barges followed eventually, with mountains of gray-white powder.

"Where's it goin'?"

"Creole City. Forty-seven miles." he replied, gazing up into the sky. It felt warm for December. "Where you headed when you go?"

"Still lookin' for my friend. Thought he mighta been in Biloxi."

"What he doin' dere?"

"Was shrimpin' maybe."

Perlie nodded.

"Had some trouble in New Orleans. Thinkin' he's hoppin' trains now."

He held his plate and stood with some difficulty. His feet were swollen and his bones ached. "Devil's Town, my momma say. Ain't nothin' dere be right."

A third barge passed by.

He touched his shirt pocket. "Gave me too much money."

"Gave you what I had to give."

He looked down at Willie, more tenderly this time. "Well, thank you, 'cuz I sho' can use it. And fo' da soup."

A warm wind stirred around them.

"Good luck wid yo' friend."

Willie stood as well. He'd need to hit the road.

They watched the river one last time.

"You been slapped every which way, haven't you, Perlie?"

Perlie looked down at his one bare foot.

"You need a ride somewhere? See your cousin maybe?"

"Tell me again, how come yo here?"

He'd almost forgotten. "I was lookin' for a church."

"What kinda church?

"The one in Happy Jack."

"Baptist place?"

"Yep."

"How come?"

He looked out. The barge was gone. "Thinkin' my momma's there. Cemetery in back, maybe. Next to a sister."

Perlie concentrated."What's her name?"

"My momma?"

"Sister."

"No idea."

The answer surprised him. "And yo' momma?"

"Sadie Graves."

He squinted, remembering the place. "Best I can think, ain't no names like dat." He looked at Willie sadly. "Place be small."

A pelican plunged headfirst from the sky, slicing through the water.

"Been washed away, man. Stones 'n' all."

Willie took a deep breath, understanding it finally. How far he'd come for nothing. "Not what I was hoping for."

The bird surfaced, lifting its bill.

"Well…" Perlie sighed, watching the river slide, "dey wid ma' momma now."

Perlie Fuchet stood by the road and watched him drive away. They'd shaken hands and said their final words, thanked each other one more time for the gasoline and the money. Something tender had passed between them. He wasn't sure what it was. He had mail to stack, cars to stop. That would be enough. And when the sun set and the day was done, he'd shuffle home, tie his lantern to the post, and listen for the wind.

# CHAPTER ELEVEN

David Sheffield knocked again. The temperature had dropped and his nose was cold.

"Sorry, Sheriff. Was in the kitchen."

He looked older. "Mornin', Halsey."

"Pretty quiet upstairs. You need Josie?"

"Please."

Halsey opened the door and backed away. "Come on in, cold out there."

The hallway smelled of biscuits and cigars.

The sheriff removed his hat. "Twenty at the house this morning. Callin' for snow today."

"Lord have mercy! Make me some Brunswick, case the power goes out."

The two men looked at each other. They'd never had a cross word.

"You missin' the Tavern these days?"

"No, sir. Ladies treat me right. Got some good hours and… you know the drill." He wiped his big, greasy hands across his apron. "Pancakes 'n' bacon… eggs on the side."

"How long you there?"

He said it like he always did. "Thirty years til the wheels come off."

"Done your time, man."

"Thank you, sir. Did the best I could for the time I had."

"All you can do."

"All you can do."

They waited a spell.

"Got the oven on."

"Smells good."

"Better pull 'em out. Good to see you, Sheriff." He turned for the kitchen. "I'll give Josie a call, tell her you're here."

He looked around. The basket was empty. "Appreciate it. And hey…"

Halsey turned back, worried. "Sir?"

"Save me a biscuit."


When Josie appeared, they moved to the parlor. She looked pretty and tired. There was coffee on the bar.

"You want some?" she asked, helping herself to a cup. "Halsey makes it fresh."

He'd go easy on her for a while, but they'd need to sort it out. "Cup a black would be fine, thank you."

She poured him a cup. "His biscuits smell good, don't they?"

"Always."

She brought him his cup and found a sofa nearby, plopping down carefully, enjoying her first sip. "Good for the soul."

Tiny embers glowed in the fireplace. He looked around, imagining the men, all horny and liquored up, her ladies in their tight evening dresses.

The room was cold.

"Want me to get your fire go'n?"

"Very kind of you, if you don't mind."

He put his cup down and stood, moving the screen back, placing two logs carefully over the embers. "Callin' for snow tonight."

"Got bellows right there if you need it."


When the flames kicked in, he added more wood and positioned the screen.

"They told me you called. Yesterday, I think it was."

"I did," he replied, returning to his chair.

"Didn't mean to put you off," she explained, sounding sleepy. "Been a busy month."

The fire crackled as they drank their coffee, waiting for the other to speak.

"What can I do for you, David Sheffield?"

He sat back to consider it.

She removed her slippers, drawing her legs up under her robe. "Thinkin' it's not about the biscuits."

He put his cup down and leaned forward. "Been doin' the best I can with this, Josie, but I told you and Cary from the get-go, you get this thing rollin', can't stop what happens next."

She watched his face harden.

"You got a doctor, I hear?"

"Every two weeks."

"And Bob Brewer in Richmond?"

"Nice man."

"Better lawyer."

She waited. "Three girls, a cook, and a housekeeper, then what?"

"And Cary Buck."

"Cary too."

He leaned forward, waiting to say it.

"What's this about?"

"'Bout you."

"Me?"

A spark of wood popped against the screen.

"And Willie."

She finished her cup, watching the fire grow.

"I got a notice from the health department to close this place down." He pulled an envelope from inside his coat and tossed it on the coffee table. "Got ten days to respond."

She gave him an exhausted smile. "Let me guess, a kitchen violation."

"Gotta read it."

"Before what?"

He grinned, enjoying her attitude. "Before we close you down for a while."

"And how long will that be? A week? Couple hours?"

"What the hell do I know, Josie? Not my deal to fix it. Y'all put this on yourselves, not me. Told you this would happen and that's what's goin' on."

She placed her cup on a small table.

"Ain't gonna stop 'cuz you got a list, if that's what you're thinkin'."

She waited for him to finish.

"Bunch a *names*." He shot her a menacing look. "Not how it works."

Her face was hard to read. He looked at the bar. "Think I'll switch to bourbon, if that's alright?"

"Knock yourself out."

He nodded, crossing the room, seeing an old clock on the wall. It was half past ten. "Want one?"

"I'm fine, thank you." She noticed the windows. It was snowing.

The sheriff returned to his chair and drank his bourbon, watching the snow come down. It was simple enough. A cozy room and a good-looking woman.

"You done talkin'?"

He smiled, enjoying her tone, feeling the booze. "Sorry to be here like this."

"Part a the job."

"Be a shitty Santa Claus."

She laughed, imagining a small child on his lap. "Make sure Halsey gives you some biscuits when you go."

"Appreciate that."

The fireplace popped loudly.

She rose from the couch. "Changed my mind," she decided, moving to the bar.

He watched the silver robe, her smooth legs crossing the room.

"Pretty out there," she said, returning with her drink. The flakes were fat and slow.

"Makes you feel like a child again."

She took a sip and gave him a look. "Won't stick, David."

"I'm sorry?"

The glass was cold in her hand. "If you had somethin', you wouldn't be the one tellin' me."

He took a deep drink. "Open the envelope, Josie."

"Got names and you know who they are."

"Pretty straightforward."

"When they were here. Who they were with."

He gave it a moment to clear his head. The bourbon was strong.

"You hear about last night?"

"No idea."

"Well, then," she shook her head resisting a laugh, "that's the problem now, isn't it?"

His jaw tightened.

"Not me." She took a sip. "Or Willie."

He drained his glass, pausing for a moment. "How long you been here, Josie?"

"Came early November."

"Six weeks."

"Whatever you're trying to say, let's get to it, shall we?"

"Already did. You're done here for a while, plain and simple. Not real complicated."

"I run a business. You run a town."

"Not the same thing, now is it? Sadie understood that."

"You think?"

"Apples and oranges."

She finished her drink, placing it on a table. "Until she didn't."

He put his glass down and stood. "Been trying to help you with this, Josie, you know that. Said what I came here to say. You have ten days."

After a moment, Josie stood as well, removing an envelope from the outside pocket of her robe, tossing it on the table next to his. "Suit yourself."

It looked thick.

"That's two thousand to make you go away. Help us when you can."

He didn't budge.

"And whenever you get to where you were yesterday, come see me first."

"And why would I do that, exactly?"

She looked him in the eye. "July twenty-fifth, 1955. Room six, upstairs. First door on the right." She stopped, letting it sink in. "Nine p.m. to five a.m. with a certain Miss Connie James. You remember her?"

His face was pale.

"Bit strange what went on. People you were with?"

He touched the safety snap of his holster.

She tightened her robe, feeling the fire. "The gentleman next door?"


When the wipers stopped, snow blurred the windshield, dampening what little light remained. Leaning back, he thought of her threats, his marriage. Cop to criminal, criminal to cop. It was all the same.

He held the money in his hands, thinking of his wife. It surprised him at first, how easy it had been. Spontaneous. He grabbed his things and opened the door, imagining it once again. Two first-class seats and some pink champagne, with the perfect strand of pearls.

# CHAPTER TWELVE

When Willie saw the Christmas lights, he pulled in for gas. The tires were off and the oil was low. He'd ask for directions when he went inside.

Entering the station, a freckle-faced teen looked him over from behind a desk. "That's three dollars for the gas and a buck for the Opaline."

Willie handed him five dollars.

The bathroom door said WHITES ONLY.

"Ain't chargin' for the air."

He wanted some candy. The place was creepy. "I'm lookin' for Woods Guesthouse on Mobile Street."

The attendant took change from his drawer. "Got your book?"

Willie played along. The last thing he needed was a shakedown. "Yes, sir, I do," he replied with a friendly smile.

He offered the money. "Down East Hardy here, third right."

"Third right," Willie repeated, opening his hand, taking it. "Appreciate your help."

Hearing it, the young man wiped his fingers on a dirty paper towel, noticing his Buick outside. His face grew cold. "Get your food cross the street."

He locked the car door and checked the gauges, pulling out slowly, counting the lights. Turning right on Mobile, he saw a hotel sign in the distance. Mel's Café was across the street. He found a parking spot, turning the key and grabbing his Green Book. Opening the trunk, an old Black man watched him from across the lot. He was used to it by now, his indignant glare.

A truck backfired nearby, startling him. Closing the trunk, he thought of Perlie's hull. How his momma washed away. He'd read somewhere that life was mostly make believe, an imitation of the truth. Taking his bag and heading in, he smiled to think of it, the mysteries and the fables. One more night in Hattiesburg with the demons, ghosts, and saints.

He tossed and turned all night. Stick had haunted his dreams, then his father, then Poppy's sweet face—all of them together at one point, inconceivably, tumbling, somersaulting down a dark, petulant river, smashing up against the rocks, one by one, before he woke, fumbling for the light in a pool of sweat.

He went to the open window, his heart still racing, removing his t-shirt, hanging it on the catch to dry. Someone was snoring next door. He caught a glimpse of his car in the shadow of an entrance light. Or was it farther down? He couldn't tell. He'd take a bath and hit the road, grab some food at Mel's. The window trembled from a passing train. He wondered if he'd always think of Stick when he heard one, or if the memory would fade, disappear into a tunnel.

The hallway smelled of cheap perfume. A voice had woken him in the night. A man's voice, he remembered clearly, reaching the bathroom door, opening it slowly.

The faucets screamed. Slipping into the water, he felt the quiet around him, calming his mind, his restless thoughts. Why had he come? What was the point of it? Caring for those who were gone. He raised his hands above the water, admiring them in the strange blue light. They were pale and thin. Cadaverous. A toilet flushed above his head. Or was it a wave? A summer squall? He tried to let go of it. Of everything.

The air was crisp, almost cold when he stepped outside, seeing a massive oak beside a streetlight. He'd need a sweatshirt, or a jacket from his bag, then warm the car up and count his money. A leaf dropped gently into the trunk when he opened it, its underside etched in a striking silver-white. He admired it in the half-light for a moment, turning it from side to side, tossing it away.

The clock at Mel's said 6:15 a.m. Willie found a stool and grabbed a menu. Looking around, it surprised him at first. The place was empty.

"Early bird gets the worm."

He looked up at the man. "Good morning."

"Start you with some coffee?"

"Thank you." He'd never had coffee before.

The man spun around and grabbed a pot, finding a cup.

Willie stared at the menu.

"Cream and sugar by the napkins. What d'you think?"

"Maybe just some fried eggs and bacon with toast?"

"White?" He slid the cream and sugar closer. "How you like your eggs?"

He remembered the way Stick liked them. "Over easy, please."

He looked at Willie for a second. "Where you from?"

"Virginia."

"Which part?"

"Albemarle County."

"Horse country."

It surprised him the way he said it. "You ever been?"

"I have."

Willie smiled, seeing his expression.

"Worked horses after the war. Kentmere Farm. You heard of it?"

"No, sir."

"Guy named Gilpin." He stopped, dragging a wet rag across the counter. "Sport a kings."

He remembered his drives with Mr. Matt and his momma down Route 22. It was another world to him then. "Lotta pretty farms there."

The man's face grew more serious, thinking of it. "Made a movie, couple years back."

Willie hadn't heard.

"Last one that James Dean did, I think." A family came through the door. He gave them a smile, pointing toward a table. "Got a girl sick today, so I best get goin'," he explained, noticing Willie's black eye.

Willie nodded. "Good, 'cuz I could eat a horse."

He laughed loudly, slapping his hand on the counter. "Name's Mel."

"I'm Willie."

"Willie Over Easy from Albemarle County," he replied, enjoying the sound of it, returning to the kitchen.


The coffee was strong. He tried some sugar. After the third sip he added cream, then sugar again. He liked the way it smelled, how it swirled around when he stirred it. He figured it was an acquired taste, something you drank from habit, or from watching others do it—like Dr Pepper, or vodka on the rocks.

A tall, skinny woman brought him his plate with two eggs and a pile of bacon. She said her name, but he was too focused on his food to hear it. The toast was next, with butter and jam, then grits, then more sweet coffee. He tried to go slow, the way he had at Perlie's, but it was hopeless. Everything tasted so good.

When he was done, he cleaned his hands with a paper napkin, noticing the tables had filled, finishing his cup, leaving some money and a tip. He felt at ease there—enjoying the way they talked to one another, coming in, going out. Christmas lights. Tinsel on the sills. Maybe Hattiesburg was more than its parts. A kinder place. More than the painful story.

He rose from the stool. A dark-skinned girl with deep-set eyes watched him as he passed. She was about his age and sitting alone. He approached the entrance, pushing against the door.

"*Willie Over Easy!*" Mel shouted, watching him go.

He turned back, feeling their eyes upon him. The cold morning air. "See ya, Mel!" He gave him a wave, heading out the door.

Sweat hit the grill and scattered. Something was burning. He wiped his brow and took a moment, remembering the fields. The hills of Albemarle County.

The clock said 7:00 a.m. He started the car and turned the heater on, considering the day. How some folks stuck together. Made the world a better place. He rolled the window down, noticing a cloud overhead.

He grinned when he saw it, thinking of Moses, feeling the wind stir.

"Hey, mister," a soft voice said.

She'd followed him out and needed a ride.

"You like what I'm wearin'?"

It was an odd question. "Yeah." She wore a long white overcoat and her jeans were tight. He noticed her boots. "Like your boots."

She looked down, admiring her boots, turning them from side to side. "Got these where I'm goin' later, if you wanna come with me." Her eyes were smoky and inviting. "Might find somethin' you like."

Willie gripped the wheel. "Come on."


When she settled in, he headed out, turning toward the highway.

They didn't talk for a while. The car smelled of hairspray.

"Nice ride."

"Thank you."

"Take a right next street up." She pulled the visor down and checked her hair. "My name's Jeannie."

"I'm Willie."

"Turn here." She flipped the visor up, swinging her knees up onto the seat as they turned. "Thank you for the ride, Willie."

"You're welcome." He noticed the neighborhood. It was mostly run down houses.

"Where you from?"

"Charlottesville, Virginia."

She looked at him more thoughtfully. His skin was dreamy. "You one a them students up there?"

He gave her a quick glance. "You mean, The University?"

"Yeah." She checked the road. "Left on Ninth comin' up."

He signaled to turn. "No, I ain't there." He winced, hearing the way he'd put it. "I mean, I'd *like* to be someday. Apply n'all." He turned the wheel. "Just need to take care of some things."

She gave him a skeptical look. He was cute. "Like finish high school?"

He laughed when he heard the way she put it. "Probably start there, yeah."

"This be it on the right. Third house."

He slowed down.

"The blue one," she said, sounding melancholy.

He pulled up to the curb and left the engine on. The house was a wreck.

She looked away and sighed. "Home sweet home."

He felt awkward suddenly, seeing her discomfort, checking the sky. "Looks like a nice day once it warms up."

She slipped her coat off. "You wanna come inside?"

"I'd like to, but I better be goin'."

She fiddled with a necklace on her chest. "My brother's still sleepin'. Got a room out back."

She was dark and inviting. "Like I said…"

"Want me to blow you?"

The word smacked him sideways.

She slid closer, putting her hand on the inside of his thigh.

Blood raced through his body as he felt it. Her breath smelled of spearmint and coffee. She slid her hand higher and stopped, smiling, enjoying his reaction. "For five bucks?"

He tried to breathe, to slow himself down, but it was too late.

She moved her hand up his leg and squeezed gently, drawing her body closer, placing her mouth near his cheeks.

Willie closed his eyes, feeling it everywhere.

"Come all this way, like to send you home happy," she whispered softly. "Ain't like you don't want it."

When he pushed her away, she didn't resist. His cheeks were flushed. Her coat had fallen to the floor.

A car passed slowly.

He stared out the window, catching his breath.

She waited for him to decide.

"I'm sorry."

"Be better inside." She picked her coat up and dusted it off.

He watched her pet her coat.

She stopped and looked at him eventually. "How old are you?"

"Nineteen."

She looked more sad than young. "How long you been doin' this?"

She saw his Green Book on the dash. "Ain't none a your business," she said, opening the door, getting out of the car.

"Jeannie."

She stopped, watching a car approach.

Willie leaned across the seat. "I'll give you the five"—he waited for the car to pass—"if you get back in and talk to me."

She watched the car pass.

"Come on."

When the street was quiet, she got in and shut the door, still holding her coat, flipping the visor down, checking her mascara.

"Don't wanna make you angry."

"I ain't angry," she said, messing with her hair.

"Your hair's real pretty."

"Thank you."

"How you get it so straight?"

She stopped, flipping the visor up. "You mind if I smoke?"

"Not at all." He rolled the windows down and turned the engine off.

She took a pack of Spuds from her coat pocket. "You want one?"

"No, thanks. Never seen those—what are they?"

"Eddie gets 'em. From Kentucky somewhere."

"I know a guy named Spud. Need to get some on the way home."

She took a drag and looked around the neighborhood. "So, what are we talkin' 'bout for my five bucks?"

"I don't know."

She turned toward him, looking more relaxed. "You want I say somethin' bad?"

"What you mean, bad?"

She twisted around and flicked some ash out her window, turning back, watching him. "Talk dirty."

They looked at each other.

"No, shoot!"

She took a drag, exhaling quickly. "You say, *shoot?*"

"What you mean?"

She stared at him and laughed. "How come you're so uptight, man?"

He laughed with her, wondering if it was true.

"Damn." She looked away, suddenly disinterested.

He thought about Poppy. "How'd you get into this?"

She tossed the cigarette, watching it bounce across the street.

"Who's Eddie?"

"None a your business." She swung her legs up onto the seat and leaned back against the door, looking into his eyes.

He looked away. She was hard to follow. "No, it's not."

"So, why the fuck you askin'?"

He had no reason.

They sat together quietly.

She found an ashtray, pulling it out. "This a nice car."

"Thanks."

She closed it.

He noticed the condition of the car, seeing cuts in the back seat. "Clean it up when I get home."

"How come you got it?"

"Friend gave it to me."

"Lucky."

There was something in her voice. "I am."

She saw the missing radio. "Where's the radio?"

"Cops took it."

She didn't flinch. "Where they do that?"

"Meridian."

She gave him a look, noticing his eye.

"Yep."

She touched the dashboard, the clock. "Bet it made a racket."

"Yeah, real sweet. Got the speakers in back."

She spun around to look, seeing them on the doors.

"Get me a new one when I get home."

They sat for a while, before she could say it. "You wanna take me there?"

"Take you where?"

She leaned her head back, turning to see her house through the window. "Where you're goin'."

He couldn't answer right away.

"I got nowhere to go."

"You finish high school?"

She settled back against the seat. "Never started."

"What you mean?"

"What I said."

He couldn't imagine it until he realized. He hadn't either.

She stared through the windshield. "I don't want this life no more."

"You mean turnin' tricks?"

She looked at him and smiled. "Guess you ain't as stupid as you look."

He laughed, enjoying her company. "Is Eddie your brother?"

"No."

"How long you been doin' this?"

"Three years now."

"You got family somewhere?"

"No."

"Someone you trust?"

"Mel's a good guy. Helps me out when he can."

He waited for more.

"Offered me a job today. Somebody didn't show."

"Take it."

She looked at him when he said it. He was sweet. The kind of boy she needed. "You think?"

"*Shit*, yes!"

They laughed.

He reached for his wallet and took out half of what he had, giving it to her.

"What you doin'?"

"Here."

She stared at the money.

"Not a lot but enough to get you by. Find a room somewhere. Mel will know. I can send you something later."

She started to cry.

"No, come on. It's good, I'm tellin' you. Been down this road sometimes and people helped me out—they always do if you give 'em a reason. And now it's me helpin' you."

She leaned into him, wrapping her arms around him, crying quietly.

He put his arms around her as best he could. She was soft and warm. "It's good, really. I got plenty when I get home. Wish I could give you more."

She let go and scooted back, mascara streaking down her cheeks.

He held the money out. "Up to you what you do with it."

She watched him for a moment, taking it eventually, wiping her face with the palm of her hands.

"Got paper napkins in the glove compartment."


Jeannie stood on the sidewalk, holding her coat. She tried to smile as he pulled away. He wasn't sure what she'd do, if she'd accept Mel's offer. He'd felt that way a million times before, lost and forgotten, trusting no one.


The gas tank was full. He found the road north, still smelling her hair, feeling their arms around each other. It pleased him to think of it, checking his speed, the rearview mirror, saying her name out loud. Without knowing it, she'd given him that, what she could from her heart, and so much more.

# CHAPTER THIRTEEN

He pulled over near the Birmingham Station to pee, racing down a steep hill into a copse of pines, fumbling with his zipper, sighing with relief, standing there forever. Trains arrived and departed slowly below him. Southern Railway. Frisco. He heard a speaker in the distance.

Stepping out from under the branches, he moved downhill to get a better look. As the trains moved, a bull walked between them, holding his baton in one hand. Or was it a rifle? He stepped further down, hearing feet on the gravel below, seeing a man race out from behind a storage shed, diving into the darkness of an open boxcar as it moved away. Within seconds, another man followed, hesitating for a moment, recognizing the bull between the moving cars, slinking back and disappearing. He thought about Stick. How he'd always wait, consider the situation carefully, before he made his move. Like a cat, he'd said when he first explained it, knowing when to pounce.

A man arrived suddenly from below dragging a tattered satchel, coming to a stop. His black face was hollow and slack. "What you doin' up here?" he gasped, struggling for his breath.

"Sorry." Willie pointed toward his car. "Pulled over up there on top. Been drivin'."

His face relaxed, looking down over the tracks anxiously, then back to Willie. "You got some change, man? Get me somethin' to eat?"

When he heard the question, he panicked. The car was still running, with his wallet inside. "Shit!"

The road got louder as he climbed. It was steeper than he realized. He heard the man behind him trying to keep up. He'd give him a few bucks and be on his way, save the rest for the long drive home.

A line of trucks flew by as he reached the top, panting, inhaling their fumes. He looked around to get his bearings, seeing the sign, where he'd parked, where he'd descended, then again before he realized, the blood in his head swirling to a stop. His car was gone.

When the man reached him, he dropped his satchel, bent over gasping, raising himself up as best he could, seeing Willie's expression finally, understanding what had happened. "Oh, man!"

Willie looked again in disbelief, numb to the world. Everything was gone. His money. His clothes. *The Grapes of Wrath.*

A truck raced by, hitting the horn as it passed, shearing their faces with cold gray dust.

"*Merry fucking Christmas!*" the man cursed, turning his head away.

The road quieted eventually.

He watched Willie pace about, reaching into his satchel, pulling out a bottle of Rebel Yell. "Here, man, have shot a this." He held the bottle up. "Help you think straight."

Willie stopped, seeing him, it seemed, for the first time.

They found a clearing off the road and drank. Willie resisted the first hit.

"There you go," the man said, seeing his face relax.

The second made him feel better, before he gave it back.

"Pretty shitty what happened, man."

Willie couldn't talk.

He took a long drink, looking around to get his bearings, then down toward the tracks, offering the bottle again.

Willie shook his head.

He noticed his thin shirt. "Be dark soon." He put the bottle in Willie's hand. "Help warm you up, come on."

Willie hesitated before swallowing hard, handing it back. He'd walk to the station and use a phone. "Need to find my car."

The man looked down at his boots.

Willie's face was flushed. "Call the cops."

"You sure 'bout that?"

"Stole my car with everything I got. What am I supposed to do?"

He put the bottle back in his satchel, taking out a raggedy old sweater. "Here," he said, offering it. "Gonna be a cold night. Put it on."


Halfway down, they stopped under the pines where they'd met.

"Can't call the cops. Listen to me! Whatever you're thinkin' it *can't* be that."

Willie shook his head in disbelief.

"Tank Bailey gonna string you up, no way round it."

"Who's that?"

"Chief a police."

They looked at each other.

"I'm tellin' you, man. You ain't nothin' to him 'cept a nigger on wheels."

Willie looked down toward the tracks.

"Lock your ass up and say you stole it."

He was back in Meridian.

"S'how it works in this town." He stopped to let it sink in. "You understand me?"

Willie nodded slowly.

"Take no pleasure tellin' you this. Need to walk away any way you can."

He looked into the man's bloodshot eyes. He was lost again.

"Can't fly, you run."

He put the sweater on, feeling its warmth right away. His name was Ernest. He'd been to see a sister in Tuscaloosa and ran out of money. He was on his way somewhere warm.

"Feel bad about your sweater."

"Ain't mine to feel bad about, brother. Found it down there hangin' on a branch. Figured I'd grab it for the road."

Willie felt it with his hands. "Well, I appreciate it."

Ernest checked the inside of his satchel. His clothes were dry. "And here you be."

He watched him, grateful for what he'd done. "Got no money to help you with. Pay for my sweater."

He gave him an odd look. "Not somethin' you planned, now was it?"

"Guess not. Wasn't thinkin' straight when I did it."

Ernest reached down into the inner side of a boot and took out a dollar bill, offering it to him. "Take this."

Willie's face fell when he saw it. "I can't do that, man. You need to keep that, case you need it later." He looked uphill, hopelessly, understanding how desperate his situation had become.

"I would, if I had to and now it's your turn, so take it."

"I can't."

The boy was tough. "Got no choice, come on."

"Not takin' your last dollar, Ernest." He stared at the ground.

"Ain't doin' it."

Ernest shook his head, bending over, sliding the money inside his boot.

"Appreciate the offer."

He lifted his satchel and stood. "Yeah, well… good men perish and the godly go quick."

Willie checked his pocket, feeling his Swiss Army knife, taking it out.

Ernest's eyes got big. "There you go!"

He sighed when he realized, admiring it in his hand. "Forgot I had it."

"That's a good one."

He closed his hand around it, thinking of Rebecca, having it with him all this time.

"Where you headed, Willie? Forgot to ask."

"Charlottesville."

"Heck, man!" he replied, quickly. "Take the L&N to Chattanooga, Southern Railway home." He looked down at the tracks, seeing something. "Play your cards right, be there by morning!"

Willie looked down, barely hearing it.

"See that chip hopper down between the timber cars?"

He moved to the edge of the trees, seeing it. "One with no top?"

"Be leavin' soon."

"How you know that?"

Ernest slung his satchel over his shoulder. "Come on!" he barked softly, taking off.

When they reached the bottom, Ernest stopped to look around, sliding beside the utility shed, inching his way slowly toward the tracks.

Willie came up behind him, holding his knife, seeing his satchel still open.

He turned his head back and whispered, "Car in the middle there, you see it?"

"Red one?"

"And don't be messin' round when you go." He faced the tracks again, looking each way for bulls.

"How you know it's goin' north?"

"See them letters?"

Willie read the letters on the side corner of the car.

"'CH' be Chattanooga and the 'N' be north." He leaned his head out, checking both ends of the train one more time. "You need to go." He turned back. "Same deal when you get there—Southern Railway, CVS, northbound and, listen to me." He checked to see if Willie was listening. "No rinky-dink hopper. Be a long ride and you'll freeze your nuts off."

They heard an engine start in the distance.

Willie stepped out from behind him, not knowing what to say.

Ernest grinned. "I know, been a pleasure. Get yourself another

car someday and the next time you walk the dog... lock the fuckin'
door!"

The chips were soft and sticky with sap. He found a spot against a
back wall, catching his breath, dropping down. He smelled of bourbon
and his feet were cold.

When the train jerked, cars slammed together, resisting each
other momentarily, before letting go, pulling away. Then faster, and
faster still. He watched the clouds pass, smelling engine fumes,
feeling sunlight against his face. Closing his eyes, hearing the rail
joints click, he touched his empty pocket one more time, thinking of
Ernest, of the knife in his satchel, glad to have left it behind.

When he opened his eyes, it was dark and the air was colder. The car
had stopped. It alarmed him at first, taking a sharp breath, hearing
voices. He smelled cigarettes.

"Not here, Jack!"

Then nothing.

"Near the reefer!"

He sank down into the chips, his nostrils just above the surface.
They were bulls, looking for someone. He wiggled his body farther
down, burying himself completely, hearing boots on the ladder,
reaching the top. He held his breath, dizzy from the turpentine.

A light passed over him. Then darkness.

"Must a jumped."

When the boots descended, hitting the gravel, he gasped for air, raising himself quickly, shaking his head of chips and dust. Listening carefully.

The train lunged suddenly, pushing him back, picking up speed. He lay there as it rocked, flashing red lights passing overhead, then darkness, hearing crossing bells.

The girls had left and Cary was alone. He stood on the porch smoking one last cigarette. The quiet was unsettling, the cold. Josie and Caroline would be back in a week; Poppy was gone for good. That was the sad part, the truth of their lives. They'd roll the dice and find another girl.

His parents were waiting, like every Christmas Eve. His father would pray, his mother would cry, his sister would ask him for money. He'd bring wine and presents and a twenty for church, avoiding his own redemption. The house had been his saving grace, an answer to his prayers. It surprised him at first, how easy it was, how satisfying-mixing money with pleasure.

He took a final drag, tossing it over the rail, watching the embers fade. He'd filled the bowls and locked the doors. Buttoning his overcoat, finding his car keys, he heard a faint and tender meow somewhere in the dark. Turning his head, he thought of Willie, wondering where he'd gone.

Chattanooga was dark when the train pulled in, coming to a sudden halt. He waited before climbing to the top, finding the ladder, feeling the cold night air. He held his breath when he landed, taking off quickly, desperately, following the letters as Ernest had said, hugging the cars as he ran, tankers, coils, reefers, hoppers, gondolas, flats, their inscriptions flying by, on and on and on. It seemed impossible, what he was doing, what little it would take before his luck ran out.

At some point, he saw it, out of breath, frantically, from the corner of his eye, racing back and reading it again, disbelieving what it said at first, then once more to be sure, finding an open doorway and grabbing the ledge.

It was empty and dry. He closed the doors, choosing a corner in the back, collapsing down against it, still panting, trembling in the dreary, dim light. He tried to remember the letters he'd seen, hearing his breathing mostly, then an engine start, brakes release. When the floorboards shuddered, his back hit the wall. It took a moment to sink in, to understand what it meant. CVS. N for North. As the train picked up speed, he closed his eyes, half believing it, whispering a silent prayer. For all that he'd lost and all that he'd found, in a boxcar sent from heaven.

# CHAPTER FOURTEEN

When the cats saw Cary's car they scattered, one or two holding their ground, crying out, smelling the bag. He left the kitchen window open as they ate, growling and hissing. There were four now. Poppy had taken one, one was found dead in the road. He lit a cigarette, sipping his coffee, hearing the clock. He'd sleep in Amber's room, enjoy the place while he could, a cozy warm fire.

When the creatures dispersed, he gathered their dishes, washing them in the sink. He'd draw a bath and read a magazine, look at all the pretty things. There was money now and more to come. He liked that part. The way they looked at him in town. Like a girl in a fancy new dress.

Something appeared in the window.

Seeing him, the dish dropped, smashing down against the floor.

When the door opened, they wrapped their arms around each other, rocking back and forth slowly.

"You smell like chickens."

Willie let go and stepped back for him to see.

Cary looked him over, horrified. "And wood."

Willie ran his hands through his scalp, watching the chips fall. He felt dirty and weak.

"And that sweater?"

He looked down, caressing it reverently with his hands. "Saved my life this thing."

"What in the world?" Where have you been?"

His face grew cold. "They took my car."

"What do you mean, took?"

"Stole it."

"Your beautiful Buick?"

He was tired and hungry.

Cary put his arms around him again, more tenderly this time. "It's just a car."

"I know."

"And now you're safe."

"I know."

They let go of each other.

Cary shook his head, seeing him again. "Josie's in Brooklyn. I need to call her, tell her you're here. She's with Caroline. I'm not sure about Amber. They're back on Friday."

A white cat appeared through the balustrade, looking for dishes.

"For fuck's sake, William! You scared me half to death."

Willie stepped back, feeling dizzy. "I need something to eat."

He served him Halsey's meatloaf with green beans, buttered biscuits, and peach jam. When he was done, he lifted his plate for more.

Cary stared at his sweater. "Take that off and put it outside. I have something in the fridge."

He hung his sweater on the railing, stopping to admire the backyard, seeing his tree next door, smelling the air. It was ripe with leaves and earth and something else, something sweet.

A slice of coconut cream pie was on the table. Taking the first bite, he closed his eyes, tasting whipped cream, then coconut, filling, Graham cracker crust, moaning quietly as he swallowed.

Cary lit a cigarette, watching him, seeing dirt beneath his fingernails.

He took a larger bite.

"I thought you were dead."

Willie stopped to see if he was serious, swallowing. "I'm sorry."

Cary tapped his cigarette against the edge of the ashtray. "You said you'd call after looking for your momma."

Willie took a final bite and put the fork down.

"You want some milk?"

"Please."

He put his cigarette down and stood, filling a glass from the fridge and returning to his chair. "Here. Would you like another slice?"

He drained the glass.

"Whoa! Slow down, honey!" He rose from his chair and repeated what he'd done, handing him the glass and sitting. "My little camel."

Willie laughed, realizing suddenly how strange he must look. He took a small sip, sitting back in his chair, noticing the kitchen for the first time.

"See your new oven?"

It was red and shiny.

"And the floor?"

The linoleum was gone.

"A guy I know had some time. I think it's cork."

There was a different phone on the wall.

"We have them in all the girl's rooms now."

It surprised him to hear it. "All of them?"

He took a final drag of his cigarette. "With intercoms."

"What's that?"

"Room to room."

"Like an office?"

He put the cigarette out and winked. "The very same. You need to bathe, young man."

Willie dropped his head, letting go finally. "I know."

Cary saw the broken plate, still on the floor, his sweater on the rail. There was so much more to ask him. Things to say.

Willie's tears surprised him, when he realized it. No more cops. No more cold.

A cat called out through the open window. Seeing him. Then again.


When he came down from his bath, they sat by the fire drinking sherry. There was no Christmas tree.

"We put your money in the safe. The photo's in your desk."

He looked around, finally clean, dead tired. "Thank you."

They watched the fire.

"Did you find her grave?"

He took a sip, enjoying the taste. "It washed away in a hurricane." He thought of Perlie. "If she was there."

"And Stick?"

"No."

"What happened?"

Willie stared into the flames. "He killed a guy."

"So it's true?"

"Maybe."

Cary waited.

"The one who knifed him in the neck."

"On the train?"

He barely nodded.

He looked exhausted. "Where did they steal your car?"

"Birmingham." He finished his glass and put it down. "With all my stuff."

A log collapsed.

Cary opened the screen and added more wood, closing it, watching the flames grow. "So, how did you get home and why didn't you call me?"

When he turned around, the room was warm, flickering in firelight.

Willie was asleep.

# CHAPTER FIFTEEN

In the morning, Cary lounged on Amber's bed, surrounded by magazines. It was noon before he heard something, a dry cough, then a toilet flush. Bouncing up, he stood in his bathrobe before the mirror preparing himself, turning side to side, sucking in his cheeks. He'd explain the money, that would cheer him up. Why the sheriff had tucked his tail.

He put some bacon on and cracked the window, watching the cats devour their final bits of fish, the tail always last. It was warm outside and the air was soft. That was odd for late December. Whisking batter, he gazed out into the yard, remembering himself as a boy for some reason, a certain lake, his grandma's golden daffodils.

Willie stared at the photograph one more time. The eyes were the same, her pouty upper lip. It was a sister, or a cousin, he figured, turning it over, tracing the handwriting with a finger. The script was different from his momma's, smaller and more intense. It didn't matter anymore. She was gone. He knew that now. Happy Jack was just a place, before it blew away.

He put the picture in the drawer, taking the stairs, admiring the rooms as he passed. Opening the front door, he stepped out onto the porch, stopping at the rail in a pool of light. A couple waved up to him from the sidewalk. It startled him at first. He waved back, noticing patches of snow under the bushes, then higher up beyond the tree tops toward Carter Mountain. The forests were bare. Rivers were full. A moon was on the rise.

Cary called out through the kitchen window. He took a moment, storing it in his heart. Closing his eyes. This would be his family now, his only photograph. "Willie Over Easy from Albemarle County," standing in the sun.


When they were done, Cary lit a cigarette, watching Willie do the dishes. He could see that he was changed in some way, still working out where he'd been.

"How old are you, Cary?"

"Forty-one."

"You ever think about what you want from your life?"

"On a regular basis, honey."

"What it could be?"

He wasn't sure where this was coming from.

"I met a girl in Hattiesburg... blowing guys for money." He turned around, drying the last plate. "She was pretty and lost, staying with an older guy."

He sounded tired.

"Took her money, most of it I'm thinking. Gave her a place to live." He paused, remembering her face when he pulled away. "Jeannie."

"Poor thing."

"Fifteen, sixteen. Hard to tell for sure." He put the plate on the counter and hung the dish towel over the edge of the sink. "I couldn't find my momma, I couldn't find my friend... 'nigger' here, 'nigger' there... a lady's boy gets lynched." He turned back to face him. "Lose my car, all my money... and before I know it I'm standing on the sidewalk looking up at our house."

They heard the clock tick.

"I'm Jeannie's guy."

Cary watched his cigarette burn. "No, you are not."

He turned away, raising the window higher, looking out. "You think what we're doing is right?"

"Depends on how you look at it."

"Selling women for sex?"

"Not when you put it that way, no."

The sky was filling with clouds. "How else would you say it?"

He took a drag, blowing the smoke sideways. "Well... I suppose you could say… we provide a service."

After a moment, Willie turned back, returning to his chair.

They looked at one another from across the table.

"I need to show you something."

"What is it?"

Cary left his cigarette in the ashtray and retrieved a book from a drawer under the wall phone, returning to his chair, laying it on the table.

"Is that Josie's book?"

"It's usually in the safe, but I brought it down to show you." He hesitated, staring at it oddly.

"You can tell me."

He slid it towards him. "Have a look."

Willie shrugged, taking the book and opening it.

"Page ten."

He found the page, then the number.

Cary put his cigarette out, leaning back, watching him carefully.

"Are you sure these numbers are right?"

"That's four weeks. She thinks we can double it in six months. We bring in another girl… raise our prices."

Willie shook his head in disbelief, reading it out loud. "Thirty-six hundred for the girls, seven hundred to get in, seven hundred and fifty for booze, then expenses…" He stopped at the bottom of the page, checking it twice to be sure: "Four Thousand and fifty dollars."

Cary leaned forward in his chair.

"That's…"

"Sixteen thousand two hundred dollars a year!"

Willie looked up.

"Turn the page."

He turned the page, finding his name. "Three thousand seven hundred dollars."

"It's in your safe."

He was numb.

"Goes in every Sunday, next to your friend's shirt."

He closed the book.

"One thing, sweetie."

He dropped his head, elated and ashamed.

"You need to change the combination."


They put their coats on and took a walk, stopping along the sidewalk next door. His tree was there. He wondered what the neighbors thought, what they'd told their children. The house that had burned with a man inside and the boy who ran away.

They headed out together. The properties were mostly the same, some well-cared for, a few neglected.

Cary stopped to admire one, shrouded in over-grown American boxwoods. "I'd like to buy this someday," he said sweetly, pointing to a gangly old oak tree beside the house. "Just *look* at that thing, so pretty and big. Kills me when I see it."

It pleased Willie, imagining his life in such a way.

"And those *roses* when they bloom," he gushed, moving again, running his fingers over a long picket fence as he walked. "For the red blood reigns…" he recited, slipping them into his coat "…In the winter's pale."

A car passed.

"What do the neighbors think?" Willie wondered out loud, watching it disappear.

"About what?"

He checked to see if he was serious. "What we're doing."

Cary's face grew tense, remembering the phone calls. "It's a whorehouse, honey—what can I say?" He looked up into the sky, noticing a line of dark clouds overhead. "On the street where they live."

When they reached the gate, the sky imploded. They squealed as they ran, splashing water everywhere, flying up the steps, nearly slipping, coming to a stop.

It took a while to settle down. Catch their breath.

"You'll need a new license," Cary realized, shaking the rain from his hair. "We can get one tomorrow if you'd like?"

Willie lingered at the rail, his heart still racing, watching the rain fall. The air was colder, instantly fresh. He thought about the money. What he'd do with it. How quickly things had changed.

Cary opened the front door and turned back, waiting for him to follow. The cats would be hungry and he needed a drink. "There are things to be done," he announced happily, feeling for his cigarettes. He paused to smile, realizing it again. "Now that you're safely home."

# CHAPTER SIXTEEN

When he came down the next day, Josie was by the parlor fire. She felt good in his arms, scented and familiar.

"Let me look at you," she said, backing away. He was thinner. Older somehow. "Cary said you looked a fright. Something about a sweater."

He laughed when he heard it. "Kept me warm when I needed it."

"Gotta fatten you up, baby."

"I'm fine."

"There's biscuits and coffee on the bar. Did you meet Halsey?"

"No, ma'am, not yet."

Josie shot him a flirty frown. "How 'bout you call me Josie from now on?"

"That works."

"Good," she answered, softly.

They sat for a while. He told her everything. What had happened when he left, how he got home. When he was done, she switched to vodka.

"The girls are still asleep. You see the books?"

"I did."

"So, what do you think?

"Thinkin' Cary and your ladies should get more."

"Whatever you want, but I think they're fine. It's how we do things these days. With room and board."

"They're making peanuts."

"It's not like that."

He took a moment to get his thoughts straight. "They need more money and a place of their own. Can't be living here all the time."

"We got no money for that kind a thing—you know that!"

"Maybe not now. But some day."

"Some day," she repeated.

"Why not?"

"They have a cook, a maid, a doctor, and a house. What else is there?"

"It's not theirs."

"What isn't?"

"Anything. Everything."

She frowned, hearing him put it that way. "That's the life we live, baby. Always been that way. Plain and simple." She waited, hoping he'd understand it. "For your momma too."

"We charge five dollars at the door, three bucks for a drink, twenty an hour and thirty after that. Three tricks a night, nothing more. Twenty-five percent for you, the girls, Cary, and me. Expenses come outta my share."

"Lord have Mercy, Willie!"

"They're people, Josie. We treat them that way. That's what's been wrong, with my momma too, what I realized coming home."

"Like people."

"Like *everyone*."

"And you?"

"Me?"

"What do *you* want?"

"What do *I* want?"

She leaned forward as he said it. "We go to all this trouble… treat 'em better, pay 'em more… like *people*… like you and me and the girl next door… what do *you* get out of this, baby? What's *your* deal?"

"Other than the money?"

"Other than that."

He smiled when he realized it. How far he'd come to do it right. "I get the best fucking whorehouse in town."

He bought a straight-eight 52 Buick series 70 Roadmaster from a man in Petersburg. Same color, same radio, low miles. The man was suspicious when he saw the money. He'd never imagined a kid so young could afford such a thing. A mulatto no less!

When the paperwork was done, Cary admired the grill, his reflection in the chrome, opening the passenger door slowly, getting in.

Willie adjusted the mirrors, moving the seat forward, starting the engine. Everything looked new. He checked the gas gauge, tested the wipers, and turned the heater on. He'd get insurance this time. Lock the doors at night.

He revved the engine, listening to its power. He had no idea what a straight eight Dynaflash engine was when the man explained it to him. Something about cylinders, compression, and shafts. He didn't care. The mats were clean and the dash had a clock. He was back in business. "Cary?"

"Yeah, honey," he answered absently, closing an ashtray, discovering the radio. "Let's go!" He turned it on.

"Hey."

Cary moved the dial gradually, searching for a station. "What?"

"You forget something?"

He landed on a Patsy Cline song, turning it up, lost in the sound. "Forget what?!"

Willie grinned, seeing him so happy. "You drove us here, man!"


When Amber saw the thing, she danced down the steps in her tight red slacks, "Lord have mercy, you done bought your car!*"* she shouted, reaching the passenger door, pulling on the handle. "Come on, baby! Gonna take me for a ride!"

They drove around the block, then into town along East Main

202 / Peter Skinner

Street, passing Union Station, then west toward The University. She oohed and aahed, touching everything, sliding closer to him at one point, pretending to be his girl. At a stop sign on The Corner, a man stared at them from his car, captivated, before they sped away.

"Saw one a these at my daddy's funeral. Wasn't black like yours. Look at this thing," she gushed, stretching her legs out provocatively, adjusting her hips against the seat. "So quiet and smooth. Like to buy me one someday."

"You will."

She looked at him funny, wanting to laugh.

"Gonna change things up, so you can."

Her eyes got big. "And *how* you plan on doin' that, Mister Big Shot?"

"Got some ideas."

She watched him more carefully as he drove. "Ideas, like what?"

They stopped at Rugby Road, waiting to turn. The car smelled of baby powder.

"We'll talk tonight."

She noticed a young student on the sidewalk looking through her window. "You got some ideas now, do you, baby?" she replied, sliding back across the seat, crossing her legs, preparing a cigarette.

"Can't smoke in here."

"Here we go." She gave him an edgy look. "We talkin' 'bout that too?"

When they pulled up to the house, Josie and Carolyn were on the front porch with Cary, chuckling between themselves at seeing them together.

He turned the engine off.

Amber sighed quietly to herself, putting her cigarettes away. "Been through it, haven't you?"

"Kinda, yeah."

She placed her hand on the door handle. He was changed from when he left. Wiser now.

They looked at one another.

"Well, I'm glad you're safe, baby."

"Thank you, Amber. Me too."

She opened the door and paused, "One thing, though."

He noticed her wet red lips and the curve of her hips. "What's that?"

She blew him a kiss and got out. "Forgot my sweets."


When he was done talking, the parlor was silent.

Cary put a log on the fire and went to the bar.

Amber looked confused. "We get more money? *That* what you're sayin'?"

Willie looked at Josie before he answered. "A larger percent, yes. Halsey cooks, Estrella does linens, Dr. Craig twice a month."

Amber watched Cary fix his drink. "Cary too?"

He grinned. "Cary too."

"'Cuz that boy been savin' my ass, tell you that." She fiddled with an earring. "Not sure what we'd do without him."

Cary joined them, finding a chair by the fire.

They looked at Josie.

"This was Willie's idea, not mine. Let's get that straight right now. He thinks you'll be happier this way. More appreciated."

Some looked down, some away.

Josie rose from her chair. She fixed a drink and put a pretty dress on. A new year was coming, the year of the Pig. She laughed when she'd read it on the train. How compassion and kindness would lead to affluence, to luck from the ancient times. Maybe that was it—share the pie, get a place of her own some day. "We open at six," she reminded them, heading to the bar. With a garden.

Cheeky Diaz was from Baton Rouge. She had a single bag and a fake fur coat.

"You Willie?" she asked, stepping from the train, smiling when he stepped forward. "Willie with a Heart a Gold?"

They crisscrossed through the town, passing The University. It was a splendid winter day, bright and cold, with views that took your breath away. She said she loved the mountains most, how they rose up in the distance. All the trees.

"Nice feeling, this place," she remarked quietly. "And your car, man. So shiny and clean!"

"Thnak you. Just got it." He snuck a look while he drove. Her face was familiar; he wasn't sure why—from a magazine, maybe, or a movie somewhere. "You look like someone," he managed awkwardly, concentrating on the road.

"Dorothy Lamour," she answered quickly, gazing out the window.

She was born in Puerto Rico outside San Juan. Her family was there. A father, a mother, and two older cousins. She'd known Josie for a week. They'd met at a bar over Christmas. She was thirty-one years old and broke.

By the spring of 1959, the rooms were full and the lines were long. Willie's GED was simple enough. Josie liked math, Carolyn knew history, and Cheeky loved maps. He studied the basics, willfully, methodically, hours each day on every subject. When the noise was impossible, he'd drive around, park the car and read, or sit alone in the Colored section of the Jefferson Library. They loved him there— the Brothel Boy, always on his own. Taking notes. Anatomy, psychology, politics, and science. Architecture, botany, history, and art. *A Separate Peace, Of Mice and Men, The Longest Day, The Tin Drum, Dr. Seuss*, Nabokov, *A Farewell To Arms*.

When the day arrived, Professor Lilly stood by the door, watching him take the steps. It had been a while since they'd met. He was different now, taller and sturdy, with a certain air of confidence.

"Good afternoon, young man," he said as their hands met. "You seem to have grown."

Willie hadn't noticed until people mentioned it. His clothes had shrunk and his voice was deeper. "Hello, Professor." He looked pleased to see him. "Thank you for meeting me today."

They stepped away from the door as students passed. "You've been quite active with your lectures, I understand."

He was surprised to hear it. "I have."

"Wonderful. This always helps."

Willie swallowed hard. His mouth was dry. "It does?"

"What they want to see."

"So, you think I have a chance?"

He saw his eager face. It pleased him to say it. "I do."

"Even with just a GED?"

They watched the students dashing to their classes.

"You're in the one percentile, Willie."

He knew it was high, but he hadn't realized.

"That is, under any circumstance, a remarkable achievement."

Emotions swept through him. He pushed them away.

"Accomplished entirely on your own, I understand."

"I had some help, but, yes, sir. Mostly on my own."

The professor gathered his thoughts. "What's the date today?"

"May twenty-sixth. Tuesday."

He winced, realizing it. "So soon." He looked around. The Lawn was empty.

Willie watched him closely, not understanding.

He turned back to face the boy. "What can I do for you, Willie?"

"Am I too late to apply? I didn't qualify until now."

He considered it before he spoke. "May I ask you something first?"

"Of course."

"Are you still in charge of the house?"

"Sort of."

He nodded. "They may ask you this."

"I know."

Professor Lilly looked away, seeing something in the distance. "Let's sit."

The bench was near an old locust tree, beside a sculpture of Homer. They settled in and looked around.

"There's a poorly kept secret here…"

A student raced by on his bicycle, interrupting.

"Regarding admissions." He glanced at Willie. "We are undisciplined in that regard." He looked away. "Lacking common ground."

Willie listened, trying understand it.

"What would you like to study? They will ask you this."

"I'd like to be a lawyer maybe."

There was purpose in his eyes.

"To help people somehow."

John Lilly could not imagine his life, where he'd come from, what he'd lived through. "Then you would be most needed."

A professor appeared from inside an adjacent pavilion, walking briskly north along the colonnades. They watched him as he disappeared.

"You teach law, Moses said."

"For some time now."

"Why?"

"Why do I teach it?"

"If you don't mind me asking."

He gave it some thought. "Well, I suppose, I'm interested in its standards of reason. The arguments. The discourse." He hesitated, revisiting the question in his mind. "It's a way of *thinking*, mostly. A *philosophy*."

"To what purpose?"

"That's a very good question." He considered it further. "Balancing the rights of an individual against the greater good, primarily."

A bird landed on a branch above their heads.

"In principle."

Willie gathered his courage. "Would you consider writing a recommendation for me?"

He looked at him kindly, easily. "It would give me great

pleasure."

Willie took a sudden breath. "Thank you, sir."

They were quiet for a while, looking around.

"You'll need another."

"Yes."

"And who might that be?"

It came to him one night when he couldn't sleep. The people he'd known. How the ones who cared could not always show it.

"Sheriff Sheffield."

The bird took off.

Professor Lilly nodded slightly. There were obstacles he would face regarding the whorehouse. The color of his skin. "An excellent choice."

"You think?"

"I do."

"But am I too late?"

"Technically, yes."

Willie's face fell.

Seeing it, he touched the boy's shoulder. "No, no, no... it happens all the time. What's referred to as a 'delayed submission beyond events.'"

"What is that, if I may ask?"

The bench was hard. He sat up a bit. "Missing transcripts for instance... inner department irregularities."

Willie wanted desperately to believe it.

"Who you *know,*" he added, with a wink.

A young couple passed nearby, eyeing Willie suspiciously.

Willie smiled back at them, understanding what it meant. "Your, 'uncommon ground.'"

John Lilly nodded in agreement, watching them go. "However, this time"—he raised a finger in the air—"to our *advantage.*"

They rose from the bench, surrounded by a fresh wave of students, some plopping down around them in the grass, others racing about in all directions.

"Their final exams," the old man sighed, eyeing the clock.

Willie stood before him. There were no words to say it properly. "Thank you for meeting with me today."

Professor Lilly stretched his back a bit and smiled.

"For your kindness, sir."

It pleased him to hear it, seeing his face. His good intentions. If there was a future for this world, it would be here, he thought. On these grounds. Whatever the challenge, whatever his task, he would make some calls, offer his hand, for this fine young man, so dearly deserving, of the chair of Moses Henry.

# CHAPTER SEVENTEEN

Charlottesville Police Department

May 13, 1959

The University of Virginia
Department of Admissions
PO Box 44
Charlottesville, Virginia

To Whom It May Concern:

I am writing today in full support of Mr. Willie Graves for admission to The University. I have known the applicant and his family for many years. He is an exceptional individual who has overcome many difficult and challenging obstacles in the course of his young life. A more qualified candidate for your consideration I cannot imagine.

Sincerely,

Sheriff David Sheffield
Chief of Police, Charlottesville, Virginia

# University of Virginia

June 1, 1959

The University of Virginia
Department of Admissions
Dean William R. Benson
PO Box 44
Charlottesville, Virginia

Dear Bill,

It is my distinct privilege to recommend and support for admission, Mr. Willie Graves, of Charlottesville, Virginia to the Class of 1963. In my forty years of service to this school, I have rarely known an applicant more promising, capable, or qualified in this regard. His dedication, understanding, and appreciation for the principles of higher education is both profound and inspirational. Please afford him your very strongest consideration.

Respectfully yours,


John L. Lilly III
Professor of Law
The University of Virginia School of Law
PO Box 11
Charlottesville, Virginia

# University of Virginia

June 1, 1959

President Sherrill B. James
Office of The President
The University of Virginia
PO Box 7
Charlottesville, Virginia

Dear Sherrill,

I am writing to you on behalf of a Class of 1963 applicant that I have come to know, Mr. Willie Graves of Charlottesville, Virginia. He is a rare and exceptional young man, uniquely qualified, with a profound and inspirational life story. Unfortunately, through no fault of Mr. Graves, his application has been delayed until now. I am happy to discuss this with you further, in person or over the phone, if that would help his cause. Thank you in advance for your kind consideration in this matter.

Jane and I send warm wishes to you and Margarette. If I miss you at graduation, enjoy your sailing in Maine.

Best wishes,


John L. Lilly III
Professor of Law
The University of Virginia School of Law
PO Box 11
Charlottesville, Virginia


cc: Dean William R. Benson

# CHAPTER EIGHTEEN

By the middle of June, the heat was up. Willie read in his room all day, listening for the mail. Halsey fixed him pancakes, Amber gave him booze.

One morning, the white cat appeared in his room. It surprised him at first, seeing it inside, jumping on his bed, curling up next to him. He went down for milk, closing a window in the parlor on his way up. He put the dish on the floor, listening to him purr. He looked skinny and tough, but sweet all the same, with golden eyes and a long soft tail.

By the first of July, the girls were worn out. "They need a break," Josie explained finally, standing in his doorway. "Best thing to do, if you want 'em fresh."

"Make 'em sound like a racehorse," he kidded, putting his book down, petting the cat.

"They're spent, baby."

His expression changed. "I understand."

She took a moment, enjoying them together. "You see the numbers?"

"I did."

She wondered if he really had.

He leaned back against the headboard. "Twenty-six hundred for the month."

"Thirty-two thousand by the end of the year at the rate we're going."

"Jesus."

When the cat jumped down, Willie rose from the bed, stretching his neck from side to side.

"I gave the girls 'til August."

He opened the safe and looked inside. It was stuffed with envelopes. "Give 'em 'til September."

"That's too much."

He took out a large envelope and closed the door, spinning the dial. "Too much what?"

"Distractions."

He approached the doorway, handing her the envelope.

"What's this?"

"Money for August."

"For who?"

"Five hundred for each of you."

She looked uneasy.

"Come on, I have plenty and nothin' to spend it on. So, take it. Go have fun."

She stepped in and put her arms around him, feeling his body against hers.

They held each for a while before letting go.

The letter hadn't come. He was tired of waiting, waiting for his life to begin.

"What can I do for you, honey?"

He admired her nipples through the robe, the way she looked at him. He didn't care anymore, what it meant, or how to say it. "There *is* one thing."

"Tell me."

"I need to get laid."

When they laughed, the cat jumped sideways, flying down the stairs. She watched it disappear, feeling her heart race... closing the door.

# CHAPTER NINETEEN

The house was locked up. He peered through the windows. There was mail on the hallway floor. He walked around back, climbing some steps to a rear porch, finding a rocker, listening to the birds. He dropped his sack and took his bottle out, rocking slowly. The place was peaceful, freshly painted. That surprised him. How good it looked. He followed the branches of a big sycamore as it reached for the clouds. The weather was changing. His neck ached. It had been a hard ride north. He'd need a shower, some clean clothes, and a good night's sleep. A cat called out from behind a balustrade; he turned to find it, noticing an open window.

# CHAPTER TWENTY

Five miles past Winchester, Willie found the driveway, stopping at the mailbox. The Pettit name had faded. He wanted to see them again, to make sense of the world. A truck flew by, startling the apple trees, flushing the air with fumes and grit. He held the wheel and considered it again, what to do, where to go. There would be fireworks at home.

He turned around and drove away. It was easier than the truth. How he'd paid for the Buick. What had happened to Stick. The knife. He left the window down as he drove, smelling cornfields and cow shit, listening to the radio. He'd be back someday when the days were warm and the nights were cool. Fish the streams and make some pies. Push her on the swing.

Charlottesville was crazy with cars. He pulled around back and parked in the alley. The clock said eight. He'd feed the cats and change his clothes, walk to the park before dark. It was good to be alone, have the place to himself. He thought about Josie, the way she'd moved when he touched her. It wasn't right, he knew that. How much he wanted her again.

Taking the stairs, he noticed a man asleep in the rocker, quieting his footsteps as he climbed, reaching the final step. Seeing the scar.

"That you, Willie?"

He gasped, realizing it.

Stick stood up, groggy.

It was impossible.

"Heard you got girls."

His voice was different.

They stared at each other.

"Thought you were dead. Or gone somewhere."

"I know."

He blinked in disbelief. "Drove all the way to New Orleans."

He gave him time to understand it.

Willie took a step forward and stopped. "Sheriff gave me a photo, so I took off to find you. New Orleans, Biloxi, then, I don't know, said you were shrimpin' maybe, or gone, 'cuz you killed that guy and I kept thinkin' I'd *find* you, or I'd ask around somewhere, and they'd tell me somethin'... *pick you up,* maybe... get you outta there." He took a trembling breath. "Saw the sheriff down there."

"Johnny Boudreau?"

He wondered if they'd met. "Said the photo put you there."

"Yep."

"That you'd run."

He didn't answer.

"What he told me."

Stick looked off. His legs were tired.

He was afraid to say it. "That you *did* it."

Stick nodded slightly hearing it.

Watching him, he couldn't tell. "I found your shirt near the tunnel."

He looked confused suddenly.

"In the trailer."


He put his clothes in the washing machine. They smelled of coal and sweat.

"Been a while since I washed 'em," Stick confessed, holding his empty sack.

Willie found him clothes to wear, closing the kitchen window and feeding the cats. It was almost dark and the heat was down. They sat on the porch with their drinks. He'd miss the fireworks. Stick was here. Nothing mattered anymore.

"Nice place you got."

"Thank you."

"With cats."

"Yep."

They drank a bit.

"Heard about this place. What you did to it."

"From who?"

People passed along the alley toward the park, some with blankets and coolers.

"Hard to hide it when the word gets out."

Willie took a sip and rocked. "Ladies took some time off. Been busy since we opened."

"How many you got."

"Four right now. Get some more later if we can."

Stick stopped rocking, listening to something.

"What?"

He waited to be sure. "Whip-poor-will."

Willie remembered them from his tree, their tiny growls.

"Bad luck when you hear one near a house, Mo said."

Willie rocked slowly, thinking of Sister Mo.

"Answer back, you die."

"Crazy ole Mo."

Stick drank a bit, rocking again. "You seen her lately?"

"Drove out when I got here. Didn't know where you were. Where to look."

"She tell you?"

He'd forgotten until now. "Said I wouldn't find you in a Buick."

Stick grinned, imagining her saying it.

"Looked old when I was there. Thinkin' she's gone by now."

"You think?"

"Maybe."

"Or lives forever."

They thought about her as they rocked. How they'd met. The things in life that make no sense.

"So…" It was hard to ask.

"Did I kill the son of a bitch?"

He turned to him, surprised by his tone. "Figured you must have. Bein' there and all."

Stick felt the booze. The cooler air. "You've grown, Willie." He slowed his rocker. "More man than boy now."

Voices drifted through the alley.

"They still lookin' for you?"

"Came to say goodbye."

The words went through him.

Stick stared up into the sky, finding an early star. "Hit the road early."

They stopped their chairs.

"You get to your friend's funeral?"

His head was spinning. "Missed it. Found his grave when I got here."

"And your momma?"

There was no point to it if he was leaving. "How you know about that?"

"Didn't find her?"

He put his glass on the floor. "No."

He could see the boy was agitated. "You still readin'?"

"Applied to The University. Haven't heard yet."

He nodded in appreciation. "I should a done more a that when I was your age. Read stuff. Not been so wild."

He wanted to go to him. Put his arms around him somehow. "You goin' to Hilda?"

"Maybe."

"You think about her?"

"All the time."

"So, how come?"

"How come what?"

"Come on, man! The first time we pulled in, I saw it. Way you acted. How you looked at each other."

He steadied his feet, turning to the boy. His face was strong and handsome. The girls would come, the money, school, but the rest of it, the *other* things, that would take time. He stood up stiffly and went to the rail.

A car door closed in the distance.

Willie rose from his chair, worried suddenly. "You hear somethin'?"

They had the night and nothing more. He'd miss the boy. What they'd found together. It would never leave him, not in a million years. Like the call of a whip-poor-will.

When the fireworks started, they hurried past the opened mail, up the stairs, squeezing through Willie's dormer window, sitting carefully on the roof, side by side, watching the sky, diamonds exploding, tumbling through the trees. Then again, and again, hearing the distant cheers when it was over. Waiting for more.

When it was quiet, they came inside and took the stairs. Passing the basket of keys, Willie noticed the corner of an envelope, wedged under a stack of magazines by the door. It had been there a while.

They moved to the parlor while Stick fixed a drink. "You want something?"

"No, I'm good," he answered, transfixed, holding the envelope in his hand.

Stick found a chair, taking a sip, looking around the room. The only thing missing were the girls. "That your letter from the school?"

Wille stared at his name.

He watched him consider it. "Well, there you go! What's it say?"

"Funny. I been waiting all this time…"

"Ain't gonna bite you, Willie. Open the goddamn thing."

He took a final breath, working his thumbnail under the flap, opening it carefully, then stopping.

Stick took another drink. "Ain't comin' out on its own, man, let's go!"

He pulled the paper out.

He watched him read it, seeing something cross his face.

Willie's eyes filled with tears.

He put his drink down, approaching him quickly, opening his arms.

Willie rose from the couch, holding him, being held, stunned, his heart pounding, trying to breathe.

They let go of each other, stepping back.

"I'm proud of you, Willie. Goddammit, son!"

He saw the tenderness in Stick's eyes. The ease of it.

"Got this on your own time. Every step, every trouble."

He dropped his head, tears spilling down his face.

"Just glad I was here to see it."

Catching his breath, he tried to look up, blurry-eyed, then down again at the letter, thinking he'd imagined it:

It gives me great pleasure to offer you admission to The University of Virginia's Class of 1963...

Dean William R. Benson

When they settled down, Stick poured him some vodka, taking the letter, reading it for himself.

"Damn, Willie," he muttered, shaking his head, looking up finally. "Sometimes it all works out, don't it?"

He stared at his drink. "I need to thank somebody."

Stick raised his glass in the air. It had been a sweet night, the fireworks, the booze. "To my young friend, Willie Graves!"

Willie did the same, still sniffling, overwhelmed.

"Gotta keep movin', man, remember that."

"Yes, sir. Thank you, Stick."

He looked at him sadly, lovingly, remembering his leaving. "Sit in one place, you get run over."


They had a peanut butter and jelly sandwich in the kitchen, hungry and exhausted, then another with beer. While Stick took a bath, Willie folded his laundry and called Cary. He'd forgotten the hour.

"This better be good, honey," he answered, sounding pissed.

"I got in."

He was half-asleep. "To the house?"

"Virginia."

The line was quiet.

"The letter came."

"My *God, Willie!*" he shouted at last.

"I start in the fall."

"*Fuck!* It's everything." he whispered suddenly, seeing the time.

"Thank you."

"This is…"

"For everything."

They were quiet, listening to each other.

"*So* beautiful!" he managed, finally. "*So* proud of you. *Very very* proud…"

He heard a second voice in the background, a man's voice, before the line went dead.


He gave his room to Stick and said good night, sitting alone on the porch, rocking mindlessly forward and back. The night had cooled and the moon was up. He'd call Professor Lilly in the morning, then walk The Lawn. Listen for his bells.

The day was done; the streets were still. He watched the stars fade over time, closing his eyes eventually, hearing frogs at first, then katydids, dreaming of her hair.

# CHAPTER TWENTY-ONE

When he opened his eyes, a Swiss Army knife rested in his hand. It stunned him at first, feeling it again, seeing sunlight through the trees, racing upstairs.

The bed was made and his clothes were folded neatly on the dresser. He sank into a chair, clutching the knife, understanding what had happened. Stick had a bottle, Ernest had a knife, someone had money, someone had bread. That was their currency, their legal tender. The business of their lives.

His heart ached, knowing Stick was gone. He cracked a window and lay down, trying to forget, waking suddenly, out of sorts, hearing the front door close.

Cary was standing at the kitchen stove, frying sausages. "Rise and shine, sleepyhead! Give me a hug!"

He felt small in Willie's arms. Warm.

"Your momma would be over the moon." He let go, enjoying their moment together. "And Ole Moses."

"Sorry I called you so late."

Cary turned the burner off, moving the pan to one side. "Don't be silly. Look in the fridge."

He went to the fridge, opening the door, seeing a box marked 'coconut cream.' "Oh, boy! When you get this?"

He checked his scrambled eggs. "Syntax, William. It's for tonight. Grab the butter."

He found the butter. "I thought they'd be closed."

"I was there first thing." He lifted the sausages from the pan onto a plate. "It was silly with pies."

Willie shut the door and approached the table, remembering Stick was gone. He put the butter down.

Cary moved to the sink, pouring grease from the pan into a large tin can. "I was a mess last night when you told me."

He felt the knife in his pocket, dropping into a chair.

"Where's your friend?"

"My what?"

He turned around to say it. "The one who drinks bourbon?"

Something shot through the open window, leapfrogging over the sink.

"*Holy fuck!*" Cary shrieked, nearly dropping the pan.

The white cat ambled slowly towards the table, hopping onto Willie's lap.

He put the pan in the sink. "I swear to God! This *thing* will be the end of me!"

Willie grinned, stroking it gently, sending his tail into the air. His face grew instantly tender. "He needs a name."

Cary watched them together. His heart was still pounding. "Lucifer."

Willie laughed.

"Thing?"

They both laughed, enjoying the idea.

There was white fur everywhere. It came to him quickly. "It's your *demon* from the South."

Willie stopped petting and looked up. "My what?

"*Mr. Cotton.*"


A door knock echoed through the hallway, sending the cat flying. The second was louder.

"*Jesus Christ!*" Cary protested, finding their plates. "*Someone* has a hard-on."

Willie rose reluctantly from his chair.

"Thank you, darling." He rolled his eyes, taking toast from the oven. "Tell them we're *all fucked out.*"


When the door opened, Sheriff Sheffield tipped his hat. The boy looked sleepy. "Mornin', Willie."

He wasn't sure why he was there. "Hey, Sheriff."

"Been a while."

"It has, son. You hear anything?"

"About what?"

"The University."

Willie relaxed when he said it. "I did."

A car drove by, slowing down as it passed.

"And?"

He tried to play it cool. "I got in."

The sheriff broke a quick smile. "You did? You got in?"

"Just found out."

"Oh, Willie!" He extended his hand.

Willie stepped out into the sunlight, taking it.

"Without a doubt the best news I've heard in a long, long time."

"Thank you, sir."

"Damn!"

He let go of his hand.

The sheriff shook his head, thinking of it. How far he'd come. "I wish Sadie could have seen it."

He nodded. It felt good to think of her that way.

"Didn't always see eye to eye, the two of us, but she meant well, she really did."

Willie looked out. It was a pretty day.

"Be over the moon 'bout this!"

"Appreciate it, Sheriff."

"It's true, what I'm sayin'. Matt Abel too."

"And thanks for the letter. Wasn't sure how you'd feel about it. Made all the difference in the world."

He looked the boy in the eye. "Happy to help."

"It did, sir. Couldn't have done it without you."

"Good, well..." He smiled again, enjoying the compliment. "Had to check my spelling before I sent it."

"Me too."

"Thinkin' your professor friend helped some."

"Yes, sir. Quite a bit."

"And that GED score of yours, Heavens to Betsy! My cousin's a secretary in the admissions office- don't think you knew that."

"No, sir. I did not."

He looked the young man over, seeing him differently now. "Your momma always said you were a reader."

"I was."

"Well, keep it up."

"I will."

"'Cuz you're on your way, son."

Willie looked down shyly. "Surprised myself, Sheriff. Appreciate you coming by."

He looked past him into the hallway. "You alone this mornin'?"

Another car drove by.

"Just Cary in the kitchen."

"Girls around?"

"No, sir. Took some time off."

The sheriff looked worried suddenly.

"What's up?"

"Need to talk to you."

"About what?"

He adjusted the rim of his hat.

Willie's heart sank, seeing his expression change.

"I got Stick Watson in a cell."

They'd cuffed him in the alley. He didn't resist. There was no point to it. The neighbor had called the night before, seeing a strange man, looking through the windows, going around back. She'd waited to be sure, blending in with the crowd, seeing them on the back porch. The guy in the photograph, Stick Watson, with the young man, Willie Graves. He'd lied about Hilda. He was on his way to see her. Zach was waiting in Reedville.

Willie's face went pale, knowing what they'd do to him. How justice came hard and sometimes at a price.

"I'm sorry to be the one to tell you, but he knew what would happen if he came here." He looked at Willie sympathetically, seeing his despair, his helplessness. "Wanted to tell you myself. I can drive you to the station, if you like? You wanna bring him a book, or somethin'?"

"A book?" he replied miserably.

"Could be a while, I don't know. Might keep his mind on somethin'."

Willie dropped his head, trying to think. He'd call Hilda, then his lawyer, or hers maybe. He couldn't remember the name. Then Professor Lilly.

"Gotta get back, if you wanna come later?"

His mind was spinning. "How much time do I have?"

"Hard to say. He's seein' a judge at three o'clock. Public defender after that. A day or two, I'm thinkin'."

Cary appeared in the doorway.

"Mornin', Cary."

"Sheriff." He noticed Willie's expression as he passed through the doorway into the house. "Everything okay?"

Sheriff Sheffield took the car keys from his pocket, lowering his voice. "Need you to take care of Willie for a few days, if you can?"

"What do you mean?"

"Keep an eye on him."

"And why is that?"

The sheriff peered past him into the hallway. There was no list to fix it. Nothing to be done. "They got his friend for murder and it don't look good."


Willie left a message for Hilda at the Tangier Inn and for D. K. Wells, finally remembering his name. He grabbed his wallet and the car keys, calling Professor Lilly on his way out. He answered on the second ring.

"John Lilly."

It took him a second to recognize his voice. "Professor Lilly?"

"Yes?"

He didn't know where to begin, or how to say it.

"Is that you, Willie?"

What he could do to make things right.

When the clock struck 3:00 p.m., Judge Barrett Martell sat behind his desk shuffling papers. A murder trial was dragging on and his wife was at the river. "Mary!" he barked, noticing the time, rising from his chair. "My file's missing and the warrant's gone!" He threw his hands up. "And *where* are my mints!"

Mary Harris entered the room. After thirty years, she knew the drill. "Your lunch ran late. The file and warrant are on your bench, Your Honor."

He stopped to think of it, then of something else.

"The mints are in your pocket."

Stick waited in the courtroom, shackled, thinking of the Chesapeake. How the light hit the water when the sun set.

"I'm Ricky White," his lawyer announced, arriving suddenly, out of breath, dropping his briefcase on the table, opening it quickly, removing a file. "I do the talking. The judge will ask you who you are, your address if you have one, if you understand the charges…" He stopped to collect himself, closing the briefcase, placing it on the floor by his chair. "Good judge, knows his stuff," he added quietly, glancing around, sitting. "Sorry I'm late."

A large bailiff appeared through a side door, strutting out and around the bench, coming to a halt. After a moment, Judge Martell entered slowly, deliberately, through an opposite side door. Mary Harris was close behind.

Stick studied him carefully. He seemed nice enough, with a look of certainty. Like a hoghead on a train.

"*All rise!*" the bailiff bellowed to no one in particular.

Ricky White closed his file and stood.

Stick stood, as well.

"*This court is now in session!*"

Judge Martell dropped into his chair, identifying Stick, then Ricky White, hearing the rear doors open quickly. It was odd, at first, seeing John Lilly with a young man in his courtroom. He finished his mint, watching them as they found their seats. A lone policeman stood in the corner at the very back. "Please be seated."

The ceiling fans hummed as the room fell silent.

The judge took a moment to look around, acknowledging the stenographer, the sparse crowd. Sheriff Sheffield was missing.

"Bailiff, do we have everyone?"

The bailiff came to attention. "We do, Your Honor."

"Thank you," he replied, referring to his notes, before turning to Stick. "Mr. Watson, sir?"

Stick sat up, not knowing what to do.

"And Mr. White?"

Ricky White flashed his courtroom smile, adjusting his tie tack. "Good afternoon, Your Honor."

"And to you, Sir."

Checking his papers, verifying the sequence of his responsibilities, he proceeded. "I have before me a warrant executed and signed by Circuit Court Judge Wilbur M. Foss, representing the Jurisdiction of Jefferson Parish, New Orleans, dated, June thirtieth, requesting the apprehension of a Mr. Richard Allen Watson in the matter of an outstanding October seventh felony offense with a subsequent petition for removal issued July first by the Office of the Attorney General of the State of Louisiana." He stopped, checking something from a separate file before continuing, "Following his arrest on July fifth, Mr. Watson has been remanded to the Albemarle County Regional Jail, pending the conclusion of this hearing until further notice."

Looking up, the judge examined Stick more closely, noticing his fatigue and disrepair. "So"—he removed his glasses—"if you would please, can you state for the court today your full name and current address?"

"Stick Watson."

The two men sized each other up. They were, roughly, the same age.

"I have no address, sir."

"Thank you. And do you understand the circumstances of your arrest, Mr. Watson?"

Stick's mouth was dry. "As best I can, sir."

The judge relaxed, trying to appear more sympathetic. "Well, the first thing you need to understand, Mr. Watson, is that this is a hearing and not a trial." He waited to see if he understood. "Our purpose here today is to determine whether or not we have the right individual and, if we do, whether or not and when to honor this request for extradition to the State of Louisiana. Do you understand?"

"I do."

"Good." He glanced briefly at Mr. White. "And if, at any time, you have a question or need something clarified, let your lawyer know and we'll do the best we can to address it properly, either now or later, when you're dismissed. Does that work?"

"Thank you, sir."

The judge sat back in his chair, taking a moment, before continuing, "So… it's my understanding you've been read your rights and appointed a public defender in this matter, is that correct?"

"Yes, sir."

"And, Mr. White?"

"Your Honor?"

"You have had time with your client to explain the matter before this magistrate?"

"I have not, Your Honor."

The judge halted. "And why is that?"

"Your Honor, I was detained earlier today in Louisa County and have only just arrived."

"I see."

"If I may, I would ask the court for a brief recess, allowing Mr. Watson and I time to review these charges, the purpose of this hearing, and, most importantly, my role as his representative."

The judge propped his elbows up onto the armrests of his chair as he considered it.

"This should not take long, Your Honor, and I apologize in advance for this request."

"Mr. Watson?"

Stick looked surprised.

"For the record, have you agreed, either verbally, or in writing, to Mr. White's representation in this matter?"

*"He has not, Your Honor."*

The room turned suddenly as John Lilly stepped out into the center aisle.

Barrett Martell dropped his elbows and leaned forward to get a better look. When it came to the practice of law, to the matter of evidence, in particular, there was none better, more thoughtful, or competent. "The court recognizes Professor Lilly."

"May I approach the bench, Your Honor?"

He gave it some thought. "And for what purpose, sir?"

"For the purpose of representing the defendant."

The courtroom grew still.

"*Representing,* you say?"

"Yes, Your Honor."

The judge hesitated, turning to Stick. "Have you been made aware of this, Mr. Watson?"

Stick turned in his chair, seeing Professor Lilly, then Willie, returning his attention to the judge. "I am now, sir."

The judge considered the request, seeing a document in the professor's hand. "And let me guess, John… is that an affidavit?"

"It is, Your Honor."

He turned to Stick one more time, trying to make sense of it.

Stick smiled. "And if I may, Your Honor?"

The judge reached for his box of mints. "You may."

"I wasn't sure when to say this."

He popped a mint in his mouth, waiting. "And what would that be, Mr. Watson?"

Stick tested his ankles against the shackles. "I tried to tell the boys who locked me up when it comes to stuff like this… with the lawyers and all…"

Growing impatient, the judge motioned for Professor Lilly to approach the bench. "And we are waiting, sir. As you can see."

When the professor joined him, Stick sat up in his chair and smiled. "My legal name's Eugene."

Once they were seated, Mary Harris shut the door and returned to her desk. She could tell they'd make quick work of it. She poured herself a cup of Lipton and started typing.

Professor Lilly scanned the file quickly. The name discrepancy was significant. The missing weapon.

Judge Martell straightened his desk, allowing him time before he spoke. He knew what was coming. Where there was law, there was injustice.

"So, John, let's start with the obvious, I suppose. No reason to dance about. We have some problems here, clearly."

Professor Lilly checked a final page and closed the file, tapping it lightly with his fingers. It had been a while since he'd argued before a judge. Or wanted to. "First of all, Your Honor..."

"Barrett, please," the judge insisted.

"Well, then." He smiled, appreciating the gesture. "Thank you. Barrett. And, again, my apologies for interrupting today. I'd only been informed of this matter an hour or so beforehand."

He waved him off. "Nonsense, John. He's a lucky man to have you in his corner. Let's cut to the chase, shall we?"

The professor gathered his file and stood, placing it on the judge's desk. "Thank you for this," he said, returning to his chair and sitting.

The two men studied one another.

"I'd like to file a motion to quash."

The judge feigned surprise. "For what reason?"

He assembled his thoughts as best he could. "Unsupportable burden of persuasion, insufficient probable cause, inadmissible, prejudicial, and improperly obtained direct, or competent, evidence. A missing murder weapon, fingerprints, illegible photo dates, witness calumny, the Fourth Amendment, reasonable doubt," he paused, "to begin with."

The judge grew instantly subdued.

"Regarding a person wrongfully named in both the arrest warrant and request for extradition"—he paused, seeing his expression—"I'll check on that, of course."

"That would be helpful, yes."

He considered it further. "Perhaps a delay is in order, at the very least."

Barrett Martell nodded. He enjoyed these moments, the cordial candor. "How much time do you require?"

"A week, two at the most?"

Finding his pen, he jotted something down. "This appears to have been badly handled by the State of Louisiana." He put the pen down, reviewing his notes quickly.

John Lilly watched him carefully. "In my opinion, the documents are not in order."

The judge listened, finding something as he read.

"With misleading statements."

He took a moment for himself, removing his glasses.

"This is not about evidence."

"I understand, John."

They regarded one another briefly.

"I may need to call a witness or two regarding these statements, if you will permit me?"

"Of course. As may I."

"Solicit our Governor."

"I understand."

"But that would be all." He took a moment to make his point. "Nothing more."

A telephone rang outside the door, then stopped.

John Lilly waited to say it. "If I may ask?"

"Please."

"Regarding custody?"

He'd almost forgotten. "Can you attest to his character, I wonder?"

"I cannot, no."

"He is both unemployed and without residence?"

"That is my understanding, yes."

"With priors?"

"Three, I believe. Vagrancy and public intoxication."

"And when was that?"

He remembered the page. "Two in 1937 and one in '39."

"Some time ago."

"Yes."

"So..." He leaned back, caressing his jaw slowly with an open hand. "To the best of our knowledge, we have an individual with insignificant priors, decades old, poorly treated by our system, illegally at times one might argue, whose single 'crime' may simply be being in the wrong place at the wrong time."

He waited.

"That about right?"

"It may be, yes."

The judge sat up, understanding it more clearly. "First thing... we need to get him home before we do more damage than we've done."

"I agree."

"Then sort it out."

John Lilly waited.

He found a section of the extradition, reading it carefully. "Bear with me a moment."

"Please."

Putting it down, his face grew stern. He took his time. "In my opinion, the warrants, as written, contain potentially false and misleading statements." He checked his calendar, writing something down before continuing. "A two-week delay is granted. You may call a limited number of non-evidentiary witnesses only. Bail will be set at one hundred dollars."

The professor smiled. "Thank you, Barrett. Your Honor. He'll be most pleased to hear it."

The judge took a moment, regarding Professor Lilly more keenly. "It's a noble thing to fight for one's freedom, John… but finer still to fight for another." When he stood, Professor Lilly did the same. "If I may…" he asked, moving toward a closet in the corner of the room, opening the door. "What's your relationship with the accused?"

"I'm acquainted with his young friend."

He removed his robe. "The *boy* in court today?"

The word jumped out when he heard it. "Sadie Graves' son, yes."

He found a hanger for his robe, placing it inside.

"He's been accepted to The University this fall."

The judge paused before closing the door, turning back to face him. "The kid who runs the whorehouse?"

Professor Lilly met his gaze.

"Sheffield says it's quite the operation. People there you wouldn't expect." He shot him a pious look, returning to his desk. "Not good for the town, though, is it? Mr. Graves, in particular, I should think." He appeared suddenly satisfied, gathering his papers. "Wants to close it down once and for all."

John Lilly considered his response carefully. The hypocrisy was one thing, but their self-righteousness made his skin crawl. Willie had given him a list of clients and testimony that the sheriff had taken money. That would help. "We'll see where it leads."

The judge looked up, amicably. "Seems easy enough. Not sure

what's taking him so long."

Seeing the hour, he became distracted by the idea of bourbon. The work ahead. It had been a while since he'd felt such things, off grounds, with a purpose. He looked at the judge and smiled. The fuse was lit. "You mean, other than the money?"

When the door opened, Mary Harris stopped typing and smiled. The men appeared pleased as they said their goodbyes. On his way out, Judge Martell stopped at her desk, reaching down, taking her hand— that surprised her.

The weekend would be busy. There'd be paperwork, letters and petitions to prepare. She didn't mind. It was part of the job. She'd reheat a tuna casserole and take her schnauzer for a walk. They enjoyed their time together. The cooler evening air. His name was Molson and he walked with a limp. Until he saw a firefly.

# CHAPTER TWENTY-TWO

The next morning, Stick and Halsey met in the kitchen.

"Nice to meet you, Halsey."

"You too, Stick." Halsey looked him over, grabbing a pot holder as he did. "Feel like I seen you before." He pulled a pan of biscuits from the oven and closed the door. "Worked a kitchen outside Memphis for a while." He placed the pan on the oven top and turned back, thinking of the place. "Maybe that was it."

Stick nodded, looking sleepy. He'd met a ton of folks hopping trains. "Yeah, you never know. Or on the road somewhere."

"Oven's *my* road, baby!" Halsey laughed, with a wink. "One biscuit at a time."

Stick's eyes locked in on the biscuits. After a couple beers, he'd skipped dinner and gone to bed.

"'Nough a that stuff. Sit on down, man! Let me feed you." He checked the clock, seeing Willie at the door. "Mr. Graves!" He flashed a friendly smile, motioning for him to sit. "Almost ten o'clock, boy. Where you been?"

"Mornin', Halsey. Smells good."

"Come on now- sit yo' ass down! Got bacon, grits, eggs, and biscuits. Coffee's on the table."

Willie plopped down in his chair noticing a jar of fresh raspberry jam. "Good deal! This *your* jam?"

"Done it yesterday."

Willie caught Stick's eye as he lowered himself into his chair. "Gonna blow you away with this stuff!" he boasted. "Best jam on the planet!"

Stick leaned in to get a better look.

Halsey pulled pans of scrambled eggs and bacon from the bottom rack of the oven. "Need to call Josie when you're done, Willie."

He poured coffee into Stick's cup, then his own. "She okay?'

"She be fine." He closed the oven door with his foot. "Thinkin' 'bout comin' back," he explained, finding two plates. "And a fella named Wells called."

"DK?"

"That's it."

"Said you got the number."

Willie sipped his coffee, watching Stick, remembering how he'd played it in court. He was more than his parts, cagey and smart, when the wolves were at his door.

Halsey served their breakfast.

Stick gazed into his plate, then up at Willie, realizing it again. What the boy had given him. "Thanks for what you done. "

It surprised him, at first—seeing his gratitude. His sudden tenderness. They'd never quit on each other. They never would. "It's nothin', Stick," he replied easily, slapping jam on his biscuit, taking a bite.

Josie was his first call. There was traffic in the background. She sounded tired and worried. He explained the situation, how Stick had dodged a bullet for the time being.

"Just let me know."

"No reason to come."

"I wanted to hear it from you."

"We're good. It's hot here."

"Here too, baby." She fanned her face with a magazine. "Talked to the girls, except Cheeky. Not sure where she went."

"They missin' me yet?"

She thought about Charlottesville, the shaded streets and mountain air. "Be missin' your big ole' Buick."

After the call, he leaned against a kitchen cabinet, imagining her body next to his. Amber was in Florida, Caroline- Pennsylvania. Poppy was gone. It made him sad to think of them all—scattered about. He stared at the plates, so perfectly stacked, glasses all in a row. Halsey had left. Stick was asleep. He'd forgotten how it worked, the business of living. Peaceful, then violent, then calm again. Shattering, sometimes, without warning, into a thousand different pieces.

D. K. Wells took the call as quickly as he could.

"Sorry, Willie." He was distracted. "In the middle of something. You okay?"

"I'm fine, sir. Thanks for calling me back."

"This about your friend?"

"Yes, Sir."

"What Hilda said. Got John Lilly on it."

"I do, yes."

His secretary handed him a document and pointed. He signed on the line and waved her off.

"He's somethin', sir."

"As good as they come."

"So, I guess, I don't need your help after all." He waited. "Unless you think I do... we do. I'd be most grateful. Stick too, of course."

"I've looked into it, Willie. Made some calls." He sat back, remembering more specifically what it was. "You've got some problems, son."

Willie gripped the receiver. "Like what?"

He stretched his legs under the desk, considering his words

carefully. He'd give it to him straight. The fickle side of probity. The uncertainty. How justice came and justice went, depending on the prize.

David Sheffield was heading home when the phone rang. Friends were in town. His wife needed peaches.

"Sheffield?!" He heard panting through the line.

"Yes?"

"What kinda cock-suckin' circus you runnin' up there, goddammit?!"

He looked at his watch.

"You let him go 'cuz his name don't fit—or some such horseshit? Jesus, man! I will not *stand* for this, you understand me?"

He'd call his wife after.

"You *listen'n'* to me, Sheriff?"

"I am."

"What kinda cockamamie shit you pullin', huh?"

"Just following the law, Johnny."

"The law!" he screamed, lowering his voice suddenly. "Let me tell you somethin' 'bout the law, or whatever the *fuck* you wanna call it."

Sheffield sat down in his chair, closing his eyes.

"You will *return* that son of a bitch to me like we asked you to when he was served, or I will *fly up there* and take that cocksucker *by the balls,* myself."

He opened his eyes.

"You understand me?"

"I do, sir."

"Good. And who the fuck's this lawyer of his? Wrong name, no gun, no witness?" He paused to catch his breath. "We got a goddamn photo and a goddamn gun, Sheffield! Fella saw him do it!"

"Didn't know that."

"You didn't know that?"

"No, sir."

"Well then, *Read the friggin' warrant for Chrissake!*" he bellowed, stopping to catch his breath. "*How the fuck you think we got the attorney general of the state of Louisiana on this guy if we didn't have the goods?!*"

He stood up and stretched. His shoulders ached.

"Think we're *makin' this shit up?*"

"Not entirely sure."

"Not entirely sure," he repeated, trying to make sense of it. "*Come* on, man! Cut me some *fuckin'* slack here, *would* ya please? Y'all *butt-fucked* the chicken and *now* you need to *fix* it."

It wasn't the language. Something was missing.

"I got an election down here. You know what that means? A *course* you do! Like that *soft as fuck* town a yours, man. Every *four* years. People wanna know."

"Know what exactly?"

"What's takin' so long to get this thing straight."

"What thing?"

"What you mean, *what thing?*"

"Thought we were talking about Eugene Watson?"

He cleared his throat and swallowed, trying to keep the story straight. "Need your help, Sheriff—plain 'n' simple. Like to clean things up down here."

He let him stew a bit, swim around in the bullshit.

"You got *ten* days to right this ship, or I'm *up there* with my deputies. You *do not* want that."

"No, sir, I do not. You got proof of what you're sayin'?"

"'Bout what?"

"The weapon? Your witness? The photo?"

"You're *lookin'* at the photo!"

"Got no date."

There was a pause on the line.

"Well, it does *now.*"

He shook his head. "Where'd the gun come from?"

"Room he slept in the night he done it."

"And the witness?"

He lowered his voice. "Brought him in last week."

"For what?"

"Burglary."

"Burglary."

"That's right."

It was backyard cookin' plain and simple. "When's the election?"

"First Tuesday in September."

"Let me see what's goin' on."

"Goin' on where?"

"'Bout what happened."

"We all *know* what *happened,* goddammit! Seems your boys have *other* ideas."

He stood up from his chair. "Well... you got your boys and I got mine, Boudreau, so perhaps we can figure this all out together."

He changed his tone. "I'd like that, David."

"Come to a mutual understanding."

Boudreau laughed. "Only thing *mutual* down here's how to cook a crawdad, man, so... cha-cha with this fucker all you want, but what I need now, no, *goddammit,* what I *insist* upon... is that son-of-a-whatever-*bitch*-his-name-is, in *my* town, *locked up,* and *read his rights*. Got *no* room for your salty fuckin' peanuts down here, you *understand* me?"

"Easy on the nuts."

"Now you're talkin'."

The line went quiet.

"I'll give the judge a call."

"What's his name again?"

"Martell. Barrett Martell."

"Barrett."

"Yes, sir."

"Some fancy names you got up there."

"I'll call him in the morning."

"Well… appreciate that. I really do."

Sheffield reached for his hat on the desk. "Part of the job, Sheriff."

"One thing. Before you go."

"Sir?"

"And I *insist* on this."

He put his hat on.

Johnny Boudreau turned to his fish, remembering what it took. The patience and the wherewithal. How it twitched on the deck when he hit it with his bat, over and over again until it stopped, finally, blood everywhere, stock-still and vanquished. "Call me Johnny."


When Stick saw The Lawn, he stopped in his tracks. "Holy shit, Willie!" he exclaimed, admiring its long, splendid colonnades, ten pavilions gleaming in the sun.

They stepped out onto the grass to get a better look, turning back to see the great Rotunda, gazing up at the clock.

A flock of mourning doves angled overhead, veering south toward Old Cabell Hall. "It's almost three, Stick. We better get a move on."

They continued on, enjoying the trees as they passed.

"You still have your dictionary?"

"Left it in Winchester."

"I remember now. On your chair."

A girl drew near, looking away as she passed.

"Forgot it when we ran."

The chapel bell rang behind them.

On the second ring, Stick stopped and cocked his head, enchanted by the sound. "Ain't that somethin'."

Willie turned back towards the tower, overwhelmed suddenly by the memory of it. His old black hands, pulling down, letting go.

They listened to it fade.

Stick shook his head in wonder. He'd never seen such a place—such a temple for learning. "Like to see your chair someday," he said, understanding it more clearly. "If you don't mind."

Clark Hall stood before them. They took the stairs quickly to the second floor, searching for the professor's office, number 354, he'd said, finding it at the end of a long, starkly lit hallway. The door was open.

"Gentlemen!" John Lilly called out cheerily. "Right on time! Come in, come in! Please!"

They entered cautiously, timidly at first, captivated by the stacks of books. There was no place to sit.

"Ah, yes," he realized suddenly, stepping away from his desk, dashing out the door.

They stood in place, waiting, hearing a door at the end of the hall open and close, then footsteps.

The professor returned with two folding chairs. "My apologies, gentlemen." He struggled to open one. "Mr. Watson?" he suggested, putting it down, handing the other to Willie. "If you would be so kind, Willie."

"Of course, sir. Thank you," he replied, taking it quickly, pulling it apart.

Professor Lilly closed the door, seeing their chairs together, side by side. "There we are." He circled around his desk, finding a large file buried in a sea of papers, lowering himself delicately into his chair. "Thank you for coming today," he began, looking up. "How you holding up, Stick?"

"I'm fine, sir. Thanks for asking. Quite the place you got here."

"Well, yes." He looked around the room, momentarily confused, before he realized. "The University... yes, of course."

"Heard about it, but never seen it for myself."

"Here we are indeed. I sometimes forget." He turned to Willie. "Your new home soon enough, I'm pleased to say."

Stick noticed the floor, cross-stitched in oak. "Well, it's a fine place and you're lucky to have him, sir."

Willie looked away, embarrassed.

"We are, indeed," the professor agreed, enjoying his reaction. "And well deserved, I might add."

Stick smiled, seeing it too, understanding how his life had

changed. "Gets after it when he wants something, this one."

The Professor nodded thoughtfully, appreciating the way he'd said it. "Yes, he does."

Willie wiggled around in his chair, hearing them go on.

"Don't back down."

John Lilly gave Willie a final look of admiration. "Well done, Willie."

"Thank you, Sir."

"Have we embarrassed you enough?"

He cracked a smile and glanced at Stick. "Yes, Sir."

"Well then…" he grinned with satisfaction, scanning the papers on his desk, "To the matter at hand."

They watched him as he retrieved a file, opening it, hearing voices in the hallway.

The professor looked up. "Willie said the girls are away. On a bit of a break at the moment."

"Yes, sir."

"Good. Forgive me, but I told the judge you'd agree to stay in town and not leave Albemarle County."

"I understand, sir. I'm around until this thing's done. Promise you that."

"All I need to know."

Willie sat up. "We both will, sir. Whatever you need us to do."

The professor paused, appreciating his earnestness. "Good to hear. Thank you, both."

"Really appreciate what you're doing for us. For Stick. Can't imagine… if you hadn't come along."

The professor's face grew more concentrated as he returned to the file. "Remind me, Willie, if you would please—the kind of law you may be interested in?"

"Don't know, really. Criminal. Civil rights, maybe? There a difference?"

He looked up for a moment, struck by the irony. "Theoretically, yes. We'll call them distant cousins."

They watched him review some pages before closing the cover. "So… let's begin." He checked to make sure he had their full attention. "And if I lose you somewhere, just stop me. I'm prone to wander, my students tell me. '*Go on* a bit', they say."

They both nodded, trying not to smile.

"So, speak up, please. Don't be shy."

They nodded again.

He placed both hands on the file. "We have *many* moving parts here—I cannot stress that enough. Some large, others rather small and, seemingly, insignificant." He removed his hands and paused. "They are *not*." He let it sink in. "The more you can tell me *exactly* what happened down there, the better. Big things, little things, things you never thought of until now, perhaps. Anything and everything. *That's* what I need to build an argument with, gentlemen. Clear, logical evidence presented dispassionately, without prejudice, repeatedly, systematically, over and over and over again until it's done. Until we *have* it!" He looked at Willie, then Stick. "And Stick's a *free* man."

Stick appeared troubled. "You wanna know if I did it?"

"I do not, sir."

"How come?"

"That is not the purpose of my responsibilities at this time."

He shook his head, puzzled.

"Nor, yours."

"So, you don't care if I done it, or not?"

"That is correct."

Stick glanced at Willie, then back at the professor.

"This is a hearing, not a trial. We need to prove that the statements they've introduced are, in some cases, misleading and false."

He listened carefully.

"That is our only opportunity."

"So, how does that work exactly?"

He wasn't sure how to answer him."How does what work?"

"When a fella's guilty and everybody knows it."

"As in a trial?"

"Yeah."

"People can be wrong."

They tried to understand it.

He smiled, seeing their reaction. "It's human nature- truth be told." He looked at Willie. "A lawyer's job is to present the *facts*. The *person,* theoretically, is of no consequence in this regard… legally speaking."

Stick nodded. "What you don't know won't hurt you."

"Correct." He gave it a moment. "We are driven by evidence, not feelings," he said, dispassionately. "In a perfect world."

Stick wanted to tell him what had happened that night. The money Hook had lost and his crazy-ass friends. How they'd rushed him at the end when he'd played his final hand. "Well, I won what I got and he lost what he had. We had words… people got between us…" He stopped. "Turned my back and the thing went off."

Professor Lilly sat up when he heard it.

"Gun belonged to another guy."

"Which guy?"

"The cop."

The professor found a legal pad and pen.

"Fat fucker." He paused. "Excuse me."

"Quite alright."

"Al somethin'."

The professor wrote it down.

"With fake hair."

"A toupee?"

"Kept slippin' forward the drunker he got."

"Did he lose money, as well?"

"He did."

"A lot?"

"I stayed off the sauce to keep my head clear that night." He tried to remember exactly. "Couple thousand."

"And John Cheshire? 'Hook,' I believe you called him."

"Couple hundred."

"Hundred?"

"Yep."

"And his friends? How many were there?"

"Two."

"Did they lose money, as well?"

"Not so much."

"Just Mr. Cheshire? And the cop? Ex-cop, excuse me."

"Yep."

He made a note of it. "Were there others?"

"In the game?"

"Yes."

"No. Some guy was watching in back."

"And what did he do?"

"Worked for the hall. Muscle man, drinks… that kind of thing."

"I see."

"Kept an eye out."

The professor sat back in his chair, processing it all. "And when the incident occurred, was he in the room?"

"He was outside."

"Doing what?"

"No idea."

Full Beaver Moon / 263

"Was there a phone outside?"

"Yep. It was like a lobby. Had a phone on the wall. And a bathroom.

"So, to your knowledge, just before the game ended, he left the room?"

"Correct." Stick looked at Willie, sensing something, not knowing what it was. "Never saw him again."

"Willie said you knew the fellow who died."

"I did."

He waited for him to explain.

"Grew up together, guess you could say. With his brother mostly. He was more my age."

"And where was this?"

"Thelma, Virginia. East a Cismont."

The answer surprised Willie. "Thelma?"

Stick threw him a look. "'Til we were teenagers."

John Lilly made a note. "Your family moved at that time?"

"Yep. Started hoppin'."

He had no idea what that meant.

"Trains."

The professor nodded his understanding as he wrote.

"Pretty much left and didn't come back."

He stopped writing and looked up. "And at what age, if I may ask?"

"Sixteen."

He looked at Willie.

"Did some trampin' after that."

"I'm sorry?"

Willie jumped in, "Hoe-boys, sir. Took their hoes with 'em and found work where they could."

"Of course, excuse me."

Stick sat back in his chair. "Been a while since we've used those words, I guess." He crossed his legs to get more comfortable.

"Not at all. I remember them quite clearly. A difficult time for all kinds of folks."

Willie gazed at Stick, appreciating his story.

"Still goin' on."

"Is it?"

"All around you, sir," he replied quickly. "Gotta know where to look."

The professor took a moment, putting his notes in the file. There was work to be done, calls to make. "We'll continue tomorrow, if you don't mind." He sat back in his chair. "Last question."

Stick was ready for a drink.

"This Hook fella?"

"Sir?"

"Willie said he stabbed you several months ago."

"He did."

He saw the scar on his neck. "There was bad blood between the two of you? As it were."

"There was."

"And what was that about?"

He took his time, thinking of it again. "I hit his brother pretty bad, long time ago."

The room grew still.

"He run off with my money once. So, I tracked him down. Let him have it."

The professor leaned forward in his chair. He was afraid to ask.

"With a crowbar."

Cary returned from Virginia Beach. He'd had enough sun and the wind was up. He wasn't sure what he could do, but he missed Willie, and Josie said he sounded changed. He met them on the front porch, enjoying Stick's firm grip, his gray-blue eyes. They reminded him of his grandfather.

"'Bout time you met," Willie declared, seeing them together finally. "Cary's the real deal, Stick. Runs the door. Keeps an eye out." He looked at Cary affectionately. "Made this place what it is today."

Cary released Stick's hand. "Like they say, honey." He spoke in a slow Southern drawl. "If the creek don't rise."

Stick watched Willie as he laughed, his face bathed in late afternoon sunlight. If Crystal Ann had given him a son, he'd be the one, maybe. Someone smarter than himself, more forgiving. Merciful. The kind of guy who'd give you a chance and put you at the door.

Willie folded the newspaper and hit the light. It was 3:00 a.m. The booze hadn't worked. His head was throbbing. He went over it again, the evidence, a witness, the gun. What Stick remembered, what he didn't. How he'd grabbed the barrel and turned it sideways, letting go when the thing went off, then running for the door. Stick's picture stared back at him from under the lamp. He looked menacing and dangerous.

RICHMOND MAN WANTED FOR MURDER

The New Orleans Jefferson Parish Police Department says a man suspected in a fatal shooting will be extradited back to Louisiana. The shooting occurred October 7, 1957, at the Black Pearl Club in New Orleans.

According to police, the suspect has been identified as fifty-two-year-old Eugene Allen Watson of Richmond, Virginia. The shooting involved a dispute between both parties during a gambling incident.

Watson was arrested in Charlottesville near McIntire Park on the morning of July 5 by members of the Charlottesville Police Department and transported to the Albemarle County Regional Jail. At the time of his arrest, he was considered armed and dangerous. He has been charged with first-degree murder in the shooting of John Cheshire III from Palmyra, Virginia. It is unknown what brought him to Charlottesville at the time of his capture.

Watson was released on bond and is scheduled to appear in court July 19 for his final extradition hearing overseen by Circuit Court Judge Barrett Martell.

A whip-poor-will called through the open window. He rolled to one side, captivated by the sound, the soft evening air. There was still beauty about, with wonder and purpose. There had to be, he thought, thinking of Stick, of his own life.

After a while, he closed his eyes and fell away, believing in the world again. If a bird could sing, then a judge could too. Like a prayer on a warm summer night.

# CHAPTER TWENTY-THREE

Halsey came early. They stared at their food, taking small bites to make him feel better.

"Good luck today, boys," he finally said, drying the last pan. "Be fine, once you know." He turned around, leaning back against the counter. They looked miserable. "Leave the plates."

"Thanks, Halsey," Stick replied, finishing his coffee and standing.

Willie did the same, checking for the car keys in his pocket.

"Heard some folks are comin'. *Daily Progress* guy, couple girls from Timberlakes."

Stick looked worried.

He shot him a smile. "It's a small town, man." He tossed his dish towel on the counter and raised himself up. "Middle a July."

The Buick gleamed in the hot morning sun. They climbed in and pulled away. Willie had washed it the day before. He said it helped him think straight.

"You polish this thing?"

"Simoniz Wax." He turned the AC up. "Looks good when you're done."

"Quite the ride," Stick agreed, sitting back, enjoying the cooler air.

Willie looked him over as he drove. "The shirt fits."

Stick looked down, touching his sleeve.

"Hope you don't mind me buying it."

"Not at all. Appreciate it." He stared out over the dash. "Everything helps."

They drove in silence for a while.

"Want some music?" Stick asked finally.

"No thanks. Too much on my mind right now."

He leaned in and turned the radio on. "Come on, Willie, we can do this."

He turned onto Proffit Road.

"Just another day."

The song was sweet and silly.

Willie gripped the wheel. "Need to talk to you."

Stick watched the houses as they passed. "Sorry?"

He turned the radio off. "Tell you something."

The boy looked tired. "You sleep last night?

"On and off. You? "

"Same."

They came to a stop on West Main Street.

Willie took his hands off the wheel, putting them in his lap. "Somethin' bad happens, we need a plan."

Stick waited.

"Way to get you out."

"Outta what?"

"Here."

"Charlottesville?"

"Yeah. Not sayin' it'll happen. Just sayin' we need to figure it out before."

A car honked lightly from behind.

Willie saw it in the rearview mirror, suddenly agitated. "Hold your horses, man, Jesus Christ!"

They pulled out, turning left through the intersection.

Stick waited for him to continue.

"Before they decide."

"Nothin' we can do, Willie."

"Sure there is! Can always do *somethin'*! Need to figure it out, that's all."

"Whatever happens and whatever don't, can't make it go away."

Willie concentrated on the road. His tank was full. There was money in the house.

He looked at him sadly. "That's the truth of it."

They drove a few blocks.

"Not gonna just sit here and watch you go."

Stick looked around, admiring a couple as they walked together. They were holding hands. The town had been good to him. Like a place should be. "Not the way the world spins."

When Willie saw the courthouse his stomach lurched. There were people everywhere. "It's a circus, man, look at that!"

It surprised him, seeing it. "We'll be alright."

Willie's face grew tense with worry. "How you know that?"

He tried to smile. Make him feel better. "Just do."

Willie shook his head, looking for the side street. "I should be helping you, Stick. Figure it out."

Stick laughed when he heard it.

"You think it's funny?"

"Funny, no."

He saw a sign for Court Square and turned.

Stick took a deep breath. His time was coming. "I'm just as worried as you are, son, but I'm older now and when you're older you take your lumps, that's all. Face the music. Not gonna lie to you—gonna hurt to lose. But either way…"

A deputy stood outside a side door as they approached.

"We'll be alright."

He wanted to scream, to hit the gas. "We ain't *losin'* man! I *swear to God*, you hear me?!" He pulled the car over and stopped, facing him. "That ole professor's gonna pull us through this thing and, somehow, I don't know how, but we'll get on with it, you and me, I swear!"

Stick smiled, seeing his bloodshot eyes, the beginning of tears. "No doubt."

"And if it all turns to shit, I'll get you outta here."

"Cake's baked, man."

"No, it ain't."

The deputy recognized their car and raised his hand.

"One thing you can do for me, though." He opened the door.

Willie's heart sank. "Anything."

He put a foot on the street and thought about it. How far he'd come. How the boy had helped him get there. "Tell Hilda I love her."

Willie drove back for Cary, numb to the world. The hearing would start at 11:00. He went upstairs to calm himself, take money from the safe. If they locked him up, he'd steal him away. He didn't care about school, or the house, or Rebecca- that could all wait. What mattered most was Stick. To be there, always, as he had been for him. That strong, sure hand, reaching out from a train.

When he lay down for a moment, Cotton jumped up, plopping beside him. Closing his eyes, he caressed him gently, enjoying his purr, his soothing presence. It sounded like water, rivulets of blood, washing his fears down a fast-moving stream.

# CHAPTER TWENTY-FOUR

The fans were spinning and the courtroom was abuzz. Cary found a seat in the back. It surprised Willie again, the size of the crowd. The rumblings. He put his head down, reaching the front row quickly, finding a chair behind Stick's empty table. He took a moment to gather himself. His shoes needed a shine. His nails were stained with car wax.

Sitting there, Sister Mo came into his head, laughing quietly, then giggling, going on about something—the weather, maybe, or was it Stick? "Ain't nothin' but *light*," he heard her say. "When duh *glass* take duh *shine*, an yo' boy be gone."

Sunlight streaked through a nearby window. Across the aisle, he saw the badge, his snively sneer. That was what she meant. Why she'd come to him. Sheriff Johnny Boudreau was licking his chops, ready to take Stick away.

When Sheriff Sheffield entered, the courtroom quieted. Willie turned, seeing him, recognizing certain faces scattered about. A Timberlakes waitress smiled when she saw him. He smiled back, not remembering her name. The clothing store guy, an old librarian, his neighbor across the street. Halsey was right. The porches were hot and the town was talking. People were looking for blood.

The crowd hushed as Professor Lilly and Stick entered from a side door. Whispering his name, their expressions grew harder. It upset Willie, seeing it. For a man they'd never known.

When they joined him, Willie stood. Stick's face was distant and cold.

"That seat taken?" someone inquired from the aisle.

Hearing it, Stick and Willie turned. Her smile was devasting.

"Got room for D. K.?"

Willie moved over to make room. He looked older than he imagined.

"Hello, Willie."

"Hello, sir."

The bailiff appeared through an open door, suddenly, making his way around the bench, stopping near the witness stand.

Hilda reached her chair, wrapping her arms around Willie.

He held on. She was still warm from the sun.

When the judge appeared, they let go.

"*All rise!*" the bailiff announced.

The courtroom fell silent.

Willie took a staggered breath. His heart was pounding. If Stick deserved a second chance, it would be now, he prayed. In this place.

"*This court is now in session!*"

The room remained still as the judge looked around, seeing Johnny Boudreau, John Lilly and Stick, then Willie for some reason. It made his skin crawl when he realized it. He looked down, wanting Hilda's hand.

Judge Martell assumed a cordial expression.

"Good morning." He paused, checking something he'd written down. "Thank you all for being here." He gave the courthouse a perfunctory look. "Once again, the purpose of this hearing is to determine the merits of an extradition request before this court by the State of Louisiana involving charges against Eugene Allen Watson on the evening of October seventh, 1957, in the Jefferson Parish of New Orleans." He turned his attention to Stick. "As we've discussed during your previous appearance, Mr. Watson, this is not a trial. Our concern is to determine the merits of extradition as it pertains to these charges." He paused, giving Stick time to absorb what he'd been told. "Nothing more. Do you understand?"

Stick took a moment to respond. "I do," he said quietly.

"We're not here to decide your guilt or innocence in this matter, sir." He paused again. "Is that clear?"

Stick clenched his fists under the table. "Yes, sir."

He acknowledged his answer. "And Mr. Lilly, to my knowledge we have resolved the matter regarding Mr. Watson's name?"

"We have, Your Honor."

"Good." Judge Martell reviewed a document briefly before continuing, "Contrary to the initial filings, Mr. Watson's name has been properly changed from Richard to Eugene Allen Watson, as indicated in the materials and petition before us."

"That is correct, Your Honor."

"And, Mr. Watson, your representative has made you aware of these changes?"

Stick nodded back in agreement.

"I will need an answer, sir."

"Yes."

"Thank you, sir. Let it be known, then, that the matter regarding conclusive identification in these matters has been resolved and we can proceed."

When a door opened, Willie turned around, seeing a policeman enter quickly, finding a place beside Sheriff Sheffield.

"So, Mr. Lilly," the judge hesitated, noticing the policeman as well. " I will make a brief statement, call a witness. You will follow, Sir."

"Thank you, Your Honor."

His face grew stern, taking a moment to emphasise its importance."Your clarity and brevity will be much appreciated."

"I understand, thank you, Your Honor."

After a moment, the judge sat up in his chair, looked out into the courtroom, and began.

Willie listened as best he could, hearing the larger points mostly. When he was done, Sheriff Boudreau moved slowly to the witness stand. His voice was low, confident as he explained the situation—how they'd gambled into the early morning, some winning, some losing, the ensuing argument, the gunshot, the bullet they'd recovered, the witness. How Stick Watson had hidden the gun in the ceiling of a boardinghouse closet, the matching bullets, and a certain Miss Tessula Cambridge's testimony. Returning to his chair, his face was flush with satisfaction, seeing Professor Lilly's expression, then Willie's sullen face.

Judge Martel closed a file, pausing briefly to collect his thoughts, before addressing Stick directly. "Mr. Watson, the petition before me requests your immediate return to the State of Louisiana to face charges for murder, substantiated by the evidence submitted to this court and to your representative." He paused, acknowledging Sheriff Boudreau. "We appreciate and thank Circuit Court Judge Foss, the offices of the Attorney General of the State of Louisiana, and Sheriff Boudreau for his considerable efforts and subsequent appearance in this matter."

Hearing his conclusion, spectators whispered among themselves. When the judge looked up, the courthouse grew quiet. "Mr. Lilly, please."

Professor Lilly looked tired as he stood, sitting back on his heels, biding his time. There was no jury, no larger body to impress. He relished the moment—the palpable silence. Cutting the engine and raising his sails.

"Your Honor," he began, stepping away from his table before stopping dramatically. "My client is innocent of these charges. He did not own, nor discharge, the firearm in question and, while present during the altercation, was in no way responsible for the unfortunate death of Mr. Cheshire." He turned, gesturing toward Stick. "And critically, at no point subsequent to those events, did my client secure a room in Miss Cambridge's boardinghouse, nor, as Sheriff Boudreau claims, hide a weapon in the ceiling of his closet."

"One moment please, Mr. Lilly."

He paused, surprised by the interruption.

"I would remind you that the focus of your arguments will pertain to false or misleading statements *only,* as described in these documents."

"I understand, Your Honor. That is my purpose."

The judge hesitated. "And mine with these latitudes, Sir."

"I understand."

He sat back in his chair. "You may proceed."

John Lilly steadied himself, considering his words carefully. "It is our view, that these events, as described, have been fictionalized, altered, and manufactured, fraudulently in some cases, by representatives of the State of Louisiana to support their position." Raising himself up, he addressed the judge more formally. "And I would respectfully submit to you, Your Honor, that under these circumstances, in the absence of irrefutable substantiating statements, Mr. Watson be cleared of these charges and released immediately at the conclusion of this hearing."

As the crowd listened, Johnny Boudreau stared into space.

Returning to his table, Professor Lilly retrieved a large manila envelope. "And one small, but significant, matter, Your Honor," he added. "If I may?"

The judge looked annoyed suddenly. "Yes, John."

"I have critical information pertinent to our argument, which has taken until now to obtain."

The two men regarded one another.

"Information, you say?"

"If I may, Your Honor?"

"Pertaining to?"

"Ballistics, Your Honor."

"Ballistics."

"Yes, Your Honor."

It took the judge a moment. "I am in possession of the same ballistics report, as, I believe, are you, sir."

"I am, yes."

He removed his glasses. "Your point, then?"

"You have *their* report, Your Honor… you do not have *mine*."

He nodded reluctantly. "I see. And the discrepancy as it relates to these documents lies where?"

Professor Lilly smiled, appreciating the question. "It is my intention to provide this court with proof that the ballistics report submitted in these documents does not match the caliber, nor the model described as the firearm discharged in this event."

The judge put his glasses on, searching for a particular document.

"As you will see, the referenced model is a Lightweight Colt Commander 1911."

"Yes. An... 'M1911 Colt pistol.'" He checked again. "Absent serial number. Unregistered." He looked up. "And your point?"

"The bullet does not correspond directly with the model in question."

"The bullet?"

"Yes."

The judge turned several pages of the ballistics report before coming upon it. "I'm confused by your point. The casings match the model described as evidence, do they not?"

"For a post-World War II, M1911 built in 1949, yes, they do indeed."

The judge shook his head, puzzled by his answer. "Therefore?"

"We are presented with a bullet, the casing from which does not, cannot *physically*, *materially*, match the make of the gun provided as evidence."

The courtroom grew tense.

"The model from which the bullet *originates* is the All-*Steel* Colt Combat Commander, *Series 70*. Same gun, different model."

The judge glanced briefly at Sheriff Boudreau.

"A *split,* not *single barrel* bushing." He let it sink in. "The ballistics report submitted to this court is incompatible with the gun it references."

Sheriff Boudreau sat up in his chair. "May I say something, Your Honor?"

They turned to him, each one, perplexed by the interruption.

"You need to wait your turn, if you would oblige us, please, Sheriff?"

"Thought that's what I was doin'."

The judge's face turned glacial. "Excuse me?"

"Obliging your court and all these good people out here."

"And we thank you for that, Sheriff Boudreau," he managed against his better instinct.

"Not at all, Your Honor."

The judge noticed journalists scribbling in their notebooks. "And for coming all this way to help us understand exactly what happened down there."

"Thank you, Judge, appreciate that," he answered back. "And I'm sorry for the interruption. Been a long couple weeks in my parish and sometimes I can't help myself when I hear Mr. Lilly there goin' on about somethin' he knows nothin' about."

The judge's face flushed. "Such as?"

"Well... let's see... ballistics, for starters." He looked over at John Lilly. "We put our best man on that, Mr. Lilly. Former specialist in his field. Knows it inside and out."

John Lilly stood his ground. "I'm sure he does, Sheriff."

"So, forgive me, but it's hard for me to sit here and listen to his good character and reputation being sullied about."

"That was not my intention, sir."

"No?"

"Not in the least."

The two men looked to the judge.

Judge Martell shook his head, mystified. "Where we going with this, gentlemen?"

The sheriff continued, turning to John Lilly "Who's responsible for this notion that the bullet doesn't fit the gun."

"Giovanni Costigan."

"Costigan?"

"Correct. Giovanni is his first name."

"Forgive me Professor. May I call you Professor?"

"You may."

"Well, I'm a cop from New Orleans, Louisiana and, as you might expect, am unfamiliar with your part of the world up here. He a local fella?"

"Yes and no."

"Which is it?"

"Born here, lives in Baton Rouge."

"Baton Rouge?"

"Correct."

"In what capacity?"

"For the past twenty years, Giovanni Costigan has been dean of the Department of Forensic Science at Tulane University."

The courtroom stopped.

"He a friend a yours?"

"He is."

"Well, how 'bout that."

"We grew up together. Attended The University."

"Don't mean he's right though, does it?"

"I would agree with you, sir." John Lilly gave the judge a fatal look before returning to the sheriff. "But it sure as hell gets your attention."

When the gavel struck, the courthouse quieted. "Are we done, gentlemen?"

"We are, Your Honor, my apologies." John Lilly answered quickly.

The judge looked sternly at Sheriff Boudreau. His patience was gone.

"Yes, Your Honor."

"You boys want to discuss this somewhere else, it's fine with me, but you will not do so in my courtroom. Do you understand me?"

"Yes, Your Honor."

"Sorry 'bout that, Judge."

The reporters made furious notes, glancing up from time to time as they did.

Judge Martell let go of his papers and grabbed his glasses. He'd heard enough. "Mr. Lilly, in my chambers, please," he announced, rising from his chair.

When the doors closed and they were gone, Stick turned back, searching Hilda's eyes. He realized it suddenly, hearing voices about- some loud, some whispering. She was everything to him now. Sunlight and water. From where he was away.

When the judge and John Lilly returned, the courthouse quieted quickly, reading their faces, watching them sit. Then silence.

It took a while for the judge to look up. "Mr. Watson, this court has considered two arguments regarding the nature and composition of the bullets used on the night of October seventh and it is the court's opinion that both arguments may, under certain circumstances, be considered plausible. The state of Louisiana has submitted a report by the New Orleans Police Department suggesting that the firearm model in question matches the recovered bullet. Mr. Lilly has submitted a report by the Tulane University Department of Forensic Science suggesting otherwise. That the casings of the bullet correspond to an earlier design of the same model, with different associative identities, by design." He regarded Stick, sympathetically. "Ultimately, sir, as I've discussed with your representative just now, this is a hearing and not a trial. As I have said." He gave Stick a moment to understand it. "Accordingly, it is not, *should not* be the responsibility of this court, to determine which argument is correct."

Stick looked at Professor Lilly. Whatever was going on, it didn't sound good.

"I will, therefore, disregard *both* arguments at this time. Any resolution involving these discrepancies will, by necessity, require future criminal proceedings, should they take place."

The courtroom stirred momentarily.

"I remind you, sir, and everyone here present, of my sole responsibility… to determine sufficient and probable cause, *only*, as it relates to your extradition. Not the accuracy, nor truth of those arguments."

Stick was lost.

"Do you understand me, Mr. Watson?"

It took him a moment. "Not really."

The judge smiled, enjoying his honesty. "The State of Louisianna will figure it out."

Stick nodded.

"I'm here to decide if they should." He waited for Stick to respond.

"I got it, thank you, Your Honor."

"A bit confusing these things." He acknowledged John Lilly.

"Mr. Lilly, are you ready to call your witness?"

"I am, Your Honor."

"And who would that person be, sir?"

John Lilly referred to his notes. "Your Honor, we would like to call Sheriff Johnny Boudreau."

When he heard his name, Sheriff Boudreau sat up in his chair, waiting for the judge's response.

"Proceed," the judge answered easily.

"With, perhaps, one final witness to follow, Your Honor."

The judge hesitated, hearing it. "Another witness?"

"Yes, Your Honor. Possibly."

"I see."

"I will be brief."

He nodded reluctantly. "Well then," he said, sitting back, "The court calls Sheriff John Taylor Boudreau as a witness."

Within seconds the sheriff assumed his chair beside the judge.

John Lilly hesitated before he began. "Sheriff Boudreau, I have a couple questions."

"Happy to help."

"Thank you."

The reporters stopped writing.

"One 'player' in the events that occurred on October seventh is a cousin of yours, is he not?"

"That is correct."

"A former member of the Jefferson Parish Police Department?"

"Correct, sir. Retired. With honors."

"With honors."

"That is correct. Spent ten years with me. Good man. Family man."

"Family man."

"That's right," he boasted, glancing out into the courtroom. "Takes care of his own."

"Takes care of his own," Professor Lilly repeated, for emphasis.

The two men regarded one another carefully.

"What happened to the gun he carried into the hall that night?"

The question took him aback. "I have no idea."

John Lilly gave him a long look. "Your testimony to this hearing, repeated in these documents, is that Mr. Watson spent the following night in Miss Tessula Cambridge's boardinghouse nearby, where, seven days later, your deputies discovered a pistol hidden in the ceiling of a closet."

"Not *a* closet, Mr. Lilly. *His* closet."

"In the room you claim he spent the night of October seventh."

"What I said, yes. Got testimony from the lady that runs the place he was there."

"A Miss Tessula Cambridge?"

"That is correct. What we found when she showed us the room. Signed a statement saying he was there."

John Lilly gave him a satisfied smile. "Thank you, Sheriff

Boudreau."

The sheriff looked around, confused.

"That will be all."

"Well, there you go," he replied, glancing at the judge in surprise, rising reluctantly.

Judge Martell gave him a nod. "Thank you, Sheriff. We appreciate your recollection of these events," he added for the record, watching him return to his seat.

Professor Lilly approached his table to retrieve a document, motioning to Sheriff Sheffield and the deputy, watching them exit quickly. "If I may, Your Honor," he continued, turning back to the judge, "I would like to call a final witness."

"I will allow it, sir."

"Thank you."

When the back doors opened, the crowd murmured quietly between themselves, recognizing Sheriff David Sheffield and a strange Black woman in a bright yellow dress.

Willie's mouth dropped open when he realized who it was.

Seeing her for the first time, John Lilly took a moment. "Your Honor," he announced, pausing for emphasis, "I would like to call Miss Tessula Cambridge of Jefferson Parish, New Orleans, as a witness."


Tessula Cambridge descended from slaves escaping Barbados

plantations or taken in raids on European estates—capsized off the coast of South America in 1635, reaching the island of Saint Vincent, miraculously, days later. Her high-pitched voice was a Spanish-English scat, punctuated, proud, and tender. She liked cats more than people, rum more than water, and dresses made of silk. Yellow was her favorite color. As she took her seat before the courtroom, Judge Barrett Martell tapped his gavel lightly on the block.

John Lilly gave it some time, enjoying the crowd's reaction, Sheriff Boudreau's sudden despair. The stage was set and he was ready for blood. For something called, *the Law*. He approached the bench slowly, deliberately. When she put her purse down, it was time to begin.

"Miss Cambridge, would you be kind enough to identify yourself, please?"

"Tessula Lucy Cambridge, 1314 Maple Street, Jefferson Parish, New Orleans, Louisiana."

"Thank you, ma'am. And are you the proprietor of a boardinghouse in the city of New Orleans?"

"What you mean?"

"The owner?"

"Yes, sir. Goin' on thirty-seven years December."

"For quite some time, then?"

"Yes, sir."

"And in that time, I presume, you've become a fixture in that community, have you not?"

"You mean, like a light?"

The courtroom stirred, some giggling.

"I do."

"Yes, sir, you could say that."

"Know a lotta people there."

"I do."

The judge raised his hand. "Brevity, Mr. Lilly, if you would be so kind."

John Lilly took a moment to collect his thoughts.

"First of all, Miss Cambridge, I want to thank you for coming all this way to answer our questions." He gestured toward Stick. "A man's freedom is at stake here and we all want to make sure we get it right. So, thank you."

"You welcome."

The courtroom was spellbound.

"Do you recognize Mr. Watson behind me?"

"The White guy?"

John Lilly suppressed a smile, gesturing again toward Stick. "Yes, the man seated there next to my chair.

"No, sir."

"*Utter bullshit!*" Sheriff Boudreau interrupted loudly.

The courtroom gasped.

Judge Martell's gavel hit the table.

"Friggin' nonsense!"

"Sheriff Boudreau, sir."

"Payin' for her plane ticket, s'all she be doin' right now."

The judge banged the gavel harder. "*Sir!*"

The sheriff looked down at his boots.

"I will have you *removed* from this courtroom if you cannot be quiet. Is that what you want?"

"No, sir, Your Honor."

The judge stared back, waiting for him to look up. When he did, the two men considered each other, before he continued. "Mr. Lilly?"

John Lilly appeared calm, returning to Miss Cambridge. "Miss Cambridge, on the night of October seventh did you, as Sheriff Boudreau has claimed, rent a room, specifically, room number twelve, to a Mr. Stick Watson?"

"No, sir."

The courtroom stirred again, before quieting.

"And did you, as you have previously stated in writing, witness the discovery of a firearm on October fourteenth, attributed to Mr. Watson, hidden in the ceiling of room twelve's closet by deputies from the Jefferson Parish Police Department?"

"No, sir."

The courtroom grew more agitated before the gavel fell.

"That will be enough, please!" the judge warned, looking out.

There was quiet.

John Lilly continued, "Are you sure, Miss Cambridge?"

Tessula Cambridge sat up in her chair, pressing her dress down against her lap. "You ever been to New Orleans, sir?"

"I have, ma'am, yes."

"So, you know how it be down there?"

The question surprised him.

"Why they call it what they do?"

"The Big Easy?"

She nodded, to herself mostly. "S'pose to mean *slow,* like they talk, like they live. From the jazz, or the booze, or the heat, I s'pect." She thought about how to put it. "Nothin' too big, nothin' too small. Nothin' too bad fo' duh take."

"The take?"

She looked at him and smiled. "Like cream down there."

John Lilly stepped back, letting her continue.

She found Sheriff Boudreau, seeing him clearly. "From the top."

The sheriff stared back, trying to contain himself.

She stayed on him. "Man make me sign somethin' wasn't what I signed. Make it look like somethin' else."

The fans turned overhead.

She returned to Professor Lilly. "Got a cousin involved, what I heard that night. Lost his dough and pulled a gun."

Johnny Boudreau folded his arms and sat back in his chair.

"Nothin' '*easy*' in that town, Mr. Lilly, sir. Why I come all this way when you ask me. Tired a the Game. Tired a the Hustle. Like livin' too long in another man's house."

The judge interrupted. "Mr. Lilly?"

John Lilly turned quickly, acknowledging the judge, before

returning to Miss Cambridge.

"You believe the sheriff's cousin was involved?

"Yes, sir."

"And that your statement has been altered?"

"Changed."

"In what way, Miss Cambridge?"

"Sat me down in the kitchen one day… asked me if I rented a room to the boy there."

John Lilly turned back to Willie, pointing. "Willie Graves, the young man behind my table?"

Willie's face flushed, feeling their eyes upon him suddenly.

"Yes, sir. Stayed with me couple nights."

"After the incident?"

"Yes, sir. Was lookin' for his friend."

"Mr. Watson."

"Yes, sir. Said he drove down to find him, see if he could help."

"Do you remember the date, Miss Cambridge?"

"End a November, somethin' like that. Nice boy. Looked worried, tired as a dog… then he left. What I told the police. Put my name to it. Switched it up later."

"Switched the names?"

"What it was, sir. Here to make it right. "

John Lilly took his time. "So, to your knowledge, Miss Cambridge, deputies from the Jefferson Parish Police Department misappropriated your signature to fit a different name?"

"How it go down there."

"Changed the boy's name, Willie Graves, to Mr. Watson's?"

"Date too."

"And the date, as well."

"Yes, sir."

"Thank you, Miss Cambridge."

She looked around, noticing where she was, the judge in particular. "Time to say it. We all tired a bein' took."

The judge addressed John Lilly. "Clearly, Mr. Lilly, we are not here to place judgment on an entire town."

He considered the question, understanding its relevance. "No, Your Honor. That is not our intention at this time."

The judge made a quick note of it and looked up. "You may continue."

John Lilly considered Miss Cambridge and smiled warmly. "Please continue, Miss Cambridge."

Tessula Cambridge looked out, seeing Black and White faces scattered about. "Be all I got to say, I guess."

John Lilly returned to his chair, standing behind it, resting his hands on the back. "Thank you, Miss Cambridge. We're very grateful for your testimony this afternoon."

She listened to him, exhausted suddenly.

"Is there anything else you'd like to add before we let you go?"

She took a short, thin breath and thought about it, looking out, seeing the sheriff, all the people. "Like ta see that Monticello... 'fore

I get myself home." She slipped her purse over an arm, understanding it finally. "Can't *change* the truth if a man don't want it. Plain and simple." She looked at the judge one last time. "Don't listen to his heart."

When the side door opened finally, the crowd returned quickly to their seats, some racing through the back door in a panic. The judge's face was inscrutable.

Willie, Hilda, and D. K. Wells dropped expectantly into their chairs behind Stick.

"Please be seated," he announced, ignoring the commotion, lowering himself slowly into his chair, putting on his glasses.

Blood pounded in Willie's head.

Hilda's heart raced.

John Lilly turned to Stick to comfort him in some way.

"Ladies and gentlemen," the judge began mechanically, checking his papers before looking up. "Mr. Watson, I thank you for your patience in this matter. Is the bailiff present?"

The bailiff, on cue, stepped out from beside the bench. "I am, Your Honor."

"Then, to all present," he continued, "the Sixteenth District Court of Virginia has reached a decision." He gave Stick a grave look. "Mr.

Watson?"

John Lilly turned to Stick.

"Please rise."

Stick rose, swallowing hard. His legs were shaking.

Willie lowered his head and closed his eyes. He thought about Sister Mo and Moses Henry. Ernest, Perlie, and Tessula Cambridge. How their kindness and their pain had opened his heart to the world. He said a prayer for Stick, for Hilda, for Professor Lilly, and, finally, for the judge. "Spare him, sir..." he recited to himself quickly, "and I will commit my life to the purpose of others, no matter how poor, how desperate..."

The judge cleared this throat.

He reached for Hilda's hand. "Or, small."

*"In the matter submitted by the Attorney General of the State of Louisiana versus Eugene Allen Watson, Penal Code 1389-1389.8 signed, October fifteenth, 1957 by the Right Honorable Wilbur M. Foss of the Twenty-Fourth Judicial District Court of Jefferson Parish, New Orleans, Louisiana, pursuant to Virginia Code number 19.2-84 and Article IV, Section two, Clause three of the United States Constitution, we find the evidence presented here today sufficient for extradition."* He glanced briefly, coldly, at Sheriff Boudreau. *"It is further determined that this court finds, however extraneous to these proceedings, probable cause regarding allegations of evidentiary impropriety and corruption within the prosecutorial, police, and*

*judicial branches of The Jefferson Parish in the State of Louisiana."* He moved his paper to the side before removing his glasses and addressing John Lilly. *"A report of these findings will be submitted to the Attorney General of the United States Department of Justice at the conclusion of this hearing."* He regarded Stick gravely, without emotion. *"Mr. Watson will be remanded to federal marshals before nine p.m. this evening and returned to the State of Louisiana, as requested."* He gathered his documents in one hand. *"Having no further business with this court"*—he reached for his gavel—*"this hearing is adjourned!"* he concluded, with a bang.

*"All rise!"*

As the courtroom rushed to life, Willie and Hilda remained frozen in their chairs, holding hands.

# CHAPTER TWENTY-FIVE

They gathered at the top of the courthouse steps in a sweeping summer light, not believing entirely what had happened. How everything had changed.

Hilda and Willie stood together, seeing David Sheffield and his deputies usher Stick into a van outside the courthouse side door. Tears streaked down Willie's face. He saw it clearly, now. How fragile the world could be, so broken and wrong. What little remained of Stick's life.

Professor Lilly extended a hand to D. K. Wells. He was a large man in a smart blue suit. They'd met once years before in Richmond. "I'm sorry, D. K."

"Not our day, John. Sadly," he replied, taking his hand, shaking it slowly. He surveyed the area before letting go, leaning in. "Some hanky-panky goin' on. In case you wondered."

The professor's face flushed.

"Boudreau's got a judge down there..." He considered Hilda in the distance. "What I'm hearing." He lowered his voice. "Did Martell a favor once."

John Lilly froze, understanding it finally.

"Nothing to be done."

They measured each other for a moment, then the street below.

"Less you got somethin' up your sleeve?"


When they separated, Hilda approached John Lilly. She looked devastated.

"You must be Hilda," he managed awkwardly.

She opened her arms to him.

It had been a while since he'd embraced a woman other than his wife. Or, one who felt so good.

"Thank you for trying," she whispered softly, letting go after a moment.

He felt his own failings, instantly, inescapably. Stick was gone, the boy was crushed, Justice was a whore. He tried to smile, to make her feel better. "Arguing the law is easy, my dear," he replied, wearily. "Winning is more difficult."


Sensing someone, Willie turned around. He was in tight, skinny pants, smoking. "Cary," he managed, stumbling toward him.

They held each other for a while, shell-shocked. Willie closed his eyes, drawing comfort from it.

"Goddammit!" Cary said eventually, letting go. "Nothing is worth saving..." he gave him a fierce look. "If you don't fight back."

Hilda drove to her dock on the Northern Neck, meeting Auggie's boat on the Corrotoman River. The inn was full and the bay was rough. The season was half over. She'd order some wood and mend her pots. Before the cold set in. Drop them in the bay.

They took rooms that night. John Lilly called his wife from the kitchen. He told her he had work to do, to watch her show, that he'd be home when he could. It surprised Willie, hearing the anguish in his voice. It wasn't about Stick, or the judge's decision anymore. It was something else, something deeper and more personal. What he once called a philosophy.

As the parlor came to life, Halsey found a table leaf in the basement. It was time to cook, to light the flames, and fill their grief with food.

Tessula Cambridge joined him eventually, smelling his sauces. She didn't mind the booze or the business of a brothel. Her cousin had one on Saint Vincent. It was near a church and the roof leaked. She liked Willie's house, the moody light, his kittens in the yard. "Can I help you, Sir?"

Surprised by her interest, Halsey offered her an apron. "I'm sorry what happened today, Miss Cambridge," he said gravely, turning to a pot.

She wrapped the apron around her waist, tying it expertly into a smart, tight bow.

"Just burns me up."

Tessula Cambridge watched him as he stirred, admiring his shiny red oven. "We'll get there someday, Mister Halsey," she replied stoically, approaching a mound of dark green basil. "When the dish be worth the wait."


After dinner, John Lilly nursed his bourbon on the back porch. It had been a rough day. He felt the heat around him, the cry of insects as the light receded. He missed his family home in the Shenandoah with its long, screened porches and deep, cold wells. Where the war was "lost," his father would say, before they put him under. Death connected us, his mother believed. To the trees, to the sky, to each other. He never understood it until later in his life, returning to their graves on a cold winter day. Touching the oak. Feeling their presence.

"May I join you, sir?" Willie inquired tentatively, seeing him deep in thought.

The professor turned, relieved when he realized. "Oh, good! We need to talk."

Willie sat beside him, holding a glass of lemonade and vodka. His mind felt blurry and slow.

The professor glanced back towards the screen door. "Pretty quiet in there."

"Cary's showing Mr. Wells around. They've gone upstairs, I think."

He took a sip of bourbon and sat back in his rocker. "Nice place you've made, Willie."

"Thank you, sir. Bit different when the ladies are here."

"Night and day," the old man quipped, finishing his glass. "I would imagine."

Willie began to rock, remembering what they'd been through. "Miss Cambridge went to her room."

When he heard her name, his heart sank. She'd come a long way for nothing.

"Will she be okay?"

He sat still, mulling it over. The improprieties of justice. The prejudice of blood. "Hard to say."

"And Stick?"

He grew pensive.

"Can we help him, sir?"

He stared into his glass. The ice had nearly melted. "We can certainly try."

It was hard to accept. "Thought that's what we were doin'."

The professor smiled painfully, putting his glass down on the floor, moving his chair back and forth slowly. "It's a process... I'm afraid."

Willie watched him. He looked older, more vulnerable in the light. "Doesn't seem to be working too well, does it?"

A warm breeze stirred the leaves. The fireflies were gone.

Willie pressed him further. "If he goes, he won't come back. You know that, right?"

"Not necessarily." He considered the idea. "But highly probable."

"And you're fine with that?"

"I am not."

Willie rocked more fiercely, recalling his prayer.

"It was a hearing, son. That's not my job."

"What the *fuck*, man?" he protested finally, dropping his feet to the floor, coming to a stop.

John Lilly stopped, as well, feeling his anger. "It's difficult sometimes. To fully appreciate."

Willie shook his head, remembering Stick's face at the end. "I don't get it."

"I understand that."

"The work you did."

He gave him time to say it.

"The point of it all."

He winced when he heard it. His impatience. "I'm afraid, as you have seen... you can't win a fight if you're not in the ring."

The white cat slithered through a balustrade.

Willie stared out into the darkness.

"Our evidence was inadmissible."

"What do you mean?"

"Immaterial to the proceedings."

"You mean, whether Stick stays, or goes?"

"Regarding his extradition, yes."

"So, I don't understand. How come the judge allowed it?"

John Lilly looked at Willie, almost tenderly. "That's a longer answer."

"Give me the short one, Sir."

The cat approached slowly, leaping onto Willie's lap. He stroked its back absently, waiting.

"He was being generous."

He stared at the Professor. "Generous?"

"Yes."

"How?"

"By allowing me some latitude."

"Like when you and Boudreau got into it?"

"Correct."

"But why? If you can't use it in the end, what's the point?"

Moths circled the ceiling light above their heads.

John Lilly leaned forward, standing carefully, finding his balance. The sheriff was late. There would be work to do in the months ahead. "We discover ourselves in trust, Willie," he answered eventually. " Of necessity."

Willie was lost.

"The law is messy, I'm afraid. An approximation, really."

"No shit."

"A good judge understands that, impartially and with patience."

"Like today."

"Like today, yes. By design, however, not intention- you must remember that. How it works. How it does not."

"What you can say, what you can't."

"Yes. The construct. The rules."

Willie nodded reluctantly.

The cat jumped down from Willie's lap, then quickly up into the professor's empty chair, dropping to one side, licking a front paw.

John Lilly admired the creature, its calm indifference. "You can counsel, you can argue. Strategize."

A car drove slowly down the alley and stopped.

"You build context, and trust... then work your way toward the heart of it." He gave Willie a stern look. " That's how it goes- how you *process* a situation like this. *Manage* it."

The car door opened and closed.

Willie's face was drained.

"It takes time to understand."

"I'm trying to. "

"It's pretty simple, really." He considered the notion one last time. "The law does *its* work... and I do *mine.*"

They heard boots climbing the steps, reaching the top.

The cat bolted.

Willie rose quickly from his chair, seeing him suddenly. "Sheriff Sheffield."

"Evenin', Willie."

Willie's legs were shaking.

It took a moment to say it. To finally let him know.

"He's gone."

# CHAPTER TWENTY-SIX

Accepting the book, Clayton Powell pretended not to care.

"What am I looking at?"

"It's a guest list."

"I can see that John, but from where?"

"Sadie Graves's place in Charlottesville."

He wiggled around in his chair.

"Belongs to her son now."

"How old is he?"

"Twenty. On his way to Virginia, I hope."

"UVA?"

"Willie Graves."

He put the book down, reaching for a glass of water.

"A very smart young man."

His face was damp. "Offer you something?"

"No, thank you."

"So…" He took a drink and put the glass down. "How can I help you?"

John Lilly remained standing. "December twentieth, 1952. Page five."

He didn't budge.

"With a girl named Summer.

"You think?"

"That's what it says, Clayton."

"And?"

"And what?"

"Ten years ago, before Christmas, I frequented a certain place, for which you are suggesting what?"

"I'm not suggesting anything."

He waited.

"*Alluding* to, perhaps."

"To what exactly?"

"Well, to begin with… the matter we discussed."

He found the file. "Eugene Watson's extradition to the State of Louisiana."

"Correct."

"Martell's made his decision."

"He's innocent."

"And, so you say."

"Without question."

The attorney general drew in a breath, remembering suddenly her long black hair.

"Bullet discrepancies, witness intimidation, falsified statements—where do I begin?"

"Not our jurisdiction."

"Of course, it is."

"You taught me this stuff, John. He goes back, has his day in court. I'm sorry, but they ruled on this thing. All I can do."

John Lilly took a file from his briefcase, handing it to him.

He checked the clock on his desk before taking it. "Have a seat, please."

"Kentucky v. Dennison, 1860—three others since then."

"I'm quite aware, John."

"Of course, you are. Please, excuse me." He lowered himself into a chair, watching him read through it quickly.

When he was done, he handed it back, swiveling nervously in his chair.

"Talk to the governor, Clayton. He's innocent and if they keep him down there, he doesn't stand a chance."

"And why is that?"

"Both the sheriff and AG are up for reelection."

His chair stopped.

"It's a hanging."

"And why this Watson fellow?"

"The sheriff's cousin did it."

"Boudreau?"

"Lost his shirt in a card game. Ex-cop. Planted a gun, doesn't match ballistics, manufactured the witness, altered Miss Cambridge's statements... not to mention Martell."

"What about him?"

"You don't want to know."

"I do not."

When the phone rang, he didn't answer.

"This is awkward, Clayton, and again... I'm sorry to barge in on you like this, I really am. I need you to call the governor and *fix* this thing, once and for all. It's his only hope."

He closed the file and sat up in his chair. "So, what does this have to do with Sadie Graves?"

"You were there."

"Forgive me, sir, but... as you have *alluded* to... I was not alone."

"Married at the time, I believe."

"We all were. And your point?"

"Expecting your first child."

"Second."

John Lilly waited, purposefully.

"Elizabeth Jane."

It was his last hope. "She was a minor."

# CHAPTER TWENTY-SEVEN

Josie stood on the porch when they first arrived. She'd missed the place, the town, the money. Cary filled her in on their way from the station—how John Lilly had gone to see the attorney general. It wasn't good. Stick was gone. Willie was asleep upstairs.

The new girl's name was Addy May. She had pretty red hair and a come-along smile. She wouldn't stay long. She worried how Willie could swing it: owning a whorehouse and going to college. She'd help him if she could, or back away, if that's what he needed. But the fucking would stop. They had a business to run.

A car passed, slowing down when they saw her. Someone whistled. She heard a radio through the open window, a slow song. Summer was done and the students were back. Like a tiger in a circus tent, it was time to turn a trick.

# CHAPTER TWENTY-EIGHT

On his first day, John Lilly met him on The Lawn. Willie's clothes were pressed, but his mind was scattered. They stood together for a while, marveling at the students, the Rotunda. He told him to be patient, to study hard. "You have it in you, son." He looked him in the eye, giving him courage as he did so. "Of that I have no doubt."

The classroom quieted when he took his seat. He thought of Moses, feeling their eyes upon him, their whispers. Perhaps it was different for an old Black man, like a deep and festering wound. He'd climb the stairs to ease the pain. Ring the White man's bell.

He glanced out the window through a yellowing elm, seeing clouds in the distance. Stick was in chains. It broke his heart to think of it. The things he could not do.

He found his new book, opening it carefully, smelling the ink and paper. *Epitome of Roman History: Cornelius Nepos*, Harvard University Press. A door closed behind him as the class settled down.

It was time to begin and start his new life. To leave the world behind.

His house became a refuge, a place to hide. When the rooms were loud, he'd take a walk, or drive to Carter Mountain. On warmer nights, he'd sit on the roof thinking of Stick, or Rebecca. He wondered where she was in school, the books she might like, if she'd met a fella.

As the weeks passed and the days shortened, The Grounds became a darker place. They called him names sometimes or whistled- looking away when he noticed. It bothered him, at first. What it said about the place. About his time there.

Early one Sunday, Addy called up to him from the stairs below. A student had been left behind. He was shitfaced, with an empty wallet. Willie appeared outside her bedroom door.

"For fuck's sake!" the young man slurred, barely able to stand. "What's the history nigger doin' here?"

Addy's face toughened, seeing Willie. "Other way 'round, baby," she answered tersely, tightening her robe. "You're in *his* house now."

When he threw up, Willie took him to the kitchen and sat him down. "What's your name, man."

"Brandon."

He offered him a glass of water. "Where you from?"

"Virginia."

"What part?"

He was struggling.

"Drink the water."

He took a swallow and looked around. His head was spinning. "This a kitchen?"

"Drink the water."

He finished the glass.

Willie poured himself a cup of coffee and sat across the table. The clock said 2:00 a.m.

"What you doin' here?"

"Want some coffee?"

He dropped his head and closed his eyes.

"Might help."

He opened his eyes, trying to focus. "Sorry, what I called you."

Willie took a sip of coffee and sat back in his chair.

"She pullin' my chain?"

"Who?"

"Lady upstairs."

"About what?"

"This bein' *your* place."

"What about it?"

He dragged his hand across his mouth slowly. "How the fuck *that* happen?" he mumbled.

"My momma gave it to me."

His hand fell away. "Wait a minute…"

He waited for him to figure it out.

His eyes perked-up. "She a whore?"

"Yep."

His face went blank. "I'm sorry."

Willie stood up, getting a beer from the fridge, opening it. "Here." He put it on the table between them and sat.

He drained the bottle, burping loudly, reading the label. "*What'll you have?*"

Willie grinned. "Pabst Blue Ribbon!"

He drove him home. The streets were empty and dark. The sun would be up soon.

"They fuckin' on Sundays?"

"Nope."

"That like a holiday?"

"What do you mean?"

He remembered the money he owed. "Never mind."

They turned left on Rugby Road.

"You can leave me here, if you want."

"No big deal."

"Appreciate what you're doin'."

Willie turned right onto University Circle, finding the house and stopping. "This it?"

"917."

He leaned over and looked up. "Nice place."

"Got a room in back. Family knows the owner." He opened the door and prepared to get out. The air was cold outside.

"Gettin' colder."

"Sorry." He drew the door closer. "I owe you money."

"Be Addy, not me."

"Addy?"

"Yep."

"She's very nice."

Willie waited. It was almost 3:00 a.m.

"I'm Brandon Casteen, III."

"Willie Graves."

He looked at Willie and shook his head. "Pretty fucked up tonight. Guys took me there and... kinda lost my way."

"It happens."

He noticed the dashboard, the leather seats. "This *your* car?"

"Yep."

He looked at Willie again. "Goddamn."

Willie turned the heater up.

"How old arc you?"

"Twenty."

"Really?"

"Yep."

"*Willie Graves,*" he repeated, enjoying the sound of it.

"See you in class, man."

Brandon Casteen III opened his door, getting out, planting his feet on the ground. He was lucky this time. "In a *fucking* Buick!"

# CHAPTER TWENTY-NINE

Hilda was fast asleep when the phone rang. It took her a while to realize.

"Hilda," she answered.

"It's John Lilly, Hilda. I'm sorry to be calling you at this hour."

It was Stick.

"I've just received word regarding Stick."

His voice was grave.

"From the Louisiana attorney general."

She bolted up, awake suddenly.

"Boudreau's in trouble."

It took her a second.

"We're working on something."

"What does that mean?"

"Have you heard from him?"

"No. Why?"

"We have a plan in place."

"For what?"

"To get him back."

She leaned across the bed, struggling to see the clock. It was midnight.

"We're dealing with *several* moving parts at the moment. But we're getting there."

"When will you know?"

"Soon enough. I have a meeting in Richmond today."

"And then?"

"And then, we'll see."

She looked around for her robe. "Does he have a chance?"

"There is always a chance, yes."

"But... an *actual* one."

"I think so, yes."

The news was stunning.

"I apologize for the hour, but I wanted you to know."

"How is this possible?"

"Which part?"

"For God's sake, John... *everything!*"

He sipped his bourbon. The fire had dimmed and his German Shepherd was asleep. It was time to say good night. "Good friends, good plot," he answered cryptically, thinking of his wife.

Willie lived in two worlds—one whole, one dark and broken. Halsey left him sandwiches in the fridge, but he rarely touched them, drinking coffee instead, or rum and Coke, with a stack of Lorna Doones.

The girls looked spent. He'd cheer them up from time to time, sneak them a joint, or take them to the movies when he could. They liked the comedies most of all, spilling popcorn when they laughed too hard, always clapping at the end. The business of pleasure was the business of woe, of the things you could not say. He understood that now, hearing their silence, driving home in the rain.

He visited Josie's room one night. It wasn't right, but she didn't care, covering the lamp, taking her time. At dawn, she smoked a cigarette, watching him sleep in her arms. He was young and determined, raw with desire. She liked that. It didn't change things between them, the business of their life. But it felt good, like something she needed, something better than her life.

# CHAPTER THIRTY

After their exam, Brandon Casteen and Willie went for a beer.

"You doin' alright?" Willie asked.

"Test was a motherfucker."

Willie nodded, exhausted. "The Etruscan thing. Not expecting that."

Brandon took a wad of bills from his coat, sliding it across the table. "Got your money, man. I'm sorry it took so long. Been on my mind all week."

Willie pushed it back, taking a drink. "Save it for next time."

Brandon winced, laughing nervously. "Really?"

He raised his bottle in the air. "Hail, Caesar!"

They walked together, hungry and cold. The Spot was packed with students.

Brandon stopped, looking in. "Come on," he decided, opening the door. "Get you a burger."

Willie followed him in. He'd seen it from the street. It was stuffy and small, with posters everywhere. When two seats opened up, they took them, sitting side by side at the counter.

Willie read the menu on the wall. The hamburger had a fried egg in it. "Are the burgers good?"

Brandon turned his head, taken aback. "You never been here?"

"Nope."

"Thought you were from Charlottesville."

"I am."

He took a sip of water, noticing an older Black man standing by the kitchen pass-through. "Well, you're in for a treat, Roadmaster." He put his glass down and raised his hand, catching the man's eye. "Ernie, my man, two Gus's and some fries please. With Cokes!"

When Brandon went to pee, Willie sat, waiting, listening to the conversations. It was good to see girls his age, smell their perfume as they passed. He looked around, noticing the crowd. They were all white, friendly, and pleased. Like the magazine ads in Meridian, Mississippi.

As their food hit the counter, they both sat up.

"There you go, Brandon," the man said, smiling. He had a missing tooth and a scar on his lip.

"Now we're talkin', man, thank you." He grabbed a bottle of ketchup, gesturing to Willie. "This is Willie."

"Nice to meet you, Willie. I'm Ernie."

Willie looked up. "Hey, Ernie."

They regarded each other for a second.

"You look familiar."

Willie smiled politely.

Someone called out from the kitchen.

He turned to go, lingering for a moment. "You the fire boy!" he said, snapping his fingers and pointing.

Willie's stomach turned.

"Been down my street a hundred times with ole Moses. *Knew* I'd seen you somewhere."

Willie forced another smile.

"Be his *sidekick,* way he told it."

People at the counter quieted, hearing him, noticing Willie.

Brandon stopped eating, listening as well.

"Got your momma's house now."

"I do," Willie replied quickly, hoping he'd stop.

"And dat big black Buick."

Brandon jumped in, excited to hear it. "The Roadmaster!" He looked around as the others listened. "Saved my ass the other night, Ernie."

"He did?"

"Yessir." He winked at Willie, putting his hand on his shoulder. "Shoulda tossed me on my ear."

Willie grinned, embarrassed, looking down at his burger.

"You boys need to eat dem burgers now. And Willie?"

He looked up.

"Me and ole Moses were close."

Willie nodded, surprised.

"He was a good man."

"Yes, he was."

They looked at each other with a sudden tenderness. "Thought the world a you."

"Thank you, sir."

"Be pleased to know what you done."

People were talking again.

Brandon listened intently as he ate.

"Twenty-two brothers in this school right now." He stopped to think of it. "Proud a you, son."

Willie nodded, lifting his burger finally. "Thank you, sir."

A voice called out from the kitchen, louder this time. "Ernie!"

"Enjoy yo' Gus, gentlemen."

Willie took a bite.

Ernie's old eyes sparkled, seeing his pleasure. "Welcome to The Spot."


The following morning, The Grounds emptied and the students fled for winter break. He packed the car quickly, gassing up, heading East to Reedville. Hilda was waiting. He'd gotten her a present. There would be others, she said. And a Christmas tree. His room was over the garden. He remembered how the rooms smelled, of pine trees and fresh-cut grass, the sound of gulls in the morning. It was more than a place, more than a memory. Tangier was a calling, moving through him always, with water, air, and light.

# CHAPTER THIRTY-ONE

From the bow, it looked like Venice, or what Willie had seen of it in a book. Clouds and mist, then Oyster Creek, the Uplands, golden Spartina listing in the sunlight. The shack was still there, the steeple, boats everywhere as they pulled in.

Hilda stood at the edge of the dock, looking up, grinning when their eyes met. Her face looked different, free from pain and her usual melancholy. Willie waved to her, smiling with relief as the bow turned and the stern slowed.

When he disembarked, dropping his suitcase, Auggie, Hilda, and Salty, stood together.

"Got the whole gang, Willie," Auggie announced, seeing his face, smiling happily.

He stopped, seeing them all, fighting his emotions.

"Come on, now…" Auggie opened his arms and stepped forward. "What are you waiting for?"

Willie held him for a second. He was still tall but not as skinny.

Hilda was next. She looked striking, as ever, opening her arms as well.

"Welcome back, darlin'."

He closed his eyes as they embraced. She was the place itself, the reason he was there.

"Glad you could make it."

He let go, embarrassed to have held her for so long. "Been a long time comin', ma'am. Thanks for having me."

As Auggie loaded his suitcase onto a cart, Willie turned to his right. He looked ancient in the sunlight.

"'Bout time you said somethin', boy."

"Salty."

A large hand shot out.

Willie took it into his, feeling his skin. It was rough like leather.

"You look good."

"Thank you, sir."

"Name's Salty."

"Salty." He tried not to smile. "Thanks for coming."

"Got your skiff when you need it."

He glanced at Hilda. "Appreciate that."

"Put her at the shack. Wrong time for larkin'. Left you a line."

It took a moment to understand him. "Thank you."

"Get yourself another shad!"

They rolled the cart to the end of the dock, unloading it into the back of Hilda's truck. Auggie's boat was nearby. He needed fuel.

Willie stood by the door as the truck idled. "White Christmas" played on the radio.

Auggie laughed hearing it, walking away.

"See you, man."

He turned back, still moving, pointing a finger. "You owe me a beer, Santa Claus."

They said goodbye to Salty and stopped at the cemetary to see his wife. The stone was aboveground. He stood with Hilda, looking down, reading the name.

MARGARET SUSAN CROCKETT
Born: February 2nd, 1886
Died: December 20th, 1956

There was a blank space beside her name. He thought about his birthday dinner, how they'd sat together, her eyes twinkling when he tickled her the most.

"She really arm wrestle Stick?"

"Kicked his ass."

He shook his head, trying to imagine it.

"A Gloucester girl."

"Massachusetts?"

She scowled. "Shit, boy!"

He winced, realizing it.

A cold wind slapped their backs. They closed their coats and looked around. There were more graves than houses.

"You hungry?"

He read her name one last time.

"Come on."


The boats were in and the tourists were gone. The Blue Café was empty. They found a table beside an old woodstove. Hilda tossed a log in, holding her hands over the top.

Willie removed his coat and sat.

She tested the joints of her fingers slowly, finding her chair.

Dot Pruitt popped her head out from the kitchen. "That you, Hilda? Didn't hear you come in."

Hilda perked up. "Hey, Dot."

She noticed Willie. "Who you got there?"

He raised his hand and grinned.

"Got Willie Graves with us this week. Friend a mine."

The woman wiped her hands on her apron. "Nice to meet you, Willie."

Willie stood.

She chuckled when she saw it. "Sit yourself down and tell me what you want. Get you some coffee?"

Willie sat. "Yes, ma'am, thank you."

She grabbed a pot off the counter. "Hilda?"

"Please."

"Cold outside, Lord have mercy!" she replied, waddling to the table, pouring their cups. "Cream and sugar there if you need it." She gave Willie a closer look. His skin was smooth as silk. "Easy on the eyes, this one."

Hilda grinned when she heard it, admiring him, as well. "You think?"

Willie stirred his cream and sugar, taking an awkward sip.

Dot stepped back, lifting her pot. "Gonna break some hearts."


They had crab cakes with eggs, bacon, and toast.

Hilda watched him eat.

"Never had crab cakes in the morning."

"More like a lunch when you're up at two."

"In the morning?"

She put a cake and some bacon between two pieces of toast. "A.M.," she replied, taking a bite.

When their plates were done, they sat back in their chairs, drinking coffee together. She put her cup down. "It's been a while since we've done this."

"Since my birthday that night," Willie remembered, suddenly troubled.

"What is it?"

He gave it a second. "I never thanked you for Stick."

A pot crashed in the kitchen, bouncing off the floor. The fire had dimmed.

Hilda rose and put a log inside the stove.

He watched her. "You heard from him yet?"

She shut the door and returned to her chair, reaching into the pocket of her sweater. "No."

He leaned closer. She was hard to read. "Not even a letter?"

There were things she could not talk about. Words she would not say. She tossed five dollars on the table and put her coat on. "Time to go."


On their way out, Hilda went back to the kitchen. Dot Pruitt stood over a bowl, peeling apples. "We're shovin' off, Dot. Money's on the table."

"You get enough, darlin'?"

"Always, thank you. Careful out there. Callin' for ice."

She continued peeling, considering it. Every year was different-sometimes early, sometimes late. "When?"

"Tonight. Got family comin'?"

Her face brightened. The channels would freeze, but it wouldn't be much. "Next boat in," she replied, hearing the door open. "With my pretty little niece, if he's lookin'?"

It was cold outside. They walked in silence for a while, enjoying the Christmas lights, the older trees. It was still a small place, putting up a fight. People passed from time to time, noticing Willie first, then Hilda, waving hello. It felt good to be among them, connected to a place.

Hilda turned onto her street and stopped. The wind was cold.

"Thank you for breakfast."

"Where you headed?"

"Salty's shed, I guess. Figure Auggie's fixin' pots."

She nodded, thinking of Auggie. "He's a good man, Willie. Workin' like a fool."

Willie found a frozen puddle. The ice was thin and gray. "Be good to see him. Help him if I can."

There was something in him—a restless grief.

He pressed his boot against the ice, cracking the surface. "You think he did it?"

"Did *what?*"

"Come on, Hilda. You know what I mean."

She looked away.

"He kills a guy maybe... maybe not? All the bullshit and the lies?"

She felt everything, suddenly.

"How hard you try to help him."

The wind strengthened.

"What do you call a man like that?" he asked, finally. "A thing you cannot keep."

She considered his question, understanding it finally. "You don't own a person, Willie."

He thought of Moses. His momma.

"Not a woman. Not a man."

The mail boat appeared off Whale Point, sounding its horn.

She gazed across the bay, feeling ice against her cheeks.

"He's not coming back, is he?"

She looked at him calmly, knowing what he wanted. What she could not say. "Or the truth."


The water was dark. The bow said *PEGGY SUE*. The door squeaked as he entered, stacks of pots, nets hanging everywhere. "You in here, Aug?" he called out, hearing a toilet flush. A curtain opened suddenly in the corner. Auggie appeared, raising a plunger in the air. "Pipes are froze to shit."

When they settled in, Willie went to work, mending pots, sitting on a wooden box. "Like this?" he asked, closing a rip, tightening it with a strand of wire.

"Willie-The-Waterman!" Auggie exclaimed, appraising his work.

The heater helped, but the shed was cold. Willie looked around, admiring the chaos. "This all yours now?"

Auggie concentrated on his pot, holding a collapsed floor between his fingers.

"Hilda said you bought him out."

"Trying to."

They worked for a while.

"Want some music? Got a radio."

"Like the quiet, actually."

"Me too."

After a while, Willie stopped. "Ask you something?"

Auggie finished his pot and stacked it up against a wall, returning with another. "What you wanna ask?"

Willie did the same, returning to his crate and sitting. "You take a loan out?"

He threaded a wire through the bottom of his pot, holding it with his teeth, reaching for a pair of shears.

"If you don't mind me asking."

Cutting the wire, he dropped the shears on the floor by his feet. "Used a bank." He looked at Willie, surprised by his interest. "First Virginia outta Petersburg. Hilda helped me some." He flipped the pot upside down on the floor. "Introduced me to a guy. Went through all my stuff." He checked his pockets. "Knew my dad." He checked his hands, examining a cut at the end of his thumb more closely, reaching into his shirt for a tin of Rosebud Salve. "From high school, my mother said." He dipped his thumb and closed the tin, returning it to his pocket. "Loaned me five grand over ten years." He stared at his crab pot. "Four point three percent."

He looked tired.

"Guy in Reedville pays me pretty good."

"Like a broker?"

"Yeah." He looked at Willie. "Sends stuff to Japan."

"No way!"

"She-crabs with eggs, mostly."

"Really?"

"On an airplane."

"No shit!"

"Said it makes 'em horny."

They cracked up, thinking of it, enjoying a nice long laugh.

Auggie looked around the shed. "I don't know, man." He checked the window. It was dark outside. "By the time I'm done, it's time to start over. Not much room to fuck around."

"How much you payin' every month?"

He took a second to remember. "Hundred and fifty-seven. Give or take."

"Then what?"

"What you mean?"

"After that."

He pushed the pot away with his foot, stretching his legs. "Another hundred, I guess. One-fifty in the spring, maybe."

Willie sat up on his box, going over it in his head.

"Pullin' in three, four hundred a month maybe. Bit more in the summer."

He took in the cold, crisp air. It felt good to be working again, using his hands.

"Bought a used dredge in August. Salty checked it out. Got some wear but seems real tight. Double my haul when the crabs are down. Take it to the Kettle."

"That the one that drags the bottom?"

Auggie messed with his hair. He'd need to change his clothes and shower before Hilda's. "It's a beast, man."

"How much that set you back?"

"Couple hundred." He stood up, collecting his shears, dropping them into a tool box.

"Gotta pay to play, Waterman," he sighed, shooting him a look. "With the crabs, I mean."


They left the shed and walked the dock, slipping on the ice from time to time.

"Glad you're back."

"Me too."

A pair of scoters passed overhead.

"Heard about Stick."

"Happens, I guess."

Auggie saw the hurt in his eyes. "Thought they'd let him go."

"Yep."

"I don't get it."

He thought of it again. "Pretty fucked up."

Auggie watched him as they walked. "What happens now?"

Willie shook his head. There was nothing left to say.

When they reached the parking lot, Auggie stopped. "You got a girlfriend?"

"Nope," Willie answered, looking around. The trees were sagging with ice. "You?"

"I do."

He turned to him, surprised. "Well, shit, man. What's her name?"

"Vale."

"Her first name?"

"Vale."

He liked the idea. "That's a cool name."

"Coleman. Vale Coleman."

"She from here?"

"Hell no! Spent the summer here on an oyster project."

"She a scientist?"

"Marine studies major, what she calls it. Third year."

"Where?"

"Virginia Institute of Marine Science.

"Where's that?"

"Gloucester Point on the York River. William and Mary runs it. Good school. Hard to get into."

A cart raced by, its back tires sliding as it turned.

Auggie slipped his hands into his coat pockets, watching it. "We're struggling here, man. Oysters are done. Crabs too."

"What I'm hearing."

He took his hands out, zipping up his coat. "Scooters Beach is gone, Low Land Creek. That sweet place we used to lark."

Willie felt the cold. "So, how do you stop it?"

"You don't. I mean, sure... they're talkin' about a wall, like a bulkhead kinda thing, but imagine that? Shit. Two miles long and a couple feet deep. Crazy talk."

The church bell rang, stopping at five. They listened to it, watching the rain turn to ice under a streetlight.

"You want a ride?"

"No, I'm good. Need to walk."

He saw the mail boat across the way. "Boat's in."

Willie grinned, blowing into his hands for warmth.

"You'll see her tonight. Told her you'd be there."

The wind strengthened.

They looked around.

"It's comin' from the Kettle."

"Think we'll lose power?"

Auggie reached into a coat pocket, finding his cart keys. "Nothin' to fear, Willie-The-Waterman," he exclaimed, suddenly merry. "Long as we got booze!"

# CHAPTER THIRTY-TWO

Pellets of ice bounced off the windowpane. Willie listened for a while, running a towel through his hair, hearing a branch snap. Auggie's car pulled in, shooting headlights through the trees, coming to a stop. His mother was with him. Looking down into the darkness, he could make out a girl.

Standing before the mirror, he brushed his hair and checked his collar. How would he know? What would it feel like? Having a girl of his own. He hit the light and opened the door, smelling candles and cedar, hearing laughter below.

When Salty saw him, he raised his glass, shouting proudly, "Our student from Virginia!"

Willie froze with embarrassment as the room quieted.

"Merry Christmas, lad!" he shouted again, approaching quickly. "Glad you could make it!"

He smelled of bourbon. "Merry Christmas, Salty."

"Can I buy you a drink, or would you like to fight?"

Willie laughed, admiring his rosy cheeks. "I'm okay. I'll get one in a minute."

"Naaaw, come on now... *what'llitbe!?*" he slurred, holding up his empty glass. "I'm drinkin'... *aManhattan.*"

A pretty girl stood before the fire. Her face was intense, framed in short black hair. "Works for me."

He rested his hand on Willie's shoulder, finding his balance. "*Ta putyouinthemood!*"


Salty's drink was strong. Willie stood with Auggie for a while, recognizing certain faces.

"That's Zach's wife, Mary," Auggie explained, nodding to a woman deep in conversation with Salty. "They're both wasted." He took a drink. "Not sure where Emily went."

The fire popped with pitch.

"Then my mom, over there... you met her once." He stopped, hearing his girlfriend's laugh. "Be right back."

Willie stood alone, admiring the distant Christmas tree. It had been a while since he'd seen one. Had a family of his own.

"Hi, Willie, I'm Vale."

He turned. She was smiling easily, happily, her eyes sparkling with light. "Hey, Vale." He offered his hand.

She took it firmly into hers, noticing his color.

"Willie's my buddy from Charlottesville, Vale. The one I told you about."

They let go of each other.

"Willie with the brains and a"—she hesitated—"house somewhere."

Auggie looked away, embarrassed.

Willie took a moment, enjoying her long red dress. "Nice dress."

"Thank you, sir." She turned from side to side, showing it off. "Made it myself."

"Really?"

"Yep." She leaned against Auggie. "You're at Virginia?"

"First year."

They all took a sip.

"Auggie said you're at William and Mary."

She took another, considering him more carefully. "I am."

She was smart, a bit coy.

"Oceanography?"

"Marine science, they call it." She finished her drink, handing the glass to Auggie. "Same species, different fish."

When they were alone, she stepped closer. "And how about you, Willie Graves?"

He waited for the question. "How 'bout me what?"

"Got a girl tucked away?"

"I do not."

Her face grew more discerning.

He looked around. The girl had left the fire.

"Like a blue fin tuna."

He had no idea. "That's me."

"From the pelagic zone."

When the kitchen door opened, the room grew still.

"My dear friends," Hilda announced, her hair askew, holding a glass of wine, "dinner is served."

The table was lit by candlelight, with a sideboard lined with dishes. As people arrived, Willie admired the great goose, inhaling a mixture of smells- cornbread, green beans, crab cakes, oysters, mashed potatoes, biscuits, sweet potato pie. Hilda motioned for Willie from the table.

"I want you to meet Emily," she said, grabbing the girl, taking her hand.

They looked at each other for the first time.

"Emily Pruitt, Willie Graves."

"Nice to meet you, Emily." He smiled as best he could. She was mesmerizing.

"Emily is Zach and Mary Sue's daughter. Dot's niece."

She had oval brown eyes under long dark brows. Willie nodded politely.

"Why don't you both sit here," she said, pointing to two empty chairs. "Keep an eye on the old folks."

When Hilda stepped away, they stood behind their chairs, quietly, waiting as people found their seats. Zach Parks, May Parks, Auggie Phillips, Vale Coleman, Pat Phillips, Salty Crockett, Fester Poons, and Gladys Crist.

"Emily Pruitt!" Salty yelled from across the way, seeing them together. "You two should have babies!"

Emily's face turned fierce. "And you should have coffee, Salty Crockett!" she fired back. "Or a long bloody nap."

Willie pulled her chair out, admiring her spunk, her long, thin body. "May I?"

She felt her insides turn. She'd never seen such a face, like a creamy caramel. His eyes were brown with hints of green. Endless and dazzling. "Thank you," she managed, raising her hem, dropping down into her chair.

.

When Hilda was seated, she tapped her glass lightly with a spoon. The table quieted, hearing it. She looked around, marveling at their faces, the room, dancing about in candlelight. "I want to welcome everyone and thank you all for being here." She leaned in a bit, seeing Gladys down the way, smiling warmly when their eyes met. "To Gladys and her divine crab cakes…"

"And my biscuits!" Gladys boasted loudly, feeling no pain.

Hilda laughed, finding Fester Poons, massive and shy, at the end of the table. "And dear Fester for his magnificent goose."

They all nodded in agreement, some turning to see it.

"And our colossal tree." She turned, admiring it, wrapped in colored lights and tinsel. "Despite the world and what we've made of it, there's a great deal for us to be thankful for tonight." She stopped, returning her attention to the table. "For our bounty... our friendships... and this island."

Willie and Auggie glanced at one another.

She paused, remembering it. "Willie and I were walking today and he reminded me of something- something I'd forgotten. How grateful I am to be here. To have had this day, this moment in my life. With all of you. In this room."

Salty turned his head away to hear her better.

"Peggy's gone. Zach's brother. Pat's cousin. Willie's Moses Henry. But their spirits live on."

Willie looked down into his napkin, thinking of Moses.

"In all of us."

No one moved.

"When the Upland is gone and the bay takes over, it won't be a wall that saves this place... an airport, or a pot." She lifted her glass. "It'll be this."

"Like the goddamn Injuns!" Salty interrupted, his eyes watering with emotion.

She took him in, like an ebbing tide, gazing around the table at each one, face by face, person by person, stopping finally at Willie. Wherever Stick was, it wouldn't be forever. He'd learn that someday. To love someone, in all ways. Without purpose. Or reason. Even when they're gone.

One by one, they raised their glasses, waiting quietly for her to say it. For the evening to begin.

"Merry Christmas to all!"

"Merry Christmas!" they cheered, answering back, hearing their voices as one.

They waited to speak. It began slowly at first, sipping wine, pushing their food around.

She was born in 1939. Her parents were strict. She worked in the summers, graduating on schedule from a college in Rhode Island. She studied art, anatomy, drawing, focused on becoming a painter. She preferred water to mountains, silence to music, books to conversation. Her favorite color was white. She drank Narragansett beer and hated jazz. She had a boyfriend once, rode a bike with a basket, and worked in a hardware store. She liked crappy weather and French movies. She had cancer when she was twelve.

Hilda's mother, Esther Scarburgh found her doctors, bought her paints, and paid the bills, left her a little money when she died. She told her to be strong, to be grateful, to stay humble, to fight for the life she'd been given.

On her fourteenth birthday, her lungs were clear; by late spring she could dance. One morning on a beach south of Providence, she watched the sun come up "like a fucking miracle," she said. And it was done.

A gallery offered to show her work. She was too attached to let them go. Her parents had given her what she needed. And Esther Scarburgh.

She looked him in the eye when she was done. "I thank them every day."


It came to him easily, feeling the wine, her glowing face. His closest friend was Moses—he was old and rang a bell. His mother ran a whorehouse; his father was a drunk. He hit him with a glass votive one night, defending himself. When the room caught fire, he ran away, too frightened to imagine what he'd done. He slept in the woods, fell into a river, washed up on the rocks, half-dead. When Stick Watson found him, he took him to a witch. She put him in a circle of burning sticks. The wind stopped. Her name was Sister Mo. In the morning, Stick was gone. She called the cops. He hitched a train to find him.

He and Stick worked apples in Winchester. He was wanted for murder. A sheriff came. They fled to Tangier. He arrived on her father's boat.

They lived in a shack off an inlet. Hilda gave him books, Auggie a fishing pole. One day, Bob Novack turned them in. Auggie helped them escape, reaching Stick's friend Oscar in the Dismal Swamp. He planted a garden, stood guard at a juke joint, danced with a hooker named Dolly. When he read in the paper that Moses had died, they hopped a train to the funeral. Stick was stabbed and disappeared. He was arrested, driven home, and released. His momma was dead. Stick shot a guy.

He drove to New Orleans looking for Stick, then Biloxi in search of her grave. A hurricane had washed it away. They stole his car in Birmingham.

He talked about his momma's list. How the law works when you squeeze it. How to play a man when he plays you back, about Meridian, Mississippi. Then Mo, then clouds, then Perlie's boat, the warmth of Ernest's sweater, the trains he rode and the stars he saw from his mighty great catalpa. That the world needed love, but not the kind you buy, or piss away on a whim. The kind you fight for.


When the fire faded and the wine was done, they huddled together. The tree remained lit. Hilda had gone to bed, popping in briefly to say good night. She was tired and pleased to see them together. They sat in silence when her door closed, watching the coals dim, dropping away

"So now I know, young Willie Graves."

He took her hand.

She could feel his warmth. His tenderness. "The green that's in your eyes."

He woke in the morning and went to the window. The trees were wet, the sky a crystal blue. The mail boat was gone. The bay was still. He wanted to kiss her again.

They avoided discussing Stick at breakfast. Hilda handed him a book instead.

"Have you read it?"

The title was *Native Son*. "No, ma'am."

She took a long sip of coffee. "About time you did."

He held it up, admiring the cover. "Thank you."

"You're welcome."

"I haven't been much on Christmas," he confessed, reaching down below his chair, handing her a present. It was wrapped in the funny papers. "Sorry about the wrapping. Was a little rushed when I left."

She laughed when she saw it, admiring the thin blue ribbon.

"Got the ribbon from your closet upstairs."

Her eyes pooled with tears.

"I know you've read it but…" He watched her, holding it like a precious thing.

She took a long breath, opening it carefully.

M O B Y – D I C K;

OR,

T H E   W H A L E

BY

HERMAN MELVILLE

AUTHOR OF

"TYPEE," "OMOO," "REDBURN," "MARDI," "WHITE-JACKET."

\*\*\*\*\*\*\*\*\*\*\*\*\*\*\*\*

N E W   Y O R K:

HARPER & BROTHERS, PUBLISHERS.

LONDON: RICHARD BENTLEY.

1851.

He waited to say it. "It's the one you gave me."

"This must have cost a fortune."

"Not really."

She turned the next page, transfixed by the font, the paper.

"There's a book dealer in town and I asked him a while back to look for one."

She shook her head in disbelief, turning the pages.

"Found it at an estate sale. Said they didn't know what it was worth."

"Thank you."

"You're welcome."

She closed the book. "It's too much."

"It's never too much when you love a thing like that."

She held it in her hands, feeling its weight. "Thank you, Willie."

"What you've done for me and Stick."

She nodded toward his book. "Read your book and tell me what you think."

He picked it up again. "I will."

She watched him go through it. "What will you do?"

"Ma'am?"

"In school."

He looked up. "What do you mean?"

"What classes are you taking?"

It took him a moment to remember them all. "Roman History, Introduction to American Government, The Constitution, Mathematics, that kinda stuff."

"Is there a purpose to it?"

The question was odd. "What do you mean?"

She considered it carefully. "Are you learning what you want to know?"

"About what?"

They heard wind against the window. Then quiet.

He thought about Meridian. Emily's eyes.

She asked again. "What to fight for."


The bay turned choppy as the boat veered west, her question still fresh in his mind. A scoter raced by, crossing the wake. Then, another. There was wind. He looked aft beyond the stern, seeing swells, feeling the stern rise and fall. The light was everywhere. Cold and clear. Intoxicating. He watched the island melt away, like Venice, as quickly as it came.

# CHAPTER THIRTY-THREE

Richmond was frozen. His heart pounded as he waited, seeing her bus pull in. He turned the key and got out, standing by the headlights. She was late.

He looked good to her, crossing the street. "His boat made a stop."

They wrapped their arms around each other, gently at first.

Her building was the next street over. He waited while she found her keys, seeing the sign beside the door:

PLEASANT'S HARDWARE

Since 1908

"Is that where you work?"

She turned the lock and opened the door. "Monday, Wednesday,

Friday," she answered, turning back, seeing his face. "Buckets, brooms, and paint."

She was glowing in the light.

"I'm up the stairs."

He moved toward her and stopped. They were finally alone.

"I'll fix us something warm."

The first thing he noticed was the size of the place, then the smell. There were paintings everywhere. They were wild with colors, laid out from one end of the room to the other. "You paint on the floor?"

She dropped her bag beside an old sewing machine and joined him. "I do."

He'd never seen such a thing.

"Some are still wet."

They were huge, on a strange white fabric.

"I paint on sails."

He looked at her, thinking he'd misunderstood.

She laughed when she saw his face. "My dad thinks I'm nuts."

"From where?"

"A yard in Reedville when they toss 'em."

He looked more closely, recognizing an eyelet on a corner.

"I cut 'em up. Sew the edges."

He approached one cautiously, bending down to get a better look. "What kind of paint is this?"

"Boat paint."

He looked back at her.

"'Sailors 'n' fools,' as Zach would say."

He stared across the floor—pools of colors everywhere, swirling about, dissolving and expanding.

"And latex."

He stood up, finally, not knowing what to say. Why it meant so much to him.

When she saw his expression she knew, standing there, so handsome and still. The color she would love.

# CHAPTER THIRTY-FOUR

He drove straight to school, parking behind a bank. American Government and The Constitution was in Old Cabell Hall- about a five minute walk from Professor Lilly's office. He stopped to visit on his way, seeing the light on, knocking quietly.

"Yes?" Willie heard him say, opening the door.

The professor stood, instantly pleased. The room smelled of pipe tobacco. "Mr. Graves, sir," he announced, happily.

Willie stepped into the room.

"On your way to Professor Hollman, I would imagine?"

It surprised him that he knew. "I am, yes."

"Introduction to American Government," he announced, enjoying the sound of it. "With your interest in the law, a perfect place to start."

"Yes, sir."

"And, *hopefully,* not your last."

Willie smiled when he heard it. "Hopefully, not."

The professor gestured to a chair. "Come sit for a moment. And Happy New Year, dear me! I nearly forgot."

Willie approached the chair, thinking of Stick. Remembering the room where they'd strategized. "Happy New Year to you, sir. Did you have a good Christmas?"

John Lilly sat. "We were in Boston with my wife's family, yes, thank you. Lovely time. Too much food, of course." He paused, glancing out his window. "And snow."

"Hilda asked me to say hello."

He placed his hands to either side of his chair and leaned back. "She's coming around. Better about it now, I suppose."

He remembered her eyes, so bewildered and blue.

"And most grateful to you."

"Not at all."

"No, sir, it needs to be said. We all are."

They looked at one another, suddenly awkward.

"Like you said that night. What you're trying to do."

Voices passed along the hallway. A door closed.

"I've telephoned Hilda. I should have called you first. We're making progress down there."

Willie sat up, hearing it.

"Incrementally... slowly, of course. You need to know that."

"What kind, sir? If I may ask."

"Of course you can, Willie, my goodness!" He leaned forward, looking for something on his desk. "Anything you need to know, that's what I'm here for." He found a file and leafed through it.

"Wish I knew how he was."

"Yes, of course. We all would." He looked up. "I spoke to the attorney general again and we're working on something."

"Something like what?"

The professor smiled sympathetically.

"It's been a while."

"It has."

"Six months and a day."

"Yes."

Willie ran his hands through his hair, rising impatiently from his chair, moving to a window. He looked out, seeing a garden below with frosted curving walls.

The professor closed his file. They had ten minutes. "I've been working on an approach."

He turned when he heard it.

"An exchange, if you will."

He waited.

"Between our two attorneys general."

"What kind of exchange?"

He considered the question carefully.

"Between us and them?"

"Something of value that both parties require in order to resolve the matter."

"To let him go?"

"Drop the charges, yes." He paused, remembering the point more precisely. "Satisfy all parties to the extent that we can."

"How long will that take?"

"I don't know exactly."

I mean… days, months… years?"

"Not years."

"Months?"

"Maybe."

"Not days?"

"Less likely."

"So…" He stepped closer. "Does he know what we're doing?"

"He does not."

"You haven't spoken to him?"

"No. I have conveyed to him through the proper channels that we're working to secure his release with no guarantees, of course. I would hate to raise a man's hopes unnecessarily."

"Well then… forgive me, sir, but how in the world do we know anything if no one's spoken to him?"

The question was unsettling.

"For all we know he could be dead!"

The professor looked at his watch. "I have a class in five minutes. And so do you."

Willie looked desperate.

"But, let me say this to you and then we need to go."

He stood still.

"The plan I have in place requires patience, negotiation, and time."

He looked at Willie to be certain he understood. "As we discussed on the porch that evening, you build context, then work to the heart of it."

Willie studied him carefully.

"It's a matter of great delicacy and not without risk, you need to trust me in that regard. We must proceed carefully, cautiously and with the utmost discretion." He paused, to consider it. "This is a little... shall we say- out of bounds."

"Yes, sir."

"Below the belt, occasionally. I'm sorry to put it that way, but you weren't born yesterday, now were you?"

"No, sir."

"Good."

They took a final moment together.

John Lilly leaned forward in his chair and stood. "You must respect the process, Willie."

Willie stood as well. "I do. I will."

"Because there is *one* thing you can hope for when this is over. When I have played my *final* card."

Willie took a short breath, fighting everything he was feeling.

"That we prevail!"

The weeks were long, his mind steeped in other things, dreaming of Emily, fearing for Stick. He felt alone. Silent and odd. Some had read books he'd never heard of. Others spoke Latin and French. He made no friends, dodging conversations, returning home each day, locking his door at night. It felt like a mountain, an ocean between them. Page by page, night by night. Working to prove he belonged.

# CHAPTER THIRTY-FIVE

On the first warm day, he took a drive. He'd missed his car, the sound it made. He headed west along Route 250, up toward Afton Mountain. Seeing it in the distance, he pulled over, rolling the window down. A valley stretched before him in endless shades of green. The air was sweet. He'd forgotten such things. Rambling streams. Budding orchards. There was purpose in the world. Ancient forces. Ridges laced in stone.

When he'd had enough, he raised his window and turned the car around, checking the time. Emily was waiting and the girls were coming home. A crow drifted by, disappearing slowly into the foothills. He watched it for a while, enjoying the moment, the peace of it, and gently pulled away.

Parking at the curb, he saw the front door.

Amber met him on the porch, tossing her cigarette over the rail. "You alright, baby?"

He read the notice.

"Need to call your lawyer. We all inside."

He read it again:

NOTICE OF CLOSURE

FOR VIOLATION(S) OF

VIRGINIA HEALTH AND SAFETY CODE AND/OR

ALBEMARLE COUNTY CODE

Violation (s):
Alcohol
Commercial Oven

BY ORDER OF THE

HEALTH OFFICER, CITY OF CHARLOTTESVILLE
DEPARTMENT OF HEALTH SERVICES
Mr. Jeremy W. Cruickshank, Deputy Director


March 2nd, 1958 DO NOT REMOVE UNDER PENALTY OF
LAW
Inspector D. Dabney      Albemarle County Code 13.12.080B,
8.04.


She gave him some time before she spoke. "Put it up this mornin' before we got here. That ole cop and Josie got into it pretty good. Thought she might smack him."

"Sheffield?"

"Told her to calm down, or he'd run her in. Said to give him a call."

He'd need the professor. And D. K. Wells.

She approached him, cautiously at first, wrapping her arms around him. "I know, I know. Always a bigger somethin'."

He held her for a moment, trying to make sense of it.

"You have a good time on that island out there?"

His head was racing.

"Eat you some crabs and bang you some girls?"

He smiled, letting go, noticing her hair. "I need to call Cary."

"They're in the house, baby." She played with her hair, tousling her bangs. "Been waitin' on you."

"Got your hair done."

"My sexy bangs, did you notice?"

"I did."

She felt a chill suddenly, tightening her coat. "Took the train down yesterday. Josie's a mess."

A man walked slowly down the sidewalk, looking up suspiciously as he passed.

He'd call Sheffield when he could. "Better get inside."

"Got a girl in yo' heart."

He turned to her, distracted. "What?"

"See somethin' in yo' eyes."

The kitchen smelled of bacon.

"Just in time," Halsey said, pouring batter on the griddle.

Amber turned to go. "I'll be upstairs for a while. Make some calls."

Josie's hair was up. She'd been crying. "Ask Addy if she's hungry. Tell her Willie's here."

Carolyn sat up in her chair, looking forsaken. "Hello, Willie."

"Hey, Carolyn."

Josie unclipped her hair, trying to smile. "You have a good time?"

"I did."

"Good." She looked at him sadly. "You know what this is about?"

He shook his head, seeing their faces.

"Well… sit yourself down, darlin'." She lifted her coffee cup. "Let ole Halsey fix you up."

Halsey worked his spatula under the final pancake, sliding it carefully onto a plate. "Mr. Willie."

"Hey, Halsey, how you doin'?" He found his chair and sat, reaching blindly for some coffee. "You doin' okay?"

Halsey turned, seeing them together, the worry in their eyes. "Never better, only butter."

They drowned their plates in syrup. Then silence. The coffee was strong. When Addy May came down, she joined them, half-asleep, swirling bacon through her plate."Hey, Willie," she said eventually, licking syrup off her fingertips.

Halsey moved to the sink, looking out the window as he washed his pots and pans. The cats were about. There were more with the cold. He'd pour them some milk and leave a plate of Spam.

When she was done, Josie lit a cigarette. "You all okay?" she asked, blowing smoke over their heads, noticing the time.

They nodded back silently.

She took another drag, exhaling quickly. "We'll get this fixed," she assured them, half believing it, tapping the ashes into an ashtray.

Willie took a final bite, putting his fork down. Nothing was working in his head.

Addy May pushed her chair back and stood. She'd called a guy she knew. He lived in Stanton.

They looked up.

"Cary said he's leaving," she announced casually, taking her plate to the sink.


When he reached his room, he dropped his bag, hearing the front door slam, then footsteps moving quickly up the stairs.

"I put your money in the safe," Cary explained, flying in, out of breath.

Willie sat on the bed. He looked pale and frightened. "What the fuck happened?"

He winced when he heard it, pacing about, finding a chair. "I've been away, honey."

He'd never seen him this way. "And now you're back."

"Yes."

They paused, noticing each other finally.

"I was not expecting this."

"I know."

"Or you leaving."

Cary froze.

"Not telling me."

Cotton entered casually, seeing Cary, then Willie, jumping on his bed.

He watched the cat, licking a paw. "I know."

Willie checked his own hands, seeing scratches from the crab pots.

"We've been closed for a while... and I didn't realize until now."

"Realize, what?"

He looked at Willie, his eyes filled with remorse. "I should have told you."

"Told me what?"

"Oh, fuck, Willie."

Willie waited.

"A car came the other day. You were in class. Some men got out, walked around. I knew it was bad. You could tell by the hats, their cheap little suits. Feds, maybe? Or who-the-fuck knows? *People.* People who *do* these things."

"Things like what?"

"How do I know? It's... how they *looked.*"

"What did they want?"

"Nothing. That was the strange thing."

"What do you mean, *nothing.*"

He moved to a window. "They walked around, watching the house for some reason. I was in the parlor, behind a curtain."

Willie waited for him to explain.

"They were smiling."

"Smiling?"

"Yes. Together on the sidewalk when they were done. Smoking. I don't know... as if something... *good* had happened—that's what I was thinking when I saw them." He scratched his arm nervously. "I don't know."

"Then what happened?"

He stopped to remember it, shaking his head. "They got in their car and drove away." He watched Willie pet the cat. "Like it was over."

"What was over?"

When Cary sat, the cat hopped down, going to him, jumping up into his lap.

Willie watched them together.

His hands were shaking. "I should have told you."

It was too late now, whatever it was. Something had gone terribly wrong. "Where you going?"

He stroked the cat, tentatively at first. "Mexico."

"Why Mexico?"

The cat turned over on its side. Cary smiled, seeing it, petting him more tenderly. "It's such a mess."


His friend was older. He'd made money in hotels around Baltimore, then Boston, then San Francisco. They'd met at a club in Richmond.

"He swept me off my feet, honey," he confessed, looking helpless. "No tomorrow without him."

"When was that?"

The cat jumped down and left the room. "November."

He stretched his legs, seeing Willie's bag. "We were walking to his hotel that night and he took my hand... the moon was out, I don't know... something about beavers or animals or whatever it was..." He paused, remembering it. "And I laughed when he said it, because, of course, I was thinking of our house."

Willie smiled.

"And then I realized— I'd forgotten your birthday."

Neither spoke for a while.

"Are you going to be okay if I go?"

"Of course, I am."

"It's just so strange. Like when we met. And with Thomas."

"Is that his name?"

His face brightened. "Thomas Logan Robbins."

They took a moment together finally.

"I'm happy for you."

"Isn't that a lovely name?"

"It is."

The phone rang downstairs, then again before stopping.

"Why Mexico?"

"He's always wanted a little Mexican casita. That's what they call it. Something... old and mysterious."

Willie imagined the place.

"He's good at this. I've seen pictures. I can't wait to get my hands on it and make it our own. Three bedrooms. Terra-cotta floors. You should see it when we're done."

"I'd like that."

"He has a boy somewhere. I haven't met him yet. He wants to come visit us."

"He was married?"

"Twenty years ago, in Baltimore."

They heard rain through the window.

"He's very sweet and he cares for me. And when I'm with him... I feel like myself, which is odd, because, I mean, my God, what *am* I if I'm not *that*."

"Yourself?"

"I haven't been. Not for a long time actually."

"What do you mean?"

He thought about it. "You know how... when you're little, you're always yourself?"

"I guess."

"When you *play*... when you *watch* the world? And then you lose it somehow? Along the way?"

It made sense.

He looked calm for a moment, almost peaceful. "I'm *me* again."


Willie rose from his bed, closing the window.

"When are you leaving?"

"Tomorrow night."

He turned back, stunned to hear it.

Cary's eyes sparkled. "There's a courtyard with a fountain."

Willie tried to smile, thinking of his happiness.

"And night-blooming jasmine."

He approached Cary slowly, waiting, reaching into his pocket.

"What are you doing?"

"Here," he said finally, placing something in his hand.

Cary's face flooded with emotion, seeing it. It was still warm. "My very own Swiss Army knife."

"*Te extrañaré.*"

"What does that mean?"

"It means, I'll miss you."

# CHAPTER THIRTY-SIX

He was late the next morning. Brandon turned when he saw him, flying down the hallway. "Roadmaster!" he shouted, "White Spot at twelve!"

The lecture wandered on, pausing for questions, then answers. The sheriff was coming. He thought of Emily, her long and slender body, naked beside him. Then the house. Someone had double-crossed them, played him like a chump.

The White Spot was busy. He found a table in the corner and removed his coat. A girl looked away when she saw him, then another.

Ernie arrived, grinning with delight. "Willie, ma man."

"Afternoon, Ernie."

His grin lingered. "Back fo' mo'?"

Willie smiled, enjoying the way he put it. "I am."

He eyed the customers at the counter. "Well… we're always here, when you need it, man." He stayed for a second, looking down into his eyes. "Be a bran' new day."

When he told Brandon what had happened, his mouth dropped open, disbelieving it at first. "I mean, screw those people, man, you're The Roadmaster!" He pounded the table with his fist. "They *fuck* with *you*, you *fuck 'em back!*"

Tables quieted around them.

Brandon took a bite of his Gus Burger, calming down as he chewed. "That's what I say."

When they were done, they walked to Willie's car. It felt like snow again.

"Thanks for lunch."

"Thanks for the ride."

A salesman watched them through the Mincer's door.

"Can't believe this fucking town."

"What do you mean?"

"Closing you down."

"What they do sometimes."

He looked him over. "Like who?"

Willie kept walking. He was a nice guy- rich and simple. "You got a suntan."

"We went to Florida."

"You're darker than me now."

Brandon cracked up, pushing Willie's shoulder. "My dad's got a boat down there."

"Really?"

"And a *condo.*"

Some girls made eyes at Brandon as he passed, whispering something between themselves. He turned and watched them go. "That's Connie Smith," he pointed out, "from our Roman history class. You haven't noticed her?"

"Nope."

"Third row? Short skirts."

He wondered about Emily. If men spoke of her that way.

Brandon saw himself reflected in a window. His hair looked good, his shoes. He felt the cold suddenly, buttoned up his coat. "Like to tap that sweet ass someday."


David Sheffield met them in the parlor. The fire was lit. A guy named Frank was coming for Addy May.

Josie could hardly stand it. "So, the *day* we come back, you just... *show up... shut us down,* is that it? Don't *call,* don't *tell* me what you're doin'?... After *everything* we done? *All* that money? *All* that cash? Just *slipped* your mind?"

"Where are the girls?"

"Upstairs." She was ready to pop. "What difference does it make, where the girls are!?"

"And Cary?"

"At home, packing."

"Where's he off to?"

She threw her hands up, going to the bar. "None of your fucking business."

He watched her pour a drink, hoping it might help. "Willie, shut the door, if you would, please?"

Willie hesitated.

"We need to be alone, come on."

"Sit, Willie!" Josie snapped, raising her voice again. "*I swear to God!*"

Willie looked down, struggling to understand it.

Josie collected her drink, closing the sliding door between the parlor and the hallway, turning back. "Happy now?"

"Thank you."

She took a long sip of vodka. "I have something to say."

"And what is that?"

She took another sip, then another. "This better be good."

He gathered his thoughts, stalling for the right words. "I had no idea…"

"Bullshit!"

"Until they called me in."

"Who did?"

"The attorney general."

"Clayton Powell?"

"Clayton Powell, yes."

Josie's glass was almost empty. "To say what?"

He looked at Willie. "To make me a deal."

Their faces went blank.

"I close the house and Stick walks."

Willie's fingers formed into fists.

"If I don't, there's a trial down there… he's done."

Josie finished her drink and moved next to Willie. "This is bullshit and you know it."

"That's what happened, Josie."

"I don't believe it."

"I give you my word."

She sat back against the sofa, shaking her head. "And why would he do that?"

He looked at Willie again. "He gave 'em the list."

"Who did?"

"Lilly."

Josie's body stiffened. "What list?"

"Come on, Josie, *Sadie's book*."

Willie stared at the fire.

"Colson, Powell, Senior Judge Preston, Mayor Tibbs."

Willie tried to remember them all. There were too many.

"John Lilly."

He thought he'd misheard him. "What?"

"You heard me."

It was impossible. "I've been through that thing a million times. He's not in it—not *once*." He looked at Josie. "Not *my* John Lilly. No way!"

"He used a different name."

When Willie heard him say it, he knew it was true.

The fire popped.

The Sheriff waited. "I'm sorry, Willie."

Josie took Willie's hand, putting it in her lap.

He watched them together, knowing what it meant. "They all got together and cooked this thing up."

Willie looked up. "And Johnny Boudreau?"

"Boudreau?" He grinned when he said the name. "Sent that boy packin'."

"How they do that?"

"Lost the election."

He thought about his stupid fish. The smile.

"Two AGs, backroom the deal. Stick comes home."

John Lilly had played his hand.

"We spoke about this a long time ago, son. What might happen."

He'd tried to be so tough.

"What they've always wanted. Told you that."

Josie let go of his hand and got another drink, pouring one for

Willie. "Here, darlin'," she said, offering him the glass.

He took a drink, watching the ice float around. "What was his name?"

"Who's name?"

"The professor when he came here."

"Oh. I don't know." Darron somethin', I think. Maybe. Darrow?"

"Clarence Darrow?"

"That's it. Kinda stood out when I saw it."

He drained his glass.

Josie slipped her shoes off. She'd start packing in the morning.

Willie felt the booze running down his shoulders. "'Something of value,'" he remembered him saying. "That's what he said."

A telephone rang, stopping quickly.

"Son?"

He put the drink down and looked at the sheriff. He was old and fat. The room was cold.

"After they told me, I called Jerry Cruickshank and it was done. I'm sorry, Willie. I really am."

A chill ran through him. He rose to his feet, noticing the fire, thinking of his momma.

David Sheffield stood as well, gathering his hat. "So..." He waited for the right moment. The kid was crushed. "You want the good news?"

Willie added a log, watching the fire grow, his eyes flickering with flames.

"He's in my truck."

He looked roughed-up and wasted, seeing the notice on the door, then Willie, flying down the steps.

Willie stopped when he reached him, out of breath, not believing it.

His lip was split, his nose bent and broken. He dropped his paper bag and grabbed him, holding on tight.

He smelled of alcohol and chewing gum. It didn't matter anymore, how he'd gotten there, his fractured face. He was free again. Eugene Allen Watson, from Thelma, Virgina, was finally home.

# CHAPTER THIRTY-SEVEN

They put him in Addy's room. He'd eaten half a pot roast and drank a couple beers. Josie gave him ointment for his lip.

"Nothing for you to do but rest, Stick."

"Thank you, ma'am," he replied, closing his door.

The girls were in the parlor. It would be a long night, or a short one, they couldn't tell.

When Willie came in, the fire was raging. He poured himself a vodka and found a place to sit. He looked worn out.

"Like to kill that Mister Lilly man," Amber started, enjoying her rum.

It was hard to wrap his head around. John Lilly at a whorehouse.

"Ain't no way to treat you... *do* you like that."

Willie nodded, taking a drink.

"An' this cat shit David Sheffield, swear to God." She noticed Willie. "You alright, baby?"

"I'm fine."

"You need a plan, baby," she explained, playing with her hair. "Way through this."

They looked at the fire, realizing how quickly things had changed.

"'Cuz, this black bootie needs a bed."

Josie poured herself another drink, returning to the sofa. "Carolyn's leaving for Pennsylvania," she announced, curling up against the pillows.

Carolyn smiled half-heartedly and took a drink.

"Got family outside Philly and there's a fella she knows. Owns a bunch a cows."

Amber's eyes lit up. "Gonna milk 'em, or fuck 'em, honey?"

Carolyn screamed when she heard it, leaning back against the sofa. She was drunk.

"Have *yo' sef* a *steak!*"

Willie joined in. They all did. It felt good to laugh. Resist the gloom.

When they stopped, Carolyn fiddled with her sweater. "He's a nice man with a big old house. Got a lake on it."

Amber bobbed her head. "There you go."

"Wife's gone. Kids are grown."

They considered it, all of them, what they would do.

Amber raised her glass. "You deserve it, baby. You surely do."

Amber went for ice. Willie fed the fire.

"What you gonna do, Amber?" he asked when she returned.

She threw him a look. She was tired of the game. "Be alright."

They watched her, all of them at once.

Willie found a chair by the fire and sat. "I never asked you—where you from?"

Josie and Carolyn sat up, waiting for an answer.

"Momma's from Atlanta, Daddy's from Deetroit." She finished her drink and stood, assuming a sexy pose. *"The Queen a Soul!"*

Josie put her drink down and lit a cigarette. "She's from Idaho."

Willie looked at Josie, then Amber.

She gave him a wink and headed to the bar. "Gonna fix me some gin and light me a smoke… tell you all 'bout it."

Her parents ran a kitchen outside Pocatello. She was their only child. They disappeared one night.

"How old were you?"

"Ten, eleven." She took a drink.

He thought about his fire.

She lit a cigarette and settled in.

"Where'd they go… if you don't mind me asking?"

One hot summer night they went to the movies and never returned. They packed her things and put her on a bus to Atlanta. Her uncle's name was Curt.

The room was quiet.

He was mean and the house was rough. At fifteen, he charged them money. At eighteen, he charged them more.

Willie gripped his glass tightly in his hand. "And your parents?"

She didn't answer right away. "Met a fella with the FBI one time. Gave me a number to call." She stopped, blowing smoke, watching it disappear. "Just kept ringin'."

Josie's face turned sad. "And your uncle? What happened to him?"

Her bangs had dropped and her drink was done. It was time to make some calls. She put her cigarette out and walked to the door, turning back. They looked wasted in the light, strangers once again. She thought about their time together, what had come of it in the end. "I cut him up and hit the road," she answered quietly, heading for the stairs.


When they were gone, he watched the coals fade, thinking of her story, of his own. Wherever he'd strayed, there was always someone. That was the good part, the kindness he'd found. People like Ernest.

Perlie Fuchet.

The parlor was chilly. He thought of Emily, wanting to tell her, to be with her again. It wasn't his house—not even his momma's. Their keys were in the basket.

Josie's door was open when he passed. He put his head in. She was standing at an open window.

"Hey, darlin'," she whispered, turning to him. She'd been crying.

He went to her, stopping halfway. Mascara ran down her face.

"Heard about your girl."

"I'm sorry, what I've done."

"Wasn't you."

"I fucked it all up, Josie."

She went to him, putting her arms around his waist. "Wasn't anyone."

"It was me," he answered quickly.

She pulled him closer, putting her head on his shoulder.

"Did what he asked to get him back."

She closed her eyes, missing him in her arms. "Tell me her name."

Her breath was warm against his neck. She smelled of cigarettes. "Emily."

They held each other.

"He did it for you, baby."

"Who?"

"Professor Lilly."

"How you figure?"

She let go, looking up into his eyes. "Get your school done, Willie. Promise me that."

He took a moment, seeing what it meant to her. "I promise."

She smiled when she heard it, understanding it finally. "Make a life for yourself."

She looked small to him. Lost and broken. "I'll figure it out."

"We'll be fine, baby."

"Maybe ask around."

She wiped her cheek of mascara. "No."

He looked away. It was true.

She walked to the window, enjoying the trees, the sudden shade of spring. "There's nothin' you can do."

They waited together one last time.

"When a person wants you gone."


He called her in the morning at work. She sounded far away. "It's Willie."

"Who else would it be?"

He liked the way she talked. The calm in her voice. "I need to see you."

"Well…"

He heard a voice in the background.

"You got the car, man."

She was distracted. "When are you done?"

"Hang on." He heard footsteps. "Five o'clock."

"Five?"

"Take you to the movies," she said, hanging up.

He sat in the kitchen, thinking of her body. How willing she'd been. Then again, over and over until it stopped, spent and laughing, watching their sweat dry in the sun.

He poured a cup of coffee and went to the phone. Stick was asleep and the doors were closed. They'd be down soon. He picked up the receiver and dialed.

It took a while to reach him. "Mr. Wells, it's Willie Graves."

"Hello, Willie."

"Did you hear what happened?"

"I did not, sir."

"They closed our house."

"Excuse me?"

He explained it to him, how he'd been squeezed, the yellow sign across the door.

"So, let me get this straight. You said, John Lilly?"

"Yes, sir."

"On your momma's list?"

"Yes, sir."

"Well, I'll be."

"I know."

"Hard to believe."

Willie thought some more. "Is the decision final?"

"Final's a relative term, Willie. I'd say, yes… but we need to think about it. See what we can do."

"I'd like to sell the house."

He listened. "Okay."

"Can I do that?"

"Of course, you can. As a house, of course. Not the business."

"Split the money with the girls. And Cary."

"Excuse me?"

"Split the money with Cary and the girls."

The line went quiet.

"Sir?"

"I'm here."

"Can I do that?"

"Which girls are you referring to, if I may ask?"

Josie, Carolyn, and Amber."

"And Cary Buck?"

"Yes."

"What about you?"

He hadn't thought about it.

"Treat you all the same."

"You're right."

"Don't you think?"

"Use the money for school, I guess."

"Not sure about the girls, though. Or Cary. Maybe him."

"Wasn't me who made the money."

"I understand, but I think…"

"Paid the price."

"Well…" He considered it quickly. "When you put it that way."

"I'm done, Mr. Wells."

The line was quiet again.

"Using them the way I did. My momma too."

"You understand what you're doing, son?"

"I think so."

"Giving them the proceeds of the house."

"Yes."

"Minus the taxes."

"And everything in it."

D. K. Wells sat back in his chair. "Cary said you had a property next door?"

He'd forgotten about his tree.

"Not worth as much, of course."

"I need to think about that, sir."

"Take your time. A lot to consider here, son."

"Yes."

"You want me to handle this for you?"

"Yes, sir. If you would, please."

"Not Bob Brewer?"

"Just you, please. After everything we've been through."

"Happy to help you if I can."

"Thank you."

Cotton came into the kitchen, looking around.

"Do you have a real estate agent?"

"No, sir."

"I'll make some calls."

"Thank you."

"You're welcome, Willie."

They both waited.

"Shall I draw up the papers?"

"If you would, please."

"I'll need their names."

"You want them now?"

"Sure."

He thought about them all. The ones who were gone.

"Josie Carr. Carolyn Pajula. Amber Black."

"C-A-R-R?"

"Yes, sir."

"Pajula with a 'J'?"

"Yes, sir."

"I'll need their social security numbers. Where to send the checks."

"And Cary Buck?"

"His, as well."

"I'll have them call you, if that's okay?"

"Works fine. I believe I have yours."

Cotton jumped on the counter by the sink.

"One thing."

"Yes, Willie."

"The money in my safe."

"You have a safe?"

"I do. And a bank account."

"How can I help you?"

"Is it legal?"

"In what way?"

"Can I keep it?"

"Well, I should think so. How was it acquired?"

"From the business."

"All cash?"

"And a gun."

He considered it.

"Josie keeps the books."

"You'll owe taxes. Have you paid them?"

"I don't know."

"That's a problem."

It didn't surprise him to hear it.

"You could start another business."

"How does that work?"

"Put it somewhere else.

"You mean, hide it somewhere?"

"Diversify."

"So, no one can find it?"

"Correct."

Cotton saw a bird outside the window and froze. "Or give it away."

When the bacon was crisp and the table set, he heard them on the stairs, flipping his pancakes, watching the edges sizzle. His heart was free and his mind was clear. That surprised him. The ease of it. He lifted the pancakes onto a platter, imagining his new life, how quickly it had changed. Never better, only butter.

# CHAPTER THIRTY-EIGHT

When their plates were empty, he poured the last of the coffee and sat down. Stick had taken a walk.

"I need to say a few things," he started.

Amber lit a smoke. Her face was puffy from the booze. "Here we go."

It surprised him, how she'd said it.

"Don't look at me that way, baby. Tell me what you got to say and let's get a move on." She took a drag and blew it out. "You givin' Miss Amber that Buick?"

"No."

"Thought so."

"Giving you the house."

She smiled and gave him a wink. "Whole thing? Or just the kitchen?"

Josie saw something in his eyes.

Carolyn saw it too.

"Gonna sell it and give you the proceeds. One-fifth for everybody."

Their brows furrowed, not believing him at first.

"Get your money when we do."

Carolyn looked at Josie.

Josie leaned forward. "What are you saying?"

"And Cary."

"Why?"

"Belongs to all of us, Josie. Not just me."

No one spoke.

"I realized it a while ago. In Mississippi, maybe... met a girl down there. Or, with Poppy before she left, I don't know."

Amber's eyes hardened.

"Then this."

He took a sip of coffee, noticing their faces. They were different suddenly. "It isn't right."

They looked away.

"The way it makes you feel... makes *me* feel."

Amber put her cigarette out and took her plate to the sink, staring out the window.

He watched her shoulders stiffen. "The men."

"Don't bother me none."

"I don't believe that, Amber."

She watched the clouds above the trees. They were flat and fast.

Josie and Carolyn waited. She was more than unpredictable.

"*Like* what I do. How I *do* it." The sun hit her face. She turned from it, facing them. "Don't need no *handout*."

"Not what it is... what I mean."

She checked the pockets of her robe. "It's alright, baby. Know what you mean and how you mean it." She shot him a softer look. "Time for The Amber to roll."

He glanced quickly at Josie, then back to Amber.

She walked to him, looking down as he looked up. He was a sweet young man. Kind in the heart and strong in the head. "You take that money and you get through school. And when you're done, you call me. Tell me how it all worked out."

Her eyes were tough and tender.

"What you doin' next door?"

"What do you mean?"

"With that ole tree a yours?"

When she said it, he understood. It was everything he needed.

She passed around the table, collecting her cigarettes. "I love me some men 'cuz I love me some money. Ain't nothin'more."

They watched her reach the door, turning back.

"Been down this road my whole life long. No pity-poo for me please."

He tried one more time. "You want to think about it?"

"'Bout what?"

"About taking what you've earned."

She took a breath, her face flushed with rage. "You ain't *listnin'* to me! *None* a you!"

They froze in their chairs.

"Won't be yo' *nigga*, plain 'n simple!"

The word went through him.

She touched her curls and turned to go. "No *rich* man's *fool*."


When she was gone, they sat together. The cat was behind the toaster, asleep. The clock ticked quietly.

Willie took his plate to the sink, trying to make sense of it.

Josie stretched her arms over her head. Everything hurt. "I need to call the station. Get my tickets."

Carolyn stood slowly. "Me too."

Willie stared into the sink. "D. K. Wells needs your social security numbers. I told him you'd call." He looked up through the window. "Number's by the phone."

Carolyn appeared beside him with her dishes. "Let me. You've done enough."

Stick would be walking. They needed time together. He thought of Amber again. The way she'd said it.

"Go!" she insisted, lowering her dishes into the sink, pushing him away.

The air was soft. It had been a while since he'd noticed such things, felt a season turn. At the end of the block, rounding the corner, he saw Stick from a distance, head down, coming toward him. He looked thinner without his coat on.

They stopped when they reached each other, pleased to be together.

"You heading back?"

"Just walkin'." He looked around, admiring the neighborhood. "Saw your cat lady."

"She's nuts, that one."

"Ran away when she saw me."

They laughed, heading down the sidewalk from where Stick had come. A car approached as they walked, the driver waved as it passed.

They turned east. The houses were older, with larger yards.

Willie slowed down. "Cary likes that one." The boxwoods needed pruning and the house was shot. "The roses out front."

Stick admired a certain tree. "Big old oak leafin' out."

Willie stopped with him, seeing it. "How old you think it is?"

He checked the trunk, the crown. A section of the top had broken off. "Don't know —maybe eighty years? A hundred?"

"Sure is pretty."

Stick nodded, moving along. "Seen some time."

They stopped at the entrance of a small park. A dog ran up, sniffing

Stick's pants, dashing away.

"You ever had a dog?"

"I did."

"Where?"

"In Thelma when I was little."

"What kind was it?"

"Just a dog."

"What you call it?"

"Mister Pickles."

Willie grinned. He liked the idea. Stick as a boy. "How come?"

Stick's face relaxed, thinking of him again. "Looked like a pickle."


They headed back, taking the long way.

"How'd it go with the ladies?"

"Fine, I guess."

"What happened?"

"Nothin' much." He thought about what she'd said. "Except for Amber."

A truck passed quickly, heading into town.

"What about her?"

"Told 'em I was selling the house."

He looked at Willie, surprised to hear it.

"Splitting the money between them and Cary."

They turned a corner.

"Why you doin' this?"

He considered it again. "I don't know. Guess I'm just tired of the bullshit. The business they're in."

"*You're* in."

They stopped, seeing his car at the end of the street.

"It's not right making money this way. I've known it all my life."

They looked at each other.

"I want you to take the money in my safe."

"What makes you think I need money?"

"How much you got?"

"Got plenty."

"How much?"

"None a your business."

"Come on, man."

"Two hundred."

He smiled when he heard it.

Stick looked around. The street was quiet. "Livin' like a king."

They stood for a moment.

"Was it rough in prison?"

"It was fine."

"They knock you around?"

He checked the sky. "Happens."

"How come?"

His lip was still swollen. "Right place, wrong time."

His eyes looked beat. "Judge was wrong to send you there."

"What they do sometimes."

He'd never asked him—how the gun went off. What he'd done with the money. "Doesn't make it right."


They started walking.

"Hilda okay?"

"She's fine. Saw her at Christmas. Salty and Auggie were there too."

"You?"

"I'm good."

"Heard you got a girl."

They'd never spoken this way before.

"Emily Parks, yeah." He thought of them together. "We'll see where it goes."

"Zach's daughter."

"Yep."

"Worked the gas dock some. Pretty, what I remember. Where she live?"

"Richmond."

He missed Crystal Ann. Their sweet little house.

They walked a bit.

"What you gonna do now?"

He took his time before he answered. "Think I'll sit a while."

"What you mean?"

They stopped.

Stick's face softened, giving in to it finally. "Lose the road. Find some work."

His answer surprised him. "And Hilda?"

A child cried out from a nearby yard.

"Can't take your money, Willie."

"Why not?"

"Didn't make it."

"I didn't either—what I told 'em. Not my money, not my house."

Stick looked down. His boots were shot. "Better for me that way."

Willie waited for more. "How come?"

He took his time, considering the question. "You took care of me and I'm grateful for that." He looked up. " We'll call it even."

"What you did for me."

He started walking.

"Come on, man," Willie persisted, following him. "Got plenty in the bank and the place next door."

The weeds were up and the tree was bare. They entered the yard, stopping.

"You remember this place?"

"I do."

402 / Peter Skinner

"Like to build a house here."

They looked around. There were bushes and trees about.

"One of these days."

"You still in school?"

"I am."

"Good for you, son."

"Spring break's comin' up.

Tiny birds worked the ground.

"Then what?"

"I don't know. Be a lawyer, maybe."

Stick looked at him strangely.

"Somebody's gotta do it."

"Why's that?"

Willie turned to him, suddenly bothered. "Get you outta jail."

Stick looked away.

"It's not the same for you and me. Bein' Black. Bein' White." He remembered the garden. Her gentle face. "Watch your son hang. Cut him down." He looked to the catalpa. "Keep on livin'."

Stick's eyes flushed suddenly, hearing him say it.

"There's no justice in the world if there's no one left to keep it."

A breeze moved through the branches.

"I used to climb this thing and wonder what the world was like. Was it big, or was it small? Were there monsters? Were people nice to each other?"

Sunlight stretched across the yard, casting shadows everywhere.

"It's *all* a that." He turned to Stick. He looked spent and broken. "That's what you showed me, in your own way." He'd never seen him feel so much. Listen so hard. "We're in this life together."

Standing on his momma's land, he understood it finally. What he'd learned, what he'd lost. If a person could love him in the end. If he could love them back.

Looking up, he imagined his children someday, climbing higher and higher, each step a certain victory, a longer view. Reaching the top, they'd look out over the world, their little hearts pounding, imagining their life, as he had done: seeing cities, seeing friendship, seeing stars. Wanting everything. And then the moon.

# CHAPTER THIRTY-NINE

She'd thought of him all day. They skipped the movie and turned the lights down. There was wine in the fridge and some chicken with grits. When they were done, they put their glasses on the floor, lying back in each other's arms.

"I love the way you touch me."

"Where?"

"Everywhere."

He put his fingers lightly between her legs.

"Especially that."

They lay together.

"What was the movie?"

"*Jules and Jim*. It's in French."

"You speak French?"

"A couple words. But no. Not really."

"*C'est de la glace?*"

"What's that?"

"Is this ice cream?"

"*C'est de la glace?*" she repeated perfectly, enjoying the sound of it.

"*Et voilà.*"

She traced his nose with her finger.

"Did you break this?"

"I don't think so. My cheek maybe."

"How?"

"In Mississippi."

"What happened?"

"I'll tell you someday."


She went for water.


"When's you're next class?"

"Monday."

"What are you reading?"

"Just school stuff. You?"

"I paint when I can. That's it."

He felt his heart beating. "There's so much going on."

"Like what?"

"Do we have more wine?"

"That's it."

"I should have brought some."

"Tell me."

He stared at the ceiling, not knowing where to start.

He told her about Hilda, about Stick, and then the house. How Amber said no.

"Why would she do that?"

"I don't know. I pissed her off."

"You offered her a house."

"Part of it, yes."

"That's different."

"How?"

"Like a business transaction."

"I guess."

"From what you made together."

He waited to say it. "The professor sold me out."

"The house, yes. Not you."

"Said it wouldn't be pretty and it wouldn't be straight."

She thought about it. How to help someone when they needed you most.

"It took me a while to understand. The deal he made." He ran his hand down her back. "The price he paid."

She waited. "You need to see him."

"I will."

"Thank him for what he's done."

He took his hand away.


It was late.

He spoke of Cary Buck eventually, what he'd done to the place, to Willie's grammar. How he'd fallen in love with a guy and gone to Mexico.

"Who's the guy?"

"Met him at a club in Richmond."

"A gay club?"

"Older guy. Married once."

"He'll be back."


Their eyes grew heavy.

"What's your favorite class?"

"History."

"Why?"

"It's like your paintings."

She didn't understand.

"You see the edges first, then the rest of it all at once… together sometimes, or separately. Swirling around until it stops."

"Dries."

"Begins again."

He rolled into her. Everything fit.

"Did you sleep with Josie?"

"Josie Carr?'

"You talk about her sometimes."

"A few times."

"Did she teach you things?"

"Like what?"

"What do you think?"

He grinned, hearing it. "Not really. Maybe."

"Like what?"

"I don't know. How to relax. Let go." He caressed her hair with his hand. "Without being afraid."

She took his hand and kissed it softly, then again, holding on to it, closing her eyes.


In the morning, she went to work. He lay in bed for a while, smelling her pillow, noticing a painting tacked to the wall. Her colors were insistent and wild. Translucent.

When it was time, he got dressed and walked to the door, leaving a note on a large piece of paper by her sewing machine. The letters were big. His heart was overflowing.


PAINT!

When she read it, she stopped completely, feeling his touch. Her parents wouldn't like it. She didn't care; she'd tell them anyway. They had found their way. Since the world began. From the edges first, all at once together.

Photo: Jen Fariello

Peter Skinner is the author of three previous works of
fiction and two plays. He lives in Virginia.

# ALSO BY PETER SKINNER

WHITE BUFFALO

THE BELLS OF MOSES HENRY

THE EDGE OF FARALLON

THE EDGE OF FARALLON (play)

NADA BROZ (play)

For more information about Peter Skinner, please visit his website,

www.peterskinner.com